BRINDLE

BOOKS

http://www.brindlebooks.co.uk

WELLINGTON'S DRAGOON 2:

SECRET LINES

BY

DAVID J. BLACKMORE

Brindle Books Ltd

Copyright © 2022 by David J Blackmore

This edition published by
Brindle Books Ltd
Unit 3, Grange House
Grange Street
Wakefield
United Kingdom
WF2 8TF
Copyright © Brindle Books Ltd 2022

Acknowledgements

Once again I must thank the members of our little writing group in Howden for their continued enthusiasm and support. Our meetings are always stimulating, and the occasional writing exercises we give each other are always a useful challenge. Writing can be a lonely occupation, and the group is somewhere I can discuss my writing in the knowledge that comments will be helpful. I am also indebted to Janet McKay for her valuable contributions during long after dinner discussions. Thanks are due once more to Gillian Caldicott for reading everything, and seeing the wood for the trees, as well as my typos. Neil Hinchliffe has again been helpful and encouraging.

I am grateful to my friends in B Troop, 16th Light Dragoons, and elsewhere in the world of Napoleonic re-enactment and research, who have enjoyed the first book, To The Douro, and not picked me up on any details, much to my relief.

I am still riding two or three times a week, frequently on Johnny, who appears on the cover of this book, and "To the Douro". My thanks to Mark Atkinson of Atkinson Action Horses for making this possible.

Finally, my thanks to my publisher, Richard Hinchliffe of Brindle Books, for making this possible, and Emma, for the photos.

Introduction

"Secret Lines" is the second book in the "Wellington's Dragoon" series, relating the adventures of a young officer, Michael Roberts, in the Sixteenth Light Dragoons during the war against Napoleon in Portugal and Spain, and in the final campaign of Waterloo.

The 16th Light Dragoons is a real regiment, the only one to serve under Sir Arthur Wellesley, Viscount Wellington in this book, and later the Duke of Wellington, from when he took command in April 1809, all the way through the Peninsular War to its end in 1814, and again in the Waterloo Campaign of 1815. Michael Roberts, is a complete invention, as is Emyr Lloyd and many, but not all, of the NCOs and dragoons of the regiment. All the other officers that appear served in the Regiment. William Tomkinson left us one of the finest diaries of a cavalry officer from the period.

The "Secret Lines" are today known as the Lines of Torres Vedras, the double line of massive fortifications that still stretch from the river Tagus to the Atlantic Ocean. They were built on the instructions of Wellington, and, remarkably, the French army under Marshal Massena, that was bent on driving the British army into the sea and occupying Portugal, had no inkling of their existence until they came within sight of them. They got no further.

This book continues the story of the Sixteenth Light Dragoons, and others, real and imaginary, and tells of Michael's part in keeping the Secret Lines exactly that. Emyr Lloyd continues to pepper his conversation with Welsh, such as 'chwarae teg,' meaning fair play, and 'diolch yn fawr,' meaning thank you very much, frequently shortened to just 'diolch'. Major Stanhope continues to make life difficult for Michael, mostly because of a young Portuguese woman. There are revelations, spies, and romantic entanglements, as well as plenty of action.

Secret Lines

Chapter 1

Three weeks into July, over thirty leagues into Spain, and looking for the French army. Lieutenant Michael Roberts tried to stretch and ease himself in his saddle. His regiment, the Sixteenth Light Dragoons, walked steadily on, across the featureless, treeless, rolling plain, eight half squadrons, one behind the other, over five hundred men. To their left were the Fourteenth Light Dragoons, the other half of the brigade commanded by General Cotton. They had been riding since four in the morning, and as the cool of the night passed, it began to get hot.

In the last two months, since they had left Oporto, Michael had learnt more about being a regimental officer than he had in all the previous year since he had joined the army. In those two months there had been no fighting, but a lot of marching. A lot of unnecessary equipment had been abandoned. The regiment no longer bothered with tents. They either had billets, or slept out, and if it rained, they got wet. There had been a lot of opportunity to learn and practice the skills that made campaigning easier and the regiment more efficient. Taking out a patrol, manning a picket, organising billets, keeping horses fed, watered and fit, it had all become second nature. Michael had got to know the men and horses of his troop better, to know their strengths and weaknesses. With the other officers of the squadron, one of the regiment's four, they had formed a mess that always made the best of what was available, whether it was feast, or more frequently, famine. Jose Parra, hired by Michael in Oporto, had proved himself a good groom, and got on well with Lloyd, his batman, much to Michael's relief. Officers, dragoons, servants, it had become an extended family.

At the head of the regiment rode Major Stanhope, now in command in place of Colonel Anson, who had been given his own brigade. He ordered a halt, and Michael dismounted his men and eased himself out of Duke's saddle and on to the ground. He untied a wineskin from his saddle and took a long drink of the lukewarm water in it. Water was a problem, finding enough for the men and the horses. Somewhere away to their right lay the Tagus river, and the Spanish Army under General Cuesta that they had joined up with yesterday. Michael had seen them, and not been too impressed. The infantry was a curates egg, good in parts, the cavalry had looked ragged. Many of the troopers had no boots, some were even barefoot, and their saddles and tack looked bad.

Another ten minutes passed, and then they mounted again and resumed the steady walk towards the town of Talavera, where they expected to find a French army. The men were already tired. The last few days had been long ones, and food and forage were in short supply. Last night they had been kept in the saddle for Cuesta to review the whole army. Michael had been lucky, and had not been on picket duty during the night. Those who had were struggling to stay awake.

Towards midday the distant sound of musketry and cannon fire came drifting across the Spanish countryside, and it seemed that the Spanish had found at least part of the French army. Michael watched as a staff officer cantered across to Cotton, leaving a trail of dust hanging in the still, hot air. They spoke briefly, before he cantered off again, and Cotton halted his horse and his brigade. Once again they dismounted. Water was taken, but frugally. No one knew when they might be able to replenish their canteens. Michael lifted the front of his tarleton helmet, and released the sweat trapped under it, which trickled down his face. He wiped it away, the silver braid on his sleeve rasping across his face, catching on the three days of stubble.

After a long wait they were ordered back into the saddle and set off again. This time they seemed to be moving further to their left, and the distant sounds of firing were more to their right than straight ahead. Behind them great clouds of dust hung in the air, showing where the infantry divisions were marching. Gradually the sounds of firing and cannon grew louder, and Michael could see clouds of white smoke far away to his right, drifting gently across the countryside. The brigade held its course, roughly to the north east, continuing its steady walk across the plain.

A small stream gave the brigade an opportunity to water the horses briefly, and refill canteens. While his horse drank, Michael saw Cotton talking to Major Stanhope and Colonel Hawker, commanding the Fourteenth. After a few minutes, the small group broke up and Stanhope rode back the Sixteenth and let his horse drink. He spoke to the adjutant, Lieutenant Barra, who mounted and rode through the regiment, speaking briefly to the squadron commanders. After he had spoken to Ashworth, the captain waved his officers to join him.

"Well, gentlemen," said Ashworth, "it would seem that the Spanish have run into a division of French dragoons and are making rather heavy weather of it. Anson's brigade has been ordered to try to turn the French right, we are to continuing moving after them in support. Quite where the main French body is, no one seems to know. That's all, gentlemen, take your posts, please, and let the men know what I have told you."

By mid afternoon, the view towards the sounds of fighting had become distorted by shimmering heat haze. For a while, the sounds of battle faded, and then suddenly and briefly they rose again in volume. Men looked at each other without speaking. It sounded as if the Spanish had found the main French force, and the French had turned at bay. Michael tugged out his watch, it was just four o'clock. The brigade continued its stop, start journey across the hot, desolate plain. The firing gradually faded away to nothing. A little after seven o'clock, a staff officer came riding up to Cotton, and at last the brigade learnt that it could halt and bivouac. Away to the right, Michael could just make out the town of Talavera. A nearby stream provided water for men and horses, but it was another hour before the Regiment's baggage and supplies reached them, along with the officers' servants, including Francisco, Michael's young Portuguese servant.

The horses were unsaddled, one squadron at a time, given a brief rub down, and then, with the prospect of imminent action, saddled up again. The men sat or sprawled at their horses' heads, reins in hand. The Regiment's officers gathered together in front of the lines of men and horses and made the best of the cold food and warm wine produced for them, standing around, chatting quietly, and, like their men, the reins of their horses in hand. At last, the sun began to sink, and the day lost some of its dreadful heat. As they ate and drank they were joined by Cotton, who told them what he knew.

"The French have pulled back across the Alberche river, a few miles the other side of Talavera. Anson's Brigade and the Third Division are to our front, opposite the French right. The Spanish are beyond Talavera in front of the French left. The French position is good, but too long, and consequently thinly held. Sir Arthur, I beg his pardon, Viscount Wellington," there was laughter as Cotton forgot for a moment their commander's new title. Cotton smiled and started again. "Viscount Wellington intends to attack tomorrow at first light, along with the Spanish. The brigade must be ready to advance at five o'clock. We have to be in position by first light at six. There is high ground across the Alberche, and the country is not suitable for cavalry, so we will be acting in support of the infantry."

As the sun sank lower in the sky the officers strolled back to their squadrons. Michael found Parra waiting for him with his other, and favourite horse, Johnny, ready to exchange him for Duke. Michael thought for a moment. "I'll stay on Duke tomorrow. We had a very easy day today, he's quite alright." He reached forward and stroked Johnny's nose, and the horse pushed back at his hand. "Yes, good boy, Johnny, good boy." He reached up and scratched the horse between his ears, and got a light push on his chest as a reward. "Alright, lad," he laughed, "alright, you behave now." He felt Duke's reins go slack as the horse stepped forward next to him. He and Johnny sniffed at each other, and Michael stroked Duke's nose. Michael could not help but smile. The company of horses was definitely good for a man.

It was a strange night. Somewhere, only a few miles away, was a French army, one that would be attacked in the morning. Yet the night was still, hot and quiet. Men spoke in low subdued voices, some stretched out and snored, others sat and lost themselves in thought. Horses shuffled, equipment bumped and rattled, there was the odd hard word from dragoon to horse, more soft ones whispered quietly.

Michael lay in front of Duke, the long curb reins in his hand. He tried to sleep. His mind was a battlefield between sleep brought on by a long day under a scorching sun, and alertness caused by the thoughts of what tomorrow might bring. His thoughts turned to the fact that, unlike everyone else in the Regiment, he had yet to charge against the enemy. He wondered if he was finally going to see action with his comrades. Through no fault of his own, every time they had been in action so far, he had been elsewhere. It rankled with him. He knew what he would have to do, he didn't know what it would be like. He didn't know how scared he would be. His imagination ran riot with possibilities, death the least of them. He was worried he would forget his training, let himself and the Regiment down. He was scared he would fail. He looked with envy at nearby dragoons, snoring gently. Eventually, for a little while, sleep took him as well.

Michael was woken by Lloyd gently shaking his shoulder. "Wake up now, sir, it's just after four, and you've just time to have a bite before we have to form the squadron, sir."

Groggy after too little sleep, Michael sat up and took the bread and cheese offered by Lloyd. There was a cup of brandy as well. "Thank you, Lloyd, much appreciated."

"My pleasure, sir, and while you have your breakfast, would you be so kind as to just hold Edward while I take a little stroll, sir? Then I can be doing the same for you."

All around the same was happening, as dragoons held each others' horses and disappeared into the darkness to where a shallow trench had been dug. "Of course,' said Michael, taking Edward's reins, and biting hungrily into his bread.

Well before five o'clock the regiment was breakfasted, and all stood by their horses ready to mount. There was a hint of light in the sky as Cotton rode out of the dark and spoke to Stanhope. Then the orders came, and the regiment mounted, formed again into a column of half squadrons, and once again started to walk across the Spanish plain towards the East. As the light grew they could make out the Fourteenth, paralleling them away to their left. A mile further forward and they halted. From behind came the sounds of drums and soon they were being passed by long columns of redcoated infantry marching to take the lead. Two whole divisions, near ten thousand men, snaked past them in half a dozen or more columns, spread across the plain. A battery of artillery rumbled by, six heavy guns, teams of horses, ammunition wagons, sweating gunners. Somewhere not far ahead was the Alberche River, and across it the French were waiting. Another infantry division appeared, there were now three divisions of British infantry moving into position, waiting for the signal to attack.

A half mile or so in front, across the flat countryside, glimpsed through the few trees scattered about, Michael could just make out the lines of redcoats as the battalions stood ready. He had a perfect view from his position on the left of the leading half squadron. A few yards to his left sat Captain Ashworth, and a few yards in front of him Major Stanhope. Michael felt reassured by their apparent calm and nonchalance. They waited. Nothing happened. Men and horses began to get restless. Every man was tense with expectation, and the horses could sense it. Half an hour passed. Not a single shot was heard, nothing moved except the sun climbing steadily in the clear blue sky, the temperature rising with it.

Cotton was sitting on his horse, slightly ahead of the brigade and halfway between the two regiments. Next to him sat Captain Cocks of the Sixteenth, Cotton's aide de camp. Michael saw Cotton turn in their direction and heard him call out, "Stanhope, you can dismount." He turned and shouted the same across to Hawker.

At Stanhope's command the regiment opened its ranks so the men could dismount. Once on the ground, and stood at ease, a quiet hum of conversation broke out in the ranks as speculation began about the unexpected delay. It soon died away for want of information, and men sat or lay at the head of their horses. Michael sat down, and Ashworth led his horse across and joined him.

"This is rather unexpected, Roberts. God only knows what's happening."

"Yes, sir, but perhaps Viscount Wellington does?"

Ashworth laughed. "I expect all will become clear, eventually." They lapsed into silence.

Half an hour later they saw Cocks ride off towards the south. Michael lay back on the hard, stony ground, his head in the shadow of Duke. He must have dozed off because he was suddenly aware of Ashworth scrambling to his feet and saying, "Cocks is back". Michael propped himself up on his elbows and watched as Cocks reined in his horse next to Cotton and spoke to the brigade commander. Cotton lifted his face to the heavens for a moment, and then slumped into his saddle. He must have said something because Cocks turned his horse and trotted across to where Hawker was watching with interest. Cocks spoke to Hawker and Michael saw him look startled and then shake his head. Cocks trotted across to Stanhope and spoke to him. He heard the Major's voice ring out, "Bloody Spanish…" and then tail off. Cocks shrugged apologetically and rode off back towards Cotton.

Stanhope turned to face the Regiment. "Squadron commanders to me!" Ashworth walked the short distance, leading his horse and one by one the other three squadron commanders joined them. Moments later Ashworth was back, shaking his head in disbelief. He looked at Michael.

"It's the Spanish," he paused. "The bloody Spanish didn't turn up. They decided, Cuesta decided he didn't want to attack today. Wellington is furious and the whole damned thing is off until tomorrow." He shook his head again. "As if the French will wait around for that."

The rest of the day passed slowly and uneventfully. The baggage was up with the regiment, so at least they had the benefit of what supplies it carried. Francisco dug out some stale bread and old cheese from Michael's supplies, along with a bottle of warm wine. He also brought Michael another wineskin of water. A squadron at a time they unsaddled and groomed the horses. A picket line of vedettes was established halfway towards to the Alberche River, beyond the infantry who had fallen back from their advanced positions in order to bivouac on the plain. The sun was as hot and unrelenting as ever. There wasn't much to eat or drink for the men, nothing for the horses. Flies swarmed around, relentlessly. It was a trying time for all, tempers frayed, and horses became fractious.

Towards five o'clock the day was beginning to cool a little, and Stanhope called all the officers together. "We can't sit here doing nothing. It's cooling down a little, so I want you to go and exercise your squadrons. Put them through half an hour's steady work, no more, less if you think it right, just walk, a little trot. I want every horse cantered and stretched a bit, but no more than a quarter mile, if that, you all know your horses and what's best for them. Then dismount and walk them until they've cooled off. After that, we will take a chance on it staying quiet, and unsaddle and rub them down. We will have to see what we can manage about feed and water. Carry on."

An hour later the regiment was back resting, but the usual sense of good humour had returned. The Regiment's commissary officer turned up with some biscuit and a few casks of wine, and was greeted with good humoured cheers as it was distributed among the ranks. Then word came back from the picket that there was no sign of any French on the opposite bank of the river, their position seemed to be some eight hundred yards further back, on high ground overlooking the river. Cotton took advantage of the opportunity. One troop at a time they rode down to the river to water the horses, the men spread out in skirmishing order, they didn't want to attract any artillery fire. Spread out along the riverbank was a green coated company of the 5th/60th Rifles, watching carefully for any French skirmishers. When it was the turn of his troop, Michael found himself standing next to an officer of the Rifles while Duke drank. The man, a Lieutenant like Michael, nodded amiably to him and grinned.

"Take your time," he said, "we've not seen hide nor hair of the French, save the odd picket right up there." He indicated a ridge in the distance.

"That's good to know," Michael replied, and relaxed a little.

Even so, standing in the open on the riverbank was a little nerve racking, but every horse got its fill of water, and the men filled their canteens.

The night was a restless one, full of the sounds of artillery moving, and men marching. At two in the morning the regiment mounted, and soon after moved cautiously forward, across the dark countryside. Near to the river they were halted and dismounted to wait. Eventually the light began to appear in the sky, and as the sun rose it revealed a line of British infantry, stretching away to the brigade's left, advancing to ford the river along a three mile front. To the right they could see Spanish infantry crossing the river by a bridge and by fords.

Michael was once again at the head of the regimental column and could see the infantry as they made their way over the gently undulating plain, and crossed the river. They began climbing up towards the ridge, towards the French position, the lines snaking and curving a little, like a red ribbon in a gentle breeze. Like everyone else, Michael was waiting for the crash of cannon and the ripping sound of musket volleys, but they didn't come. Somewhere he could hear a bird singing. The reason for the silence was soon clear, the French had gone.

In the middle of the afternoon the regiment was still stationary, waiting for orders, speculating as to what had happened and what would happen. They were at least able to water the horses in the river. Then they saw the Spanish army marching off in the direction the French had gone. Quietly, they readied themselves to follow, but still no orders came. Then they saw the British infantry returning and crossing back over the Alberche. They were not marching in pursuit of the French after all.

Later in the afternoon the regiment moved towards the town of Talavera, and bivouacked amongst the olive groves to the north of the town. Lines were stretched between the trees, and the horses tied to them in the welcome shade. For the first time in four days they unsaddled the horses and gave them a thorough grooming. Bareback, they rode the short distance to a nearby small river, and rode the horses in. Amidst a lot of shouting, laughing, and splashing the horses were washed off, and then walked back to the camp. Michael took the opportunity to change horses.

It was all a welcome relief, but food and forage were both in short supply and the whole army was on half rations. It slowly filtered through the army that Viscount Wellington had refused to advance any further until the Spanish came up with the supplies they had promised to provide. No one thought it likely that would happen, the French had already stripped the countryside of what little there was. But if there was little food, the regiment was together, and that evening all the Regiment's officers dined together. They sat on rocks and logs with plates balanced on their knees while their servants poured what wine they had into a variety of cups and mugs. It was a convivial gathering.

Michael looked around at the three dozen men gathered together, everyone of them a familiar character, known, liked, or at least respected, even Stanhope. Michael had to admit, a little grudgingly, that Stanhope was a very professional and competent officer. For the rest, they ignored each other beyond any unavoidable regimental business. The Honourable Lincoln Stanhope, younger son of the Earl of Harrington, did not approve of Michael and he considered that Michael had no place in the regiment. He held that only a proper gentleman could be a good officer. He did not believe Michael to be a proper gentleman, he considered him as coming from trade, because Michael's father had worked for Baron Quintela, one of Portugal's wealthiest merchants. He certainly didn't like Michael's forays into the world of espionage. That, however, didn't stop him making full use of Michael and his fluency in Portuguese and Spanish.

As for all the others, Michael might not have fought with them yet, but they knew he had brought the rabelos, the wine barges, down the Douro so that the army could cross the river and retake Oporto, and that was good enough for them. In the last two months he had got to know them well, and not just the officers of his troop and squadron. A few of the lieutenants and cornets were even on first name terms, and all were proving to be capable. He had struck up quite a friendship with Will Alexander and Henry van Hagen. William Osten, a German Baron, no less, had turned out to have a very dry sense of humour behind his Germanic countenance. Tom Penrice was always ready for a bit of fun. As usual, the two Georges were sitting together, as if their nicknames, Old George and Young George, bound them together. Not far away, Ashworth was chatting to Captain Lygon, the Honourable Henry Beauchamp Lygon to be precise. Ashworth was sitting cross legged, while Lygon, a tall man for a light dragoon, stretched out his full length on the dry, parched grass. The Sixteenth was turning into a good regiment, and Michael felt that this was where he belonged. Yet he also knew he might have to leave them, to answer another call. He determined to remember this evening.

The next morning started quietly enough, a little bread and cold, salted beef for breakfast, and a mug of very indifferent coffee. Michael was due to replace a picket of the Regiment that was lying out on the high ground across the Alberche, watching the road the Spanish had taken. Just before ten o'clock Michael pushed Johnny across a ford of the river, followed by Sergeant Evans, Lloyd, and another eleven dragoons, all from his troop. They found the picket on a high point from where they had an uninterrupted view across several miles of the plain. Michael was talking to Lieutenant Alexander, who he was relieving, when a dragoon called out.

"Rider, sir, coming fast."

They watched as the rider arrived at another picket, on lower ground between them and the Tagus. There was a moment's pause, and the rider was on his way again.

"That's interesting," said Alexander, "I think we will just wait here with you a while."

Half an hour later and they saw the familiar figure of Viscount Wellington, accompanied by a small group of staff officers, riding in the direction of the Spanish. As they watched them go, they were joined by Major Stanhope.

"Gentlemen," Stanhope greeted them and acknowledged their salutes, "Mister Alexander, if you are quite ready, perhaps you would be so good as to take your picket back now, and rejoin your troop?" Alexander always seemed to be getting into trouble. "The regiment is forming this side of our bivouac. I'm not sure what is happening, but Mackenzie's Division will be up here soon. Once they arrive, Roberts, you can come back as well."

What had happened, Michael learnt later, was that the retreating French had been reinforced, doubling their strength, and, realising the British were not with the Spanish, had turned on their pursuer. Now outnumbered in turn, the Spanish were making a hasty retreat back to Talavera. When the first of Mackenzie's Division appeared on the high ground, Michael could just make out a cloud of dust several miles away, the Spanish hurrying back.

Michael took his men back down to the river and across the ford. As they descended the gentle slope he could see the brigade formed and waiting, the men dismounted. On the near bank of the river they rode through the infantry division of Sherbrooke, moving into a position to support Mackenzie, and cover the retreat of the Spanish.

The day turned into yet another interminable wait, frustration mixing with nerves to put Michael on edge.

Through the afternoon the Spanish army came hurrying into view, but much to the surprise of the onlookers, they bivouacked on the far side of the river. The Sixteenth remained in the same position, sending men off in small numbers to water their horses, others to bring up provisions from the baggage, which had been sent some miles to the rear. Michael was standing alongside 'Old George' Thompson. "Ye know, George," said Michael, "I really don't understand why they are taking so long about it. I mean, you'd think old Cuesta would get his army across the river double quick, rather than wait to be attacked with it behind him."

Thompson glanced at Michael, and then turned back to watch the Spanish. "Hmm, yes, but I think things might begin to happen quicker tomorrow, and I lay odds you'll see the Spanish scuttle across the river fast enough."

Chapter 2

'Old George' was right. After a long night, the Spanish army began to cross the river by the bridge and the fords. Michael watched their allies with a vested interest in them, but thought they looked in very poor order, it was not a comforting thought. By noon, most were across, when French cavalry began to appear. As the last of the Spanish hurriedly crossed the river, the two British infantry divisions began their withdrawal back across the river. Cotton's brigade was also ordered to retire. The Sixteenth finally left the area they had been in for the last few days, and moved towards a prominent hill that lay to the north of Talavera.

As they marched, the sounds of a fierce fire fight reached them from behind. Volleys of musket fire crashed out, and anyone who glanced back could see clouds of white smoke billowing out. But they kept on regardless, walking at a steady pace, until they were finally ordered to halt, and the brigade was turned about to face the French. The two regiments were still in column of half squadrons, and Michael could see what was happening back towards the Alberche. As he watched, he saw Mackenzie's Division fighting its way back to join the rest of the army, drawn up on a line between Talavera to the right, and the hill to the left. Then Anson's Brigade of light cavalry appeared to help the infantry, and eventually they arrived in the British position, falling through the front line of infantry to form a second line.

To Michael's right he could just see the left flank of the Spanish army, which occupied the ground down to Talavera, and the town itself, on the bank of the Tagus. In front of him were two brigades of infantry, one behind the other. To their right he could just make out the infantry of the Guards' brigade. The Fourteenth Light Dragoons had shifted their position, and were now immediately to his right. Looking to his left, he could see Fane's brigade of heavy cavalry drawn up not far away, and beyond them Michael could see redcoated figures on top of the hill.

The French were quick to bring their artillery into play, their opening shots making everyone start and the horses to twitch and spook. Michael tried not to react, to sit calmly, and not give Johnny the idea that there was something to be worried about. Then the artillery fire built to a continuous, distant roar, with huge clouds of white smoke hanging in the hot, still air, and the horses settled again as the noise became a steady background rumble. By about seven o'clock, with the sun beginning to sink and cool, the French were visible in great dark, masses, and they began pressing forward in the direction of Talavera. They were still some considerable distance short of the town and the Spanish when, suddenly, a tremendous volley ran along the entire front line of the Spanish army, a great ripping sound, throwing up a long, billowing, line of smoke, that hung in the air. It did no harm to anyone, the Sixteenth's horses barely twitched an ear, but all at once there were masses of Spanish infantry running to the rear. They were shortly followed by Spanish cavalry, who soon after returned, herding the infantry back into place. Michael glanced at Ashworth, just to his left, who caught his eye and rolled his eyes skyward with out a word.

The Brigade finally moved a good way back from the infantry, in amongst some olive groves, and settled for a long night. Every man was at the head of his horse, which once again remained saddled, and stood, sat, or lay down to try to sleep with his reins in his hand. The baggage had been sent well to the rear, as had the officer's second horses. Michael would see the battle through on Johnny, for which he was glad. His other horse, Duke, was a splendid animal, a discreet gift from the Duke of York, who Michael had saved from an assassination attempt by

French agents. He had been offered large sums of money for Duke, but if it came to a fight, Michael would pick Johnny over any horse to carry him safely. The evening lacked the conviviality of the previous evening, there was little food, all the officers were at their posts with their squadrons, the atmosphere was subdued.

At about midnight every man in the regiment was brought to his feet as fierce firing broke out on the top of the hill where the left of the British line was anchored. Crashing volleys lit up the night sky, but no one had any idea what was happening, other than the French had apparently launched a night assault on the hill, which was the key to the whole position held by the British and Spanish armies. Eventually the firing died away, and, as no orders came, it was assumed the line had held.

A little later, as everyone was getting settled again, so far as was possible, another huge volley crashed out, this time from in front of the regiment. Immediately everyone leapt to their feet again, and given the direction of the firing, Stanhope ordered the regiment to mount. Then all was silent again. Stanhope waited, it stayed quiet, the only sound crickets chirruping away in the dark, and he gave the order to dismount. The regiment had no sooner dismounted than firing broke out again, this time from the direction of the Spanish.

Back amongst the olive groves Michael could see very little, just occasional flashes of light as volleys crashed out here and there. There was no chance of getting any sleep, everyone's nerves were on edge, and every man held firm to his horse's reins, ready to mount.

Just after dawn fighting broke out again on the hill top, but the curve of the hill hid everything, except huge clouds of white smoke marking the position of troops firing. Stanhope ordered the regiment to mount. Away to their right, the Fourteenth did the same. Through it all the French artillery kept up a steady bombardment, and now and then a stray cannon ball would fly overhead with a strange buzzing sound. After an hour and a half or so, the firing from the hill died away, the cannon fire decreased, and there seemed to be a lull. A staff officer trotted out of the trees, passing across the regiment's front. Stanhope called out to him and asked him what was happening?

"The French are cooking a meal!", came the reply.

Stanhope ordered the regiment to dismount. It was extremely frustrating. The belt of olive groves to the front made it impossible to see what was happening. In the respite, however, the regiment's Commissary officer appeared and was able to issue some bread and wine to everyone. The day was getting hot, and there was little water, only what was carried in canteens, and no chance of replenishing it. Michael could not begin to imagine what it was like for the infantry on the hill, fighting hard, mouths full of powder from biting cartridges open, and under incessant artillery fire.

In the afternoon the French artillery renewed their efforts, and soon after the sound of infantry fire came from in front. Still the brigade stood and waited. Then Michael heard a series of crashing volleys from in front, and the sounds of cheering that could only come from British infantry. Cotton ordered the brigade to mount. Michael took out his watch, it was just after half past three. Minutes later a staff officer burst from the olive trees and galloped to Cotton. A pause, and then Cotton put his horse into a walk towards the sounds of battle and waved for the regiments to follow him.

Major Stanhope's voice rang out loud and clear. "Sixteenth! March!"

The regiment advanced in column of half squadrons, Michael's leading, Ashcroft in front of him, following exactly the path picked out by Stanhope. The line was constantly broken and reformed as they moved slowly through the olive trees, men ducking and cursing, halting, and then pushing back into place.

Suddenly they were clear of the trees, Michael could see everything, and he felt his heart start to race as he took in the scene before him. A few hundred yards or so to his right front was a solitary brigade of British infantry, a mere three battalions standing in line. Falling back towards them were the scattered battalions of a whole British division, broken into groups from depleted battalions to half companies and smaller. Pressing hard on them were thousands of French infantry, and away to the left, he could see French cavalry advancing steadily, and threatening to charge. It was a desperate situation.

Once well clear of the trees, Stanhope calmly ordered the regiment to form line. Michael's half squadron was the left hand one, and halted, giving him time, too much time, to watch the rapidly deteriorating situation in front of him. As each of the following half squadrons got clear of the trees it wheeled right by threes, marched across the back of the regiment, then wheeled left by threes back into line, and advanced to line up on Michael's half squadron. Quickly the regiment formed its full line of four squadrons. Further to the right Michael could see the Fourteenth doing the same. Once the line was formed Stanhope gave another order, "Sixteenth! Draw", a brief pause, "Swords!" As one over five hundred glittering sabres were drawn. "Slope, swords!" And the sabres were rested on the dragoon's shoulders. Michael's hand nervously opened and closed around the sword grip, his white glove dirty and soft with sweat. The air was thick with drifting smoke, with its distinctive, sulphurous smell.

On the Regiment's right, Michael could just make out the Fourteenth moving forward to protect the open left flank of the infantry brigade to their right. Then Cotton galloped up to Stanhope, spoke briefly, and turned away to ride towards the Fourteenth. Stanhope gave his orders.

"Sixteenth!" A pause. "March". The Regiment began to walk forwards, and then, after a few paces, "Left," pause, "Incline," and every man turned his horse some thirty degrees to the left. Now the squadrons were still moving forwards, but also crabbing to the left, each man with his left knee behind the right knee of the man to his left, the front of each squadron still aligned as before.

The Sixteenth moved forward and left, slightly up hill. As they inclined the line and walked forward, Michael felt dreadfully exposed, he was the leading man on the Regiment's left, and he could see the dire situation they were steadily walking into. A brigade of infantry had fallen back, leaving a wide, inviting gap in the line, and into that gap the Sixteenth were calmly riding. Michael forced himself to remain still in the saddle, to regulate his pace, to keep his alignment, and to ride steadily forward into the battle.

Stanhope called out, "Forward", and everyman turned back to his right, straightening the direction of the line so it was moving straight forwards. A few yards advance allowed the squadrons to recover their alignment. Then Stanhope halted them, right in the middle of the gap. Behind the protective screen of the squadrons, the infantry started to gather themselves together and reform.

For a long quarter of an hour the regiment stood, plugging the gap in the line. The French artillery turned their attention to them. Cannon shot began to strike home, bringing down horses and men, throwing up gouts of soil, stones and dust where they struck the ground, while more went buzzing over head. With every minute that passed another horse or two was brought to the ground as a cannonball tore through the ranks, some disembowelled, others screaming and thrashing, legs broken, until a pistol shot put an end to the pain. Dragoons fell with their horses, some rolling clear, some uninjured, some crying out in agony or just lying still. Michael saw a dragoon in his squadron ripped from his horse as a cannonball tore through him, blood spraying all those around him. Miraculously, his horse was untouched. A young dragoon threw up, hanging off the side of his horse, retching with an empty stomach. And still the Regiment stood there, fighting to control horses sent plunging by near misses and horses falling by them, closing the gaps that appeared, moving to avoid the fallen horses, but moving neither forward nor back, steadfastly holding their ground. NCOs and officers shouted out instructions to keep the line closed. In front, Stanhope sat, immobile, with never a backward glance. Michael was now too busy managing the alignment of the squadron to feel any fear, but he saw men he knew pulled clear of their fallen horses and sent to the rear, many with leg injuries, others were just pulled to the rear and left lying under the burning sun, flies swarming to the drying blood.

For some reason the French failed to advance on the gap, and, suddenly, a British battalion came running down the hill and took up position in front of the Sixteenth. Then the French artillery switched their aim to the infantry, and the casualties stopped. So far as Michael could see they had lost perhaps half a dozen men killed, as many wounded, and three times as many horses, all without moving an inch.

To the right the retiring infantry was now streaming past the standing brigade, and then halting and trying to form themselves into organised units. To Michael's astonishment they were cheering as they did so. Then the French, a whole division of infantry, launched themselves at the British line. A savage firefight broke out, and musket balls and cannon balls began to fly over the Brigade, and some found their mark as more men and horses went down, but mercifully few.

The infantry in front of the Sixteenth were also now engaged in a dreadful, fierce firefight, shrouded in thick, white smoke, the French invisible save for the flash of their muskets. British cannon on the hill top added their fire to the fight. Soon, everything was obscured by great, white clouds of smoke, which was periodically pierced by the flash of massed volleys that ripped across the front. The smell of sulphur filled the air, clouds of smoke rolled gently over the Regiment, drifting along on a gentle breeze.

Michael looked to his left for the other cavalry brigade, Fane's, but there was no sign of them. He had no idea when or where they had gone, but it now looked as if Cotton's Brigade were on their own. Up on the slopes of the hill a fire started, and it swept quickly through the dry grass and sage bushes that grew on the hillside. It crossed ground where there had been fighting, where wounded men lay, and Michael was glad that the noise of battle drowned out all other sounds.

Gradually the superior firepower of the British infantry began to tell, and the infantry who had fallen back began show some semblance of order. Finally, the French started to fall back, slowly at first, and then they were gone. The firing died away, except for the continuing roar of the artillery, but, eventually, that too began to lessen. Finally, as dark descended, Major Stanhope gave the order to return swords, and dismounted the Regiment where it stood, on the same ground, amongst its casualties.

As the Sixteenth passed the night, it seemed to Michael as if it would never end. Men lay at their heads of their horses, both men and horses exhausted, hungry, and, above all, thirsty. Few managed to sleep. Michael's head was full of the images of the day, recalling over and over again the sight of men he knew being killed or maimed, one moment full of life and vitality, the next moment gone. He recalled the screams of men and horses. He thought of the words his grandfather had spoken to him, that wonderful Christmas almost two years ago. He could hear his voice. "There is no rhyme nor reason on the battlefield, only savagery and fortune, good and ill. You will lose friends and horses in brutal ways, and without warning." Now he understood.

Canteens were long empty, the little food that was produced by the commissaries for them was a third of the usual ration, for the horses there was nothing. Although they lay several hundred yards back from the scene of the main fighting, the sounds of shouts, screams and crying could be heard. The regiment's own casualties were light, and, once dealt with, their surgeon and his assistants had gone forward to see what help they could give. A few more wounded horses were dispatched by the farriers once the Veterinary Surgeon decided nothing could be done. The carcases of horses were stripped of saddles and furniture, and dragged a little way clear of their position. It was hard work, and of limited success. Six men had been killed, despite the regiment not engaging any enemy. Lieutenant Bence and five men were wounded. Remarkably, two men were simply missing. There were more horses killed than men, near to twenty. Michael and Johnny were both unscathed, but longing for water, Michael's lips were dry and cracked.

As the next day dawned Michael wearily got to his feet and looked at his men. They were all dog tired, hungry, thirsty, and dirty, some sported bandages, but every man stood at his horse's head waiting for the order to mount. He suddenly felt an overwhelming sense of pride, of belonging, and knew there was nowhere else he wanted to be. Cotton appeared, somehow managing to look immaculate, as if he was attending a review, Michael had no idea how he did it. He rode up to Stanhope, and spoke to him for a few minutes. Then Cotton rode over to Ashworth, with Stanhope walking alongside, leading his horse.

"Good morning, Ashworth." Michael could just hear Cotton's greeting.

"Good morning, sir."

"It would appear that the French have withdrawn in the night. Be a good fellow, take your squadron, and go and find out."

"Yes, sir."

"And water your horses the first chance you get."

"Yes, sir."

Cotton rode off in the direction of the Fourteenth. "Take it steadily, Ashworth." Stanhope smiled at Ashworth, and led his horse away.

Ashworth ordered the squadron to mount, closed up the two deep line, wheeled the squadron by threes to the left, which meant Michael was the leading officer, and took the squadron in column through the infantry to their front. It was slow going. There were bodies everywhere, British and French, and work parties were searching through them, looking for the wounded, gathering the dead together. The sun was not yet very high in the sky, but high and warm enough for clouds of flies to have appeared. There was already a sweet, sickly smell in the air. None of the squadron had eaten since the night before, and there were some pale faces.

Gradually the bodies thinned out, and a quarter of a mile or so beyond the British line, Ashworth halted the squadron. He turned his horse to face Michael. "Lieutenant Roberts, take Sergeant Evans and six men, and ride ahead. We will make for where you had your picket, when was it?" He paused, "Three days ago? No matter, you know where I mean, and I'm sure that I don't need to tell you take advantage of the first water you find." He gave Michael a wry smile. "And, please, be careful."

Michael took Evans and his six men, including Lloyd, and once clear of the front of the squadron he put them into a single skirmish line, well spread out, with himself in the middle of the line. On his orders they took their short, stubby carbines off the saddles, hooked them to their carbine belts, and loaded them. When all were ready, they moved off, carbines at the ready. At first they made their way through yet more olive groves, every man fully alert, but with visibility limited to a few yards by the trees. Michael halted the line, and spoke quietly to the nearest dragoon, "Pass it on, quietly, dismount."

Once on the ground they could see under the spread of the olive trees, and with their carbines rested in the crook of their arms, they were able to lead their horses forward with more confidence. There was not a sign of any French. The olive trees gave way to vineyards, and Michael ordered his patrol to mount. They could now see a good distance, and nothing moved anywhere. Everything was still, getting warmer, quiet save for the occasional buzz of an insect, the creak of saddles, or the tap of scabbard on spur. When they were, by Michael's reckoning, about half way to the river Alberche, they came across a narrow stream, of crystal clear water meandering its way through the vineyards. Michael halted the patrol to take advantage of it. He told off two dragoons to dismount, and while their comrades held their horses, to collect and fill all the canteens. He looked at his watch. It was nearing ten, and already getting hot. Then, two by two, he let all his patrol dismount and drink their fill direct from the stream, watering their horses at the same time, but careful not to let them drink too much.

While they were drinking, Ashworth and the rest of the Squadron caught up with them.

"Any sign of the French, Roberts?" Ashworth asked.

"Nothing at all, sir."

"Very good, you press on, we will follow your example, and make the most of the stream."

With more caution now, Michael led his patrol forward again, across the flat plain, towards the Alberche. As they moved out of the vineyards, his view became obscured by the trees and coppices that spread in all directions. Suddenly he could see the ground in front of him dipping away and down, and he signalled the patrol to halt. Slowly he walked Johnny forward, his senses alert for any sound or movement. Through a slight break in the trees he caught sight of sunlight reflecting off rippling water, the Alberche. He moved Johnny forward a few more paces, and then pulled him to a sudden halt. Fifty yards away, on the other side of the river, was a green coated French dragoon, sitting on his horse, and looking straight at him, his musket in his hands.

As Michael watched he saw the Dragoon turn his head, and heard him call out. A moment later he was joined by an officer, who looked at Michael, gave him a jaunty salute, and shook a finger at him. The message was clear, so far and no further. Michael returned the salute, and turned Johnny back into the cover of the trees, and the waiting patrol.

"Sar'nt Evans, there looks to be a cavalry screen along the other side of the river, they saw me, but just suggested I go no further, very politely, I don't think they're looking for a fight." He grinned. "Very decent of them." He got a few chuckles from the patrol. "Take Fletcher and work your way towards the Tagus, see if you can see how far the screen goes, Lloyd, take O'Rourke and work northwards for a mile or so. Go steady, keep your distance as much as you can, try not to provoke them. I'll stay here with Riley and Smith, and Williams, you ride back and report to Captain Ashworth."

Once everyone was away, Michael dismounted, handed his reins to Riley, left him and Smith where they were, and cautiously walked forward again. Now he knew where the river was he was able to approach behind cover, a little away from where he had first seen the French Dragoon. Where the Dragoon had been, with the officer, there were now half a dozen. They were just sitting quietly on their horses, a couple of them were smoking pipes. Michael walked back to Riley and Smith, and that was the last he saw of the French.

Ashworth came up with the Squadron, and established a line of vedettes along the river bank with half the Squadron. As was often the way, the French knew the dragoons were there, just as the dragoons knew where the French dragoons were, and each left the other in peace. The other half of the squadron was held back in reserve in a small clearing about a quarter of a mile from the river. Michael's patrols returned, and reported to him and Ashworth. Evans had found French dragoons all the way to the Tagus, and Lloyd said that the screen stretched more than a mile to the north. Later in the afternoon General Cotton and Major Stanhope appeared, guided by a dragoon Ashworth had sent back to report. They dismounted and joined Michael and Ashworth, who were sitting in the shade of an olive tree.

Ashworth was making his report to Cotton when reports started to come in from the vedettes that the French had disappeared. With the half squadron, Ashworth and Michael rode forward to investigate, Cotton and Stanhope with them. At the river's edge they halted, looking, listening, finding no evidence that the French had ever been there.

Cotton spoke. "Someone is going to have to go and have a look, see if they have gone, and where."

"Yes, sir." Stanhope replied, and then turned to Michael. "Mister Roberts, if you would be so kind, take your patrol, and do as the General wishes."

Once again Michael took his patrol forward. He moved slowly, nervously crossing the river, and pushing into the trees beyond. They rode quietly, spread out in a skirmish line, carbines cocked and at the ready. Eyes and ears strained for any sight or sound of the French. They saw nothing, save the occasional bird, heard only insects, and the quiet thud of hooves. It was getting dark when they finally reached the lookout point where they had been before, and watched the Spanish army returning. There was no sign of French cavalry, or a French army anywhere.

Chapter 3

Michael leaned back in his chair and looked up at the painted ceiling with its portraits of men in armour, framed by massive, gilt, timber beams. If anyone had told him six weeks ago, as they lay amongst the casualties at Talavera, that he would be celebrating his twenty first birthday with dinner in the Sala dos Duques in the Ducal Palace in Vila Viçosa he would have said "where?" and scoffed. And yet, here he was, surrounded by about twenty of his fellow officers, and relaxing with a glass of wine and a cigar after a splendid meal of game, fowl and venison. The dinner had been put together by the officers' servants, the fowl and venison having been shot in the Palace's park over the preceding two days. And it wasn't just the officers enjoying venison. There had been quite a few deer shot, and it made a welcome change from the scrawny beef on the hoof provided by the Commissary Department.

Michael took a sip of his wine and looked around the table. Sadly, there were more than a few absent faces. There were always absentees on duty, and Stanhope had chosen to stay away, but the regiment had been badly affected by an outbreak of Guadiana fever, almost a dozen officers were sick. Quartermaster Redmain and two dragoons in his troop had died. They were not suffering to the extent some of the infantry were, camped close to the river around the fortress town of Badajoz, but one of the Regiment's Assistant Surgeons had also died from it. Another had been left behind with the wounded at Talavera, and was now, presumably, a prisoner of the French. The army's wounded had been abandoned by the Spanish and all taken prisoner, save a few who had managed to flee. Mister Robinson, the surgeon, was now struggling on his own. Added to all that, Henry Bence was in Lisbon, still recovering from the musket ball he'd taken in the thigh at Talavera.

Lieutenant William Alexander sitting to Michael's left nudged him. "A penny for your thoughts, Michael?"

"Oh, I was just thinking about the change from our bivouac at Talavera, to this palace. It seems more like six months ago than six weeks."

Alexander gave a rueful smile, "Yes, I wouldn't like to go through that again. It was all a bit too close run with the French, and that bloody awful march over the mountains." Alexander was referring to the move Wellington had made from Talavera towards Soult and his army coming down from the north, only to discover, just in time, that Soult had received serious reinforcements, and that to meet him would have been a disaster. A gruelling retreat had followed, over rough mountainous paths in the August heat with the army half starved and constantly thirsty, until they reached the safety of Badajoz on the Spanish border. The regiment had lost more men and horses on the retreat and from illness than it had in the battle at Talavera.

"And now we sit here for three weeks and watch the Regiment die of fever!" Alexander took a drink. "I tell you, Michael, if we don't move soon we will be in a worse state than the Twenty-third."

Out of sight of Michael and the Sixteenth, the Twenty-third Light Dragoons had charged against French infantry at Talavera, only to find a deep, hidden stream bed in their way. In the resulting confusion and an attempt to press home their attack, they had lost almost half the regiment. "At least you seem to be unaffected by any illness. I suppose that is what comes of you being born out here?"

Michael chuckled. "That might be the case, Will, although I've never been in this part of Portugal before. But you are right, we need to move before I am the last officer standing!"

When the dinner party finally broke up there were still a few hours of daylight left, and Michael went back to his billet in the Palace, a pair of small rooms up in the roof. Francisco was busy cleaning Michael's spare boots. Leaving Francisco to carry on, he strolled down to the stables, where he found Parra. Both Johnny and Duke had suffered from the hardships of the retreat, but were looking much better for rest and reasonable fodder. Lloyd was nowhere to be seen, but Michael found him patiently walking Edward around outside as he tried to get him fit again. He left the men in peace and turned in.

A couple of weeks later Michael sat down at the small table in his quarters to give his full attention to a letter that had just arrived from his lawyer in London, Mister Rutherford. Now that he was twenty one he was his own man and had full control over his affairs. Rutherford's letter was very business like, and laid out exactly how much money Michael had, where it was invested, and what his income was from that. That included the money his uncle had been holding, and using to pressure Michael into leaving the army and joining him in his law practice in Falmouth. Mister Rutherford had put a stop to that, and had secured all the outstanding money held by his uncle. In addition he had his pay as a lieutenant, although his expenses as a lieutenant were somewhat in excess of that. Still, he was not a poor man, but neither a wealthy one. On the credit side, he had an annual income of some seven hundred and fifty pounds, and on the debit side a house in Lisbon to maintain, as well as his servants, both in Lisbon, the Santiagos, and with the Regiment. No, not wealthy, but quite comfortable, thank you. And he was painfully aware that some two thirds of the capital that gave him that income had been a bequest from Elaine.

Elaine, Lady Travers, who he had loved for a brief six months, and she him, before she was shot down in London by a French secret agent. The agent had turned out to be someone Michael had known when he was growing up in

Lisbon, Jean-Paul Renard, the son of a French diplomat. Michael had sworn to kill him, if could lay hands on him. It was a desire shared by Thomas Musgrave, the head of the British secret service, who Michael had been helping when he had met Elaine, and, fortuitously, also foiled the assassination attempt on the life of the Duke of York that had resulted in the discreet gift of his horse, Duke, from a grateful Duke.

Another letter, which had arrived two days ago, gave him more pause for thought. It had been delivered by an officer from the department of the Quartermaster General, Colonel Murray, and was a deciphered letter from Musgrave. In it he thanked Michael for the information he had obtained in Oporto regarding Renard, and his presence with the French army under Marshal Soult. He went on to inform Michael that the British Ambassador in Lisbon had been informed about Renard, and the threat he posed. He had been made aware of Michael, but without giving away his name or position in the army. The Ambassador had been told that he could reach Michael through Colonel Murray.

Michael lay on his bed and stared at the ceiling. In Oporto he had decided that he could fight in Musgrave's intelligence war, the dirty war as he thought of it, if only to avenge Elaine's death. In the last few months since Oporto, however, he had been engaged in proper soldiering, and he had enjoyed it. He had been hot, cold, hungry, thirsty, scared, excited, tired beyond belief, but he had never been alone. The Regiment had always been close. William Alexander was fast becoming a close friend, although he was going home on leave shortly. Two other officers were also homeward bound for the winter, Captain Pelly, and George Thompson. George had suffered badly with fever and was going home to recover, leaving Michael as the only lieutenant in his troop. On the other hand Major Archer was on his way out, and there were rumours that Major Stanhope was looking for a change of scenery.

Lloyd, his Welsh batman, was usually somewhere close by, if he wasn't with Michael's groom, Parra, and the horses. Those two had become as thick as thieves. As a consequence Lloyd's Portuguese had become quite passable, albeit with a Welsh accent. Lloyd, Parra, and young Francisco had all become more than just servants, they were, well, he struggled to find the words, but he did know he could rely on them completely.

As Michael lay, idly thinking over his circumstances, not once did it occur to him that he could resign his commission, return to England, and resume his old life of hunting, dining, billiards, and assemblies, and with no need to work at anything. He felt that he was where he ought to be, doing what he ought to be doing, with the people he wanted to be with.

The following morning brought good news, the regiment was ordered to move the very next day, and to Abrantes. The news brought a smile to everyone's face. They had spent nearly two weeks there before the advance to Talavera. The billets had been good, in villages just outside the town itself, and there had been plenty of fodder for the horses. Above all, it was a healthy area. This time they were going to be in the town itself.

Michael was not in the least bit surprised when Major Stanhope sent Michael on ahead of the regiment to organise and allocate billets. He might disapprove of Michael, but he made full use of his fluency in Portuguese. With so many sick to move, the regiment was going to make the march in four easy stages, Michael could do it in two days, giving him plenty of time in Abrantes before the regiment arrived. He took his horse, Duke, and was accompanied by Lloyd.

Abrantes stands on a hill topped by an old castle, and overlooks the Tagus. Michael and Lloyd approached it from the other side of the river, crossing by the long bridge of boats and riding up into the town. As they approached they were challenged by soldiers of the Portuguese garrison, and Michael was soon in the office of Colonel Lobo, the garrison commander. Lobo was delighted to find that Michael spoke Portuguese, and promised him that the quarters were all allocated, and that in the morning his adjutant would take Michael around the town so that he could mark them up.

"There is also," said the Colonel, "sufficient open ground between the town and the old castle to picket all your Regiment's horses, and it is not far from there to the river, and flat ground suitable for exercising them. The billets are all near the castle. Apart from men to watch the horses, you will not be in need of any sentries." He suggested one particular house for Michael. "Lieutenant, it is not the grandest in town, but it is one of the more comfortable houses, and perfect for an officer and a few servants."

"Thank you, Colonel, it all sounds perfect. I won't detain you any longer. If you could have someone show me to my quarters, I'll return in the morning. At nine o'clock?"

"Excellent, but, perhaps, tonight you will join myself and my officers for dinner? I will send someone to collect you in an hour."

Michael was guided to his billet by a Portuguese Lieutenant, and Michael was pleased with what he found. It was larger than he had expected given Lobo's comment, and belonged to a delightful, elderly Portuguese widow, Senhora Marquez, who fussed over Michael, and told her manservant to show them around to the stables. There was plenty of stabling, and, when they led their horses to it, they found already in residence, a stunning Arab chestnut mare.

"Now that, sir, is a very fine horse indeed," observed Lloyd.

"It is, Lloyd. I doubt it belongs to our hostess, perhaps some friend stables it here. Anyway, there's plenty of room for Duke and Edward, and Johnny and the others when they get here. I'll go and find the Senhora and see what there is for us in the house."

Michael left Lloyd to deal with the horses, and carrying his valise, made his way into the house, looking for his hostess. Dropping his valise on a hall chair, along with his tarleton, he took a guess, and opened a door off the hall.

Seated, reading, at a small table by the window was a young woman. Michael judged her to be about his age. Thick, lustrous, black hair was artfully piled on her head, her face slightly oval, her eyes deep brown, her cheek bones fine, her nose straight and delicate, her lips red and perfectly formed. Michael was suddenly very aware of just how shabby he must look after two days on the road without shaving.

Her eyes flickered over him from head to foot and back again, and then pinned him with a look of severe concentration. To Michael's further surprise she spoke in English, slowly and hesitantly. "Sir, you are the English officer come to stay with my Aunt?"

"Senhorita, forgive me for intruding, Senhora Marquez is your Aunt?" Without thinking Michael had replied to her in Portuguese. A brilliant smile flashed across her face.

"Oh, you speak Portuguese! Wonderful, now I won't have to practice my awful English on you."

Michael smiled in return, "Your English sounded quite charming, Senhorita."

She smiled, and tipped her head slightly to the side, and Michael felt his heart lurch at the movement. Memories of Elaine washed over him. She had had the same mannerism. There was a momentary silence as they looked at each other. There must have been something in his look, she frowned, and opened her mouth to speak. Then Michael was aware of movement behind him, he stepped aside to find Senhora Marquez in the doorway, and the moment was gone. "There you are, Lieutenant! I see you have found my niece. My dear, this is Lieutenant, I'm sorry, forgive me…"

"Michael Roberts, Senhorita." Michael gave a slight bow.

"My niece, Maria Barros. She and her father are here for a few days, my brother has some business near here. He should be here soon, for dinner, will you join us Lieutenant?"

"Thank you, Senhora, but I regret that Colonel Lobo has already invited me to join him." He wasn't sure, but Michael thought he saw a slight flicker of disappointment on the Senhorita's face.

"Well, never mind, tomorrow then, I insist. Now, let me show you your rooms." And the Senhora bustled off down the hall. Michael gave another slight bow to Senhorita Barros, and followed her.

Michael was given a small, but comfortable room at the back of the house, and a room was given to Lloyd and Francisco on the floor above, with a window overlooking the stables, much to Lloyd's satisfaction. Parra would be in a room off the stables, but Lloyd always liked to be near 'his' horses. As promised, Michael was collected, by the same lieutenant who had guided him to the house. Dinner was perfectly pleasant, Lobo was a good host, and his officers were good company. Lobo insisted that Michael was escorted back to his billet, and the same lieutenant was detailed to accompany him.

A soft tap at the door, and the manservant opened it to admit Michael. "Good evening, Senhor, the ladies have retired, but Senhor Barros is still up, and asked if you would care to join him for a nightcap."

"That's very kind, I will, can you take my helmet and sabre?"

The man did, and then indicated a door to Michael. "Please, Senhor, just go in."

As Michael pushed the door open, a man rose from a chair by the fire, and held out his hand. "Lieutenant Roberts? It is a pleasure to meet you."

Michael shook the proffered hand, "Thank you, sir." Senhor Barros was a man of about fifty, greying hair tied in a pigtail, Michael could see the likeness to his daughter.

"Please, take a seat. A glass of brandy?"

"Thank you, yes."

Barros turned to a side table and poured Michael a glass. "Now, would you be the son of Edward Roberts of Lisbon?"

"Yes, sir."

"Ah ha! I was correct. I did wonder when my sister told me your name and that you spoke fluent Portuguese." He handed the glass to Michael and resumed his seat. "I knew him a little. Not well, you understand, but we did business on a few occasions." He paused. "I am sorry to hear of the loss of your parents, please, accept my condolences."

Michael nodded his acknowledgement.

"And now you are back in Portugal to liberate us from the Great Tyrant?"

Michael found Senhor Barros easy to talk to, and some time passed convivially before Barros rose from his chair, Michael rising as well. "And now, Senhor, you must excuse me. I have more business to conduct tomorrow, and must make an early start, and I am sure you also have duties to attend to. So I shall bid you good night."

Michael rose early, shaved and dressed, found breakfast waiting in the dining room, but of Senhor and Senhorita Barros and Senhora Marquez, there was not a sign. A question to the manservant elicited the information that Senhor Barros had ridden off at seven o'clock, his daughter with him, and that Senhora Marquez never appeared before ten. So, Michael took breakfast alone, and then went out to the stables. Lloyd was busy with their horses.

"Morning, Lloyd, I gather others have been up and about before us?"

"Bore da, sir. They have indeed, the young lady was on that fine chestnut, and mighty fine she looked on it as well, sir. The gentleman had quite a nice bay gelding, but both a bit too fine for a cavalry horse, sir. Still, the filly is pretty enough."

Michael looked hard at Lloyd, who looked back with a straight face.

As promised, Michael was called for at nine o'clock, by the same young lieutenant, and after paying his respects to Colonel Lobo, he spent the rest of the day finalising arrangements for the regiment. Billets were identified and allocated. There was a fine, large house for Major Stanhope and the regimental staff officers, with a large enough dining room and kitchen to act as a mess. Lobo lent him some of his men, and Michael was able to get horse lines set up. That would please everyone when they arrived. The garrison had a supply of water in the castle, in huge underground tanks, but that wouldn't suffice for the Regiment's horses. They could be ridden down to the river each day, but Michael also arranged for a carter to bring up barrels of water several times a day, every day.

Eventually everything was finished. Michael thanked the lieutenant for his help, and made his way back to Senhora Marquez's house. Lloyd had passed a quiet, if productive day. He had lightly exercised both horses, and then taken the opportunity to strip down and thoroughly clean all the accoutrements and effect a few minor repairs. Damp horse blankets were drying in the sun, flounces were airing, and bridles hung, clean and polished. As the two men stood in the stable yard there was a clatter of hooves and Senhor and Senhorita Barros rode in.

Lloyd, thought Michael, was right, a very pretty filly, both of them. Senhorita Barros was dust covered, and sweat streaked her face. Some of her hair had escaped from under her stylish hat. And there was no doubting that she sat her horse very well. All in all she was a very attractive sight. Very. She smiled at him.

"Senhor Roberts, have you have had a good day?"

Michael moved to assist her, but he had barely taken three steps when she had swung her right leg clear of the side-saddle horn, kicked her left foot free of the stirrup, and dropped to the ground. As she did so Michael caught a glimpse of long riding boots before her habit dropped into place. She caught his eye, and gave him a smile that was mischievous and daring at the same time. He stopped, and grinned back. Then she tipped her head again, and Michael was lost.

By the time they assembled for dinner, Michael had recovered his equilibrium, and hoped that he could control the emotions raised by the memories Maria Barros had stirred. As it was, dinner passed off well enough, the conversation was a little stilted at times, but that was nothing remarkable between strangers. Senhor Barros was happy enough to talk to Michael about his business. It seemed that he did quite well from the production of olive oil, honey and silk, although the silk trade was declining in the face of competition from elsewhere in the world.

Senhora Marquez seemed content to let her brother keep the conversation going. Senhorita Barros said little, but every time that Michael glanced at her she seemed to be studying him with some interest. It was quite disconcerting.

Dinner ended, Senhora Marquez announced she would retire for a little rest, and that there would be a little supper at nine o'clock. Senhor Barros said he had some correspondence he needed to deal with, and that he would join them for supper. Senhorita Barros looked at Michael and suggested that as there was still some daylight left, perhaps they could take a stroll in the garden. Michael was trapped by the manners expected of a gentleman. He turned to Senhor Barros, "With your permission, sir, I should be glad to."

The garden was not large, but there was a small arbour, in clear view of the house, and soon Michael found himself seated there with Senhorita Barros. He was not feeling entirely at ease, with Senhorita Barros or himself.

"So, Lieutenant Roberts of Lisbon, our fathers were acquainted? Does that mean I can call you Michael? Lieutenant Roberts seems so formal." Senhorita Barros took the initiative, putting Michael on his back foot.

"Senhorita, if you wish…"

"No, do you wish?"

"Yes, of course," Michael replied. He felt little choice in the matter, and he thought the situation was already running away from him.

"And you may call me Maria, if you wish." She smiled. "There, now we are friends. Like our fathers." The smile vanished. "But I am sorry to hear what happened to your parents, my father told me the story today, while we were riding."

"Thank you." He paused. "Maria."

There was silence for a minute or two. Somewhere Michael could hear a bird singing in the gathering gloom. The warmth of the day was beginning to ebb away.

"I think, Michael," Maria spoke with carefully measured words, "that you have a deep, sad secret. I saw it on your face today when we met. It was almost as if I reminded you of someone?"

Michael tried to laugh. He was positively disconcerted by this young woman. He had hardly known her for a few hours, yet she had perceived that there was something hidden, and come dangerously close to the truth.

"Forgive me, Michael, I am too forward. My father and my aunt despair of me at times. I suppose it is because my mother died giving birth to me, and I was raised by my father, with my older brother. It was not always an upbringing for a lady. I ride astride better than I do aside." She laughed. "Now I have shocked you. This is not a very good start."

"No, I am not shocked, a little surprised perhaps." Start to what, he thought?

"Well, we had better go in before a search party is sent out. Now that would be shocking. But first, tomorrow, will you ride with me? Father will be busy in Abrantes all day, I know you have done all that you need to do, and I also know that your regiment will not arrive until the day after tomorrow, so you have no excuse."

"How do you know…"

She put a soft finger to his lips, and held it there for a moment. The familiarity of the action took all the words from Michael's mouth. "We women have our ways, Michael, but then, I suspect that you know that already. Now, escort me back to the house like a gentleman should."

Lying on his bed later that night Michael's thoughts were confused. Maria had sparked something inside him that he had not felt in a long time, not since had he met Elaine. She was, he had to admit, different from any other girl of that age he had met. And perhaps that was it, they were girls. Maria had the maturity, the confidence of a woman, more like Elaine, more like his friend and lover Roberta. She seemed to have a sense of humour, and of mischief, that was appealing. She was, so far as he could tell on such a short acquaintance, intelligent and well educated. That, he assumed, was her father's influence. She could certainly sit a horse well. But she was not Elaine. She might flirt with him, and he might enjoy it, but he still belonged to another.

At nine o'clock the next morning Lloyd was ready with Duke and Edward both tacked up. The Barroses' groom, Raul, was also ready, with Maria's mare and his own horse. Senhor Barros had readily agreed to Maria's suggestion that she and Michael could ride with Lloyd and their groom for protection. For whom and from who she didn't say.

From Abrantes they rode west, along the Tagus, towards the small town of Constancia, from there they planned to ride a little way up the river Zezere before making their way across country back to Abrantes. Michael and Maria took the lead, followed by Lloyd and Raul. Michael noticed that Lloyd's horse, Edward, seemed to be having a little difficulty keeping up, never dropping too far back, but never getting closer than about ten yards. Michael had a little smile to himself.

When you ride out in good company, and in fine weather, neither too hot, nor too cold, the horses seem to just eat up the miles. It was just such a September day, and Michael soon found Maria to be very good company. Within the first hour they were talking away as if they had known each other for years. He told her all about his life, growing up in Lisbon, his time in Falmouth, she laughed at his tales of hunting, he told her about how he came to be in the army, about the lighter side of soldiering. She asked about his scar, he gave her Musgrave's explanation, she looked disappointed. Of Musgrave, Renard and Elaine he told her nothing. Maria told him about her life, growing up without a mother, trying to keep up with her brother, two years older than her, about her first pony, how proud she was of her brother who was a captain in a regiment of Caçadores, the Portuguese light infantry. It appeared that she had no particular admirer.

They paused for refreshment in Constancia, then rode north, along the Zezere, a narrow valley with steep, wooded sides. A little way up the valley Maria turned up a steep track, through the trees, the horses scrabbling for purchase on soft, sandy soil. In the trees it was cooler, there was no breeze at all, and the smell of the pines was thick in the air. After a few hundred yards the ground levelled off, the trees thinned, and they emerged on to a ridge, running east, parallel with the Tagus.

Maria pointed to a hill top a couple of miles ahead. "I shall wait for you there." She tapped her mare lightly on its flank with her whip, and was into a flat gallop in a few strides.

Behind him Michael heard Raul shout "Senhorita, Senhorita." Then Lloyd called, "Best get after her, sir!" Michael stroked Duke's flanks gently with his spurs, the horse needed no further encouragement, and he was away like the English hunter he was. The Arab was a horse for endurance, and it was carrying a lot less weight than Duke, but Duke was in fine fettle, used to the weight, and settled to a steady gallop, two miles would be nothing to him. The gap was thirty yards or so, and it didn't change. He took a quick look behind, and glimpsed Raul and Lloyd a hundred yards or more behind. He wasn't sure, but he thought Lloyd was grinning.

Half way to the hill top he saw Maria look back at him, and the Arab slowed slightly, allowing Duke to gain. Slowly he pulled alongside, Maria looked at him and smiled, and they covered the last half mile side by side, pulling up the panting horses on the top of the hill. They looked at each other, and started to laugh with pure exhilaration. Slowly they calmed down, and Maria looked at Michael with an intensity that spoke volumes.

Then Raul arrived, crying out, "Senhorita, Senhorita, are you alright?" And then Lloyd trotted up on Edward, "Chwarae teg, but that was a fine contest, sir! And I'm I thinking the young lady won."

The remainder of the ride passed uneventfully, Michael and Maria riding without speaking much, but exchanging many, many looks and smiles. Lloyd kept up an incessant chatter with Raul, ostensibly trying to improve his Portuguese, and discussing horses. Truth be told, he was happy for Michael. Truth be told, despite the smiles, Michael was deeply troubled.

On their return to Abrantes, Michael found, with some relief, an invitation to dinner from Colonel Lobo waiting for him. He informed Senhora Marquez that, regrettably, he would not be joining them for dinner as duty called. Over her shoulder he saw Maria frown, and look thoughtful. Senhora Marquez said she had better speak to her cook, and left Michael and Maria alone.

"I am sorry, Maria," Michael explained, "but I can't afford to offend the Colonel."

"I understand, Michael. And tomorrow your regiment arrives, and we leave for Lisbon." She had just a hint of a sulk in her voice. There was a silence, while both struggled for words. "Shall I see you again, Michael? Perhaps in Lisbon? Do you want to see me again?"

"Yes, of course." Inside, Michael was struggling with himself. He felt he was just going through the motions to avoid hurting Maria.

"And when will that be? Oh, I know you can't say. The army could go anywhere, you could be killed." She paused. "Michael, is this a good idea?"

"I… I don't know." No, a voice screamed in his head. No, this is not a good idea. "We hardly know each other; anything could happen to me. Perhaps…" His voice faltered. He thought of Elaine.

"Perhaps we should just keep today, and make each other no promises?" She forced a little laugh. "And who knows who you might meet at your next billet?"

"Maria, please, don't speak like that." But the voice in Michael's head sighed with relief and said take the escape route.

"No, Michael? Can you make me any promises? No, I won't ask you for that. Better no promises at all."

Michael thought of the last time he had made a promise to a lady, and seized on her words. "You are right," he said, "better no promises at all." He thought he saw a flicker of disappointment, but he didn't want to hurt Maria, something that would be only all too possible. Better to stop now, before it was too late. "But I will never forget today," he threw her a bone, and felt bad.

She gave Michael a little curtsey of acknowledgement. Michael hesitated, gave a slight bow in return, and then without another word he turned and left the room.

Michael didn't see Maria again before she left Abrantes for Lisbon.

Dinner with the Colonel turned into a discussion about the regiment's needs, and the arrangements made. A late night was followed by a dawn start to finalise and check all the arrangements. Michael knew everything was ready, but keeping away from Senhora Marquez's house until he was sure Maria had left seemed like a good idea.

Chapter 4

The regiment marched in at midday, having been on the road at dawn every day, but halting to avoid the heat of the afternoon. Major Stanhope was pleased with the arrangements, and, albeit with a grudging tone, complimented Michael. The mess was quickly established, which relieved Michael of having to spend too much time in his billet. Lloyd realised things had not gone well with Maria, and kept his head down, spending time in the stables with Parra and the horses.

Within two weeks the condition of the regiment began to improve as men recovered from the fever and the horses began to recover their condition. A new Assistant Surgeon also arrived, much to the relief of Mister Robinson. As he had done before, Michael threw himself into the work of the Regiment, pushing himself hard. He kept himself away from his billet and Maria's aunt. He knew he was unable to cope with any sort of romantic liaison, not with Elaine's memory so fresh, the bonds tying him to her still so strong. Then he was summoned to the Adjutant's office, where he found Lieutenant Barra and Major Stanhope waiting for him.

"Ah, Mister Roberts!" Stanhope was holding a folded letter and something in his voice told Michael that he was not a happy man. "It seems that once again the Regiment is going to have to manage without your services. I have received orders that you are to make all haste to Lisbon, and there you are to report to Mister Villiers, the Ambassador, no less." He looked at Michael. "I don't suppose that you can explain this order?"

"No, sir, I'm afraid not."

"Hmm, I thought not. Well, I don't like it Mister Roberts, I don't like it at all. I suppose it is more of this secret malarky? You need to decide Mister Roberts, are you an officer of this Regiment, or are you a spy?" Behind him Barra rolled his eyes to the heavens. "Despite your background you have the makings of a fair regimental officer, but can we count on you, or not?"

Michael was angered. "With all due respect, sir, I didn't ask for any of this, but Lord Harcourt seems happy enough about it." Earl Harcourt was the regiment's Colonel and familiar with Michael's work for Musgrave.

"With all due respect, sir," Stanhope's voice dripped sarcasm, "Lord Harcourt is in London, and I command here, and I'll thank you to remember that."

A stony silence fell, eventually broken by Stanhope. "Well, Mister Roberts, I don't like it, I don't like it at all, but it seems that, on this matter, I have no say in the running of the regiment. So, you had best get a move on. I suppose that you will be taking Lloyd with you?"

"Yes, sir, if there's no objection."

"No, Lloyd has been a reformed character since he became your batman, which is something, I suppose. Try and keep him that way. Dismissed."

"Thank you, sir."

A flurry of activity followed, but an hour later Michael was on his way, with Lloyd, Parra, and Francisco. Michael's retinue had grown, and a pair of baggage mules had been added, now led by Francisco on Fred, the pony. With the animals all rested and fit, they made good progress, following the north bank of the Tagus until they reached Santarem where they had an overnight stop. After a late dinner, Michael relaxed with a cigar and a glass of wine, and wondered about his summons to Lisbon. Given the letter from Musgrave, he expected that he was once more about to become a participant in the intelligence war, the dirty war. He hoped it might somehow involve Renard. At least he would be able to spend some time in his home, and to catch up with Roberta.

Their unexpected arrival at Michael's house in Lisbon, early the following evening, sent Senhora Santiago bustling around the house, trying to arrange everything at once. Eventually, Michael made her stop, and concentrate on preparing food. "Senhora, Babá, no more, please, Lloyd and Francisco can arrange the rooms. If you could just get us some bread, cold meat, cheeses, anything, and a couple of bottles of wine, that will be wonderful."

Parra was introduced to the Santiagos, he had never been to Lisbon before. After they had unloaded everything into the house, Michael said to Lloyd and Parra, "Take all the horses and the mules round to Juan Moreno's, they will have to stay there, and you can let him know how the boys are." Moreno's son, Pedro, and his friend Rafael worked as grooms for the other officers of Michael's troop. A thought struck him, and he asked Santiago, "Is there nowhere we can stable the horses and mules at the back of the house? It would be useful to be able to access the house from the back as well."

Santiago thought for a moment. "Yes, Senhor, I think there might be something. I can look into it tomorrow."

"Good, if it's suitable, then we can find the owner, and discuss a price for renting."

"Renting, Senhor? Your father bought the land three years ago, and it has a storehouse on it!"

Michael raised his eyebrows. "Really?" He thought for a moment. "I think I remember where you mean. Well, so much the better. We shall see what can be done." He turned to address Lloyd and Parra.

"Lloyd, Parra, you get off now to Moreno's. Lloyd, tomorrow, first thing, I want you and Parra and Francisco to go out to Belem, and get my heavy baggage out of storage. It might as well be here as rotting in a warehouse. Then have a look at this storehouse at the back of here, see if it will make stables. Francisco, help me get unpacked, and then you can go and see your sister. You can stay with her tonight. Tell Senhorita Roberta I'm back, but make sure you are back here early tomorrow morning to go to Belem." Francisco nodded enthusiastically. His older sister, Constanca, was Roberta's maid. Michael assumed that by now Lloyd was well aware of Roberta, although he had not yet met her, and that he also knew that she and Michael were lovers as well as friends.

By the time Lloyd and Parra returned, Francisco had gone, and a meal was waiting for them in the kitchen. Michael was sitting alone in the dining room, a bottle of wine to hand, replete after a wholesome, but simple dinner. He had pushed his chair back and stretched out his legs. He was painfully aware that somewhere in Lisbon Maria was probably just finishing dinner herself. He had no idea where, and even if he did, what would he do? Had there been something real between them or was it just a passing infatuation? Had he thrown something away, or had a narrow escape? This time he was bound by not having made a promise. And he still felt bound to Elaine. It was only a year since she had died. She had written, releasing him, telling him love could come again, but he didn't know if he was ready to accept that release, or to risk heartbreak again. Well, tomorrow he had to go and see the Ambassador, he would discover if his suspicions were correct, and then, when he could, he would go and see Roberta. He needed a friend to talk to.

The following morning Michael's suspicions about the reason why he had been called to Lisbon were proved to be well founded. He had quickly been admitted to the Embassy, the guards had expected him, and he was soon in the Ambassador's office. He was a little surprised when the ambassador dismissed his secretary, leaving the two of them alone.

"Lieutenant Roberts, please. Take a seat." He indicated two comfortable armchairs near the fireplace. "Now, forgive me, but I only discovered who to expect yesterday, and I will admit that I did not expect a lieutenant of a light dragoon regiment! However, I have been given to understand by Mister Musgrave that you know by sight this French agent, Renard?"

"Yes, Your Excellency, and by more than sight, we grew up together here in Lisbon."

"Good Lord, I didn't expect that. Well, the fact is, Roberts, that he has been seen, here in Lisbon, no more than ten days ago. He needs to be caught, and caught quickly, and you are here to help do just that."

It was Michael's turn to be surprised. "In Lisbon, sir? Are you sure? I beg your pardon, sir. May I ask who saw him, sir? There can't be many people who would know him."

"Apparently an agent of the Chief of Police, do you know General de Silva?"

"No, sir."

"Well, you're going to. He's expecting a visit from a British officer who knows Renard, and I've given him your name. He will be in charge of the search for him, and you are to render all possible assistance." Villiers paused. "I don't need to tell you how important it is that we catch this fellow. He's damned dangerous and too damn good at what he does. Fortunately the Spanish guerrillas have been making it all but impossible for the French to get agents into Portugal, but this fellow can pass for a native Portuguese, as, indeed can you. Do you have civilian clothing?"

"Yes, sir."

"Good, you'll need it. Sorry to ask you to abandon your uniform, but needs must, eh? Although I suspect it's not the first time? No, don't tell me. You know where de Silva's headquarters are?"

"Yes, sir."

"Right, well, you cut along there now, as I said, you are expected, so there should be no difficulty getting in to see him." Michael rose from his chair and turned towards the door. "And, Roberts, make sure you keep me informed of everything that happens, and be careful. Musgrave seems to think quite highly of you, and I would hate to have to explain to him if anything happened to you."

"Yes, sir." Michael reached the door.

"Oh, yes, and Viscount Wellington also thinks highly of you. Now, off you go."

"Yes, sir, thank you."

Michael's mind was spinning as he walked to de Silva's headquarters. Renard in Lisbon! Could it be true? Well thought of by Musgrave and Wellington! Now that was something to put in the balance against Major Stanhope's opinion. He wondered who the Portuguese agent could be that knew Renard. Perhaps one of the other boys he had run with now worked for de Silva.

Getting in to see the Chief of Police, Lieutenant General Lucas Seabra de Silva, proved to be as quick and easy as getting in to see the Ambassador. De Silva seemed pleased to see Michael, he greeted him warmly, offered him coffee, and soon they were seated on opposite sides of de Silva's desk, ready to get to the business in hand. Michael noticed that there was a third, unused cup and another, empty, chair.

"Lieutenant Roberts, I am very glad to have your assistance in this matter. As far as I know you are one of only two people who can be trusted to identify Renard.

You, and one of my most valuable agents in Lisbon." He smiled. "And I know you can be trusted, because my agent tells me so." How on earth, thought Michael, could one of de Silva's agents tell him that? "But, first, what I need, Lieutenant, is your absolute assurance, your word as an officer and a gentleman, that you will never reveal to anyone, not even to your Mister Musgrave, yes, yes, I know him, a splendid fellow, by the way, keeps an excellent cellar, anyway, your word Lieutenant, that you will never reveal the identity of my agent to anyone?"

"General de Silva, you have my word, sir."

"Excellent." De Silva smiled. "Then, Lieutenant Roberts," Michael heard a door open behind him, "let me present you to Senhorita Roberta de Silva." Michael spun round.

"Hello, Michael."

"Roberta!" Michael was speechless as she came, smiling, into the room.

De Silva roared with laughter. "Forgive me Lieutenant, please, forgive me. Oh, the look on your face! Priceless!" He laughed again. "Yes, yes, your friend is my agent. And a very good one. Now, no recriminations, please, Lieutenant, you could not tell Roberta about your activities for Musgrave, and she could not tell you about hers for me. And now you both know, and must still be friends, I insist."

Roberta smiled at Michael, and as de Silva bent to pour her a coffee, she mouthed at Michael, "Later". Michael smiled back, and nodded.

As they sat and drank coffee, de Silva told Michael that they believed Renard had set up a small network of agents in Lisbon while he was in the city in '07 with the occupying French forces under Marshal Junot. It was probably to check on that network and to maintain it that Renard had come back, taking advantage of the British army being far away in Spain. The task in hand was simple. Find Renard, find the network, and destroy both. De Silva made no secret of his preference for Renard and his agents simply disappearing.

Later, Michael and Roberta lay in bed together at her house. Michael had known she had been married, despite calling herself Senhorita, and Roberta explained that de Silva was the cousin of her late husband, who had died soon after they were married, leaving her a wealthy widow. As a result of her being well connected in Lisbon society, she had first become a useful source of gossip for de Silva. Then she had started to supply specific information that he asked for. Soon, frankly out of boredom, she had become an active agent, and eventually a very effective agent. Her identity as an agent was a very well kept secret.

By pure chance, she had been visiting a friend when, from a window, she had seen Renard calmly strolling down the street as if he had not a care in the world. He had not looked up, had not seen her, so the one advantage they had was they knew he was in Lisbon, he didn't know that they knew. The question was, how to find him and his network? But Roberta wanted to know something else, about something Michael had told her when he had first returned to Lisbon, and now she could ask.

"Michael?"

"Yes."

"Your friend, your lover, in London?"

"Elaine."

"Yes. I know you told me that Renard killed her." She looked for the right words, but Michael spoke first.

"Yes, she was an agent for Musgrave, that is how we met."

"As I am for the General."

"Yes, I suppose so. But it's not the same, you and I, we…" he struggled to explain.

"No, Michael, it's not the same, its alright, I understand."

They were silent for a while. Then Michael started to talk.

"She wrote me a letter," Michael started, "I was given it after she died." Roberta stroked his hair while he struggled to find the words he wanted. "You see, she had made me promise never to love her, because of the dangers of what she did. We weren't supposed to fall in love, but we did, and we said nothing to each other. Then just before she died she asked me if I had broken my promise, I said I had." Michael paused, took a deep breath. "She said she loved me as well. Then she died." A tear ran down his cheek. "In her letter she wrote that she hoped we would know we loved each other. Then she released me from any ties, and told me I might, could love again."

After a moments silence Roberta spoke, "Michael?"

"Yes?"

"Thank you for telling me that."

Michael couldn't help himself, and he gave in to the need to unburden himself. As he lay in the bed, in the arms of his lover, of his best friend, and now his fellow agent, he told her the whole story of his time with Elaine, then about Maria, and the internal conflict he had suffered. Roberta listened without interruption. When he had finished he asked her forgiveness for sharing his problems with her.

"Michael, there is nothing to forgive. I have never had a friend like you, someone to love as a friend. And I hope we will be friends long after we are no longer lovers. And I would never, ever stand between you and anyone you love. Our friendship is more important than our, our, well, our affair, for want of a better way of putting it. And when you do find your true love, we will still be friends. As for Maria, or anyone else, first, you need to decide whether or not you are a free man, as Elaine told you to be. And then, Michael, you need to be careful. Be very sure of yourself before you love another again, and be sure of them. True love can come again, but it is rare."

Michael lay quiet for a minute. "Thank you, Roberta, I couldn't ask for a better friend."

"Good, now get yourself off home. It's getting late, and you are not staying the night." She kissed him. "So, be on your way, I do not want any man seeing me first thing in the morning!"

The following morning Michael joined the search for Renard and his network. He was accompanied by Lloyd, who had acquired civilian clothes with the help of Santiago and looked particularly villainous, with a broad brimmed hat and a black cloak slung dramatically over one shoulder. He also seemed to be enjoying himself as informants were interrogated and houses raided. As he said, "Duw, sir, it's better than being chased by Sergeant Taylor to get on and clean something." Roberta had found rooms on the street where she had seen Renard, and had already spent several days seated at the window, watching the passers-by, three of De Silva's men on hand should she see Renard.

After the first day, Michael was back at his house, finishing unpacking his stored baggage. He was already carrying the sword stick that Elaine had given him, and Francisco and Senhora Santiago were taking the opportunity to clean and repair all of his uniform. The storehouse had proved perfect for stabling, it was more than big enough for Michael's animals, and Parra and Santiago were hard at work preparing it with the help of a couple of carpenters that Santiago knew. At the bottom of his trunk Michael found the oilskin wrapped package. With great care he unwrapped it. He put the picture of Elaine on the table by his bed, and then reread her letter. It told him he was free to love again, but a letter was not the same as hearing it from her, and now he never could.

The second day passed much like the first, with no tangible reward for all their efforts. De Silva was getting worried that all the activity would scare Renard off. Then, on the third day, one of de Silva's men brought Michael a message telling him to go to Roberta's rooms. De Silva was there, they had possible news. An informer had mentioned an inn on the edge of the city, he had heard someone ordering a meal in fluent Portuguese, but when he had knocked over a glass, spilling his wine, he had cursed in French. The informant had been a seaman and frequently in French ports. And yes, he thought the man had a room there. The description he gave sounded like Renard.

Michael made a suggestion. If de Silva would place men, discreetly, around the inn, he would ride up as if coming to Lisbon. He would deliberately put on a French accent, and then he would make enquiries for his friend. If they just went crashing in and he wasn't there, they would show their hand, and Renard would just disappear. This way, if he wasn't there, they could quietly withdraw and wait. De Silva liked it, Roberta didn't, she didn't like the idea of Michael going in to the inn alone, but in the end they went with Michael's idea.

They were two days too late. The landlord identified Renard from Michael's description without any hesitation to suggest he was lying. The gentleman had suddenly left two days ago, and ridden off towards Spain. No, he didn't think it was suspicious that he had cursed in French. Looking for foreigners was the job of the police. De Silva explained to the landlord who he was, that it was about French espionage, how it was his duty to assist them, and what might befall him if he didn't. With that encouragement, the landlord admitted that Renard had received some visitors, and, most importantly, he said that he had recognised one of them. He readily gave them a name, and where they might be found. It was the breakthrough they needed.

Within a few hours the man named had been arrested and his rooms searched. Papers were found giving details of troops passing through Lisbon. He even admitted that he knew Renard, and that he knew he was a French agent. Under interrogation the man gave them names, and addresses. He was defiant, saying that they could arrest everyone, they would all be released and treated as heroes when the French returned. The following two days were a blur of successive raids, arrests, and interrogations as members of Renard's network were swiftly and ruthlessly rounded up. By the third day they were confident that the network had been destroyed.

Villiers expressed himself well pleased, despite Renard's escape. Much to Michael's delight, he suggested that he would like Michael to stay in Lisbon for a little longer, just in case. He told Michael that he was confident that his regiment would manage without him for a few more days. He would write to Wellington, and that would be that. Michael sincerely hoped so.

As he left the embassy Michael was surprised to hear a voice call to him, "Lieutenant Roberts, what a pleasant surprise!"

Startled, Michael turned towards the voice and saw Senhor Barros, with Maria on his arm. Her expression was questioning, her eyes, fixed on his, were watchful.

"Senhor Barros, Senhorita." Michael made a small bow.

Barros continued, "Have you just come out of the embassy?"

Michael could not deny it, "Yes, Senhor, I had a little business to conduct."

"And not in uniform?" Barros looked impressed.

"No, Senhor, not today." Michael was painfully aware of Maria's silence, and he found the situation a little embarrassing.

"Well, Lieutenant, if you are not busy, perhaps you would care to join us for dinner tomorrow? It was a shame that we saw so little of you in Abrantes. And I am sure we can offer you something better than any billet."

It suddenly dawned on Michael that Barros was completely unaware of how things had been left between him and Maria, and that he was also unaware that Michael owned a rather fine house in Lisbon. He hadn't mentioned it to Barros or Maria.

"Thank you, Senhor, but I do not wish to impose upon you."

"Please, Lieutenant, it is no imposition, I insist."

Michael glanced at Maria who tipped her head slightly, and raised her eyebrows. "As you put it like that, Senhor, I will be honoured." He was rewarded by a fleeting smile from Maria. The arrangement was soon made, and Barros explained to Michael where their house was, it was some way from Michael's, at which he felt an undeniable sense of relief.

The following morning, as Michael shaved, he considered his current situation. He had arranged to see Roberta in the afternoon, and he would have to tell her about the dinner engagement with Senhor Barros and Maria. He wondered what she would say to that. He hoped she would be kind. He was, he had to admit, also a little anxious himself about the renewal of his acquaintance with Maria. She was undoubtedly an attractive young woman, educated, and good company, but his talk with Roberta had not entirely relieved him of his doubts about his own position, and he had also taken her warnings to heart. He had avoided a possible calamity in Abrantes, for that was how he saw what he considered would have been a betrayal of Elaine, and forearmed, he was sure he could manage to do so again. If Maria really could be described as a calamity. She certainly made him question the strong sense he had of still being tied to Elaine, but so far the answer was that he still was.

After lunch, he went to see the progress of the work converting the storehouse to stables, another day and they would be completely finished. With the help of the two local carpenters, Santiago and Parra had put in a dozen stalls, partitioned off a tack room, and arranged couple of rooms in the roof for a groom. Parra had already taken up residence and that morning he had brought in Michael's two horses, Lloyd's Edward, Fred the pony and the two baggage mules. It was all very satisfactory. He left the men to carry on, it was time he was on his way to Roberta's. As he returned to the house Senhora Santiago came out, waving a letter at him. "Senhor, this has just come for you."

It was a brief note from de Silva.

"Lieutenant Roberts, come at once to my office. There has been a development, and I will need your help again."

Michael walked into the house to collect his hat and cane, he was still out of uniform, but then this was hardly regimental business. He wondered if this would prevent him dining with Maria and her father tonight. It occurred to him that it might also be something that would prevent his early return to the regiment and proper soldiering. He also realised that he found the prospect of engaging again in the dirty war of espionage rather exciting. Perhaps Roberta would be at De Silva's. Perhaps there was news of Renard. Maria and the Regiment would just have to wait.

Chapter 5

Once he arrived at police headquarters, Michael was shown quickly to de Silva's office. De Silva was alone. "Lieutenant Roberts, thank you for coming so swiftly. We have some interesting information. Please, take a seat."

"Is it news about Renard?" Michael asked eagerly, he wanted nothing more than to get to grips with him, and kill him.

"Not directly, no. You will, of course, remember the inn where Renard had been staying?" Michael nodded. "Well, the innkeeper has had someone in asking about him, and knowing what is good for him, he has let me know."

"When was this?"

"Yesterday."

"And how can I help?"

"The innkeeper said that a man came in and looked all around, carefully, and then asked for the young gentleman with dark hair who he understood to be staying there, he didn't ask for anyone by name. The innkeeper said it was if he had expected Renard to be there. He also got the impression that he didn't know what Renard looked like. So he told the man that he expected Renard back later today, that he had kept his room."

"That's rather odd", Michael observed thoughtfully. "Who might go looking for Renard without knowing him?"

"It could be a go-between for one of his agents, it's possible that we may have missed some, and they might be trying to stay out of the way. It could be some afrancesado seeking to curry favour with the French and betray our country. Or simply someone trying to sell some information and who was sent in that direction. However, it does offer an opportunity."

"It does?"

"Yes, this man is looking for someone of your age, with dark hair and a foreign accent."

"Oh!" Realisation dawned on Michael. "You want me to wait for him at the inn?"

De Silva smiled, "That is what I was thinking."

Several hours later, a rather uncertain Michael was sitting at a table in the inn's main room, toying with a glass of wine. After speaking with de Silva there had been arrangements to make, not the least being messages for Roberta and Senhor Barros. Now it was only just dark, and the ill lit room with its low, smoke stained ceiling, and scattered benches and trestle tables was empty except for Michael, a slightly nervous innkeeper, and a figure slumped in the corner, wrapped in a cloak with a hat pulled well down, and snoring gently. Michael was far from sure that there was any point to this subterfuge, but if the unknown man hoped to find Renard there, then perhaps others thought he might be there, which meant that Renard himself might return there. It was a faint hope, but Michael sincerely hoped that it would be the case, then he could kill him, and avenge the death of Elaine. It had been almost a year since she died in his arms, but the pain was still great.

The door to the inn opened and Michael looked up from his glass. Two men came in, dressed in workmen's clothes, they greeted the innkeeper by name, and ordered a jug of cheap, red wine, taking it to a table near the fire. Michael glanced at the innkeeper, who gave a slight shake of his head. Obviously regulars, thought Michael. He was beginning to think this a waste of time. He could hear the wind and rain lashing against the outside of the inn, it was a foul night and he doubted anyone would venture out who didn't need to.

The door opened again and a man in a heavy cloak and broad brimmed hat came in, dripping water on the stone flagged floor. He took his hat off, holding it in front of him. It wasn't Renard, this man was older, stockier. Michel glanced at the innkeeper, and saw him give the man the slightest of nods in Michael's direction. Michael dropped his right hand to the bench next to him, where his coat tail covered a pistol. He was sitting well back against a wall, his face in shadow.

The man approached Michael, slowly, nervously. Michael lifted his head and turned to look directly at him. As he did so, he leant forward slightly, out of the shadow, and the light of the fire fell on his face and the scar that ran down its left side, from cheekbone to jawbone. The scar he had got saving the life of the Duke of York on the night he had met Elaine. At the sight of it, the man stopped, and spoke, hesitatingly. "You are not Raposa?"

Michael could not prevent a flicker of surprise crossing his face as he heard that name. It was what the boys in Lisbon had called Renard, Raposa Negra, the Black Fox. "No," replied Michael, "he couldn't be here, he sent me to meet you." Michael hoped the man would be convinced; he was wrong.

"No, senhor, I do not think so." Behind him the hunched figure in the corner stirred slightly, and Michael glanced at it, glimpsing the muzzle of a pistol just appearing from under its cloak. Michael's glance caused the man to look as well, and he suddenly started to back towards the door, pulling a pistol from behind his hat. He levelled it at Michael, and pulled the trigger.

As the pistol shot crashed out, Michael threw himself sideways, at the same time trying to raise his own pistol. Then another shot rang out, and the man spun round, dropping his pistol and falling to the floor. Cautiously, Michael stood and walked towards him, keeping his pistol aimed at the man, who was writhing and crying out in pain. A pall of smoke hung below the low ceiling, and the acrid smell of burnt powder filled the room. The man in the corner who had fired the second shot rose to his feet, throwing back his cloak to reveal another pistol and Lloyd.

"Well shot, Lloyd, thank you. I'll cover him, you check him for more weapons." As Lloyd bent to the man, the door flew open and three of de Silva's men, who had been concealed nearby, burst into the room, pistols ready. At the sight of the scene before them they came to a halt and relaxed slightly. "Are you alright, Senhor?" their leader asked.

"Yes, but I don't know how badly wounded this man is." Michael called to the innkeeper, "Are you sure this is the man who was here before?" The innkeeper could only nod by way of a reply, the two workmen looked equally stunned by events.

"Senhor," the leader of de Silva's men spoke again, "we will take care of him, we can send for a surgeon." He nodded at one of his men, who disappeared into the night and the wind and rain. "Do you want return to our headquarters and tell the General what has happened? I think we will be a little while with this one, before we can question him." He glanced down, dispassionately, at the man writing and moaning on the floor. "If he doesn't die first," he shrugged.

Michael consulted his watch. "No, please, give the General my apologies, I have somewhere I need to be."

Half an hour later Michael was hammering on the door of the Barroses house, while Lloyd held their two horses. They were both very wet. A rather surprised servant opened the door, but seemed disinclined to let Michael in. "Look, I am expected for dinner."

"No, Senhor, dinner was hours ago, you must be mistaken."

At that moment senhor Barros emerged from a doorway and saw Michael. "Lieutenant Roberts! What is the meaning of this?"

"Forgive me, Senhor, I sent a message, did you not receive it?"

"No, Lieutenant, I did not. We waited for you as long as we could. I must say I am disappointed. Maria is disappointed, she has retired, and I am about to. I suggest that you return tomorrow to make your explanation and apologies. Good night, Lieutenant." With that he waved at the servant, who closed the door on Michael.

Michael stood staring at the door for a moment, the rain dripping off his hat and running down his face. It was cold. He turned to take the reins of his horse, Duke, from Lloyd. "Lloyd?"

"Yes, sir?"

"Let's go home."

They rode in the back way to the stables, and Michael left Lloyd with Parra to take care of the horses, but not before he saw his other, favourite horse, Johnny. Once inside he asked Senhora Santiago to bring some bread and meats, with a bottle of wine, up to the dining room, and to get some food and something to drink for Lloyd. The fire blazing away in the dining room revived him a little, and standing in front of it, while he waited for his food, he began to feel a little less chilled. After a couple of glasses of wine and some food, and he began to feel a little more cheerful.

It was good to be home, although he still couldn't sit where his father had sat at the head of the table. It was nearly two years since his parents had been lost when the ship carrying them to England disappeared. Nearly two years since he had read in his father's letter about Augusto who had been entrusted with half of his father's wealth, some twenty-five thousand pounds, or thereabouts. It was unfortunate that no one knew who Augusto was. The other half lay somewhere at the bottom of the Bay of Biscay with his parents.

Michael poured himself another glass, picked up a candle stick, and took himself up the stairs to his room. In a few days he would return to his regiment, but tomorrow he would see de Silva, he should see Villiers, the Ambassador as well, and then go to see Senhor Barros and Maria to make his apologies. As he thought of Maria he involuntarily looked at his dressing table, and the portrait of Elaine that stood on it. Lady Elaine Travers had been a remarkable woman, very remarkable, and Michael could hardly believe that she had loved him, loved him as he had loved her. On the other side of the diptych was a lock of her copper red hair. Tucked away behind that was her letter that had come with the portrait after she was killed. The letter that told him she loved him, that in death she released him from all bonds, and that he might love again, but Michael still loved her, and could not truly love another while he still felt those bonds.

The following day dawned bright, dry and mild. Michael dressed in his best uniform with white pantaloons and hessian boots rather than overalls, and, cheered by the weather, set off to see de Silva in an optimistic mood. He was soon seated in de Silva's office with a welcome cup of coffee.

De Silva had bad news. "I am afraid that the man who was shot last night died before my men could get him any assistance."

"Damn!" Michael expressed his disappointment. "Did they get anything from him?"

"No, not even his name." de Silva took a sip of his coffee. "We will find out who he is, but it is likely to take some time."

"My impression was that he hadn't met Renard before, so he might not have had much to tell us anyway."

"No, but someone told him where to go, who to ask for, and we did learn one thing."

"Sir?"

"Renard has been calling himself Raposa." De Silva grunted. "Smacks of more than a little arrogance."

"Yes, particularly as we called him Raposa Negra when we were growing up together."

"Yes, of course." De Silva was aware of Renard's connection to Lisbon and Michael. "Well, at least we have a name to ask about, but it's a shame the man died."

"He did shoot at me, sir!"

"Yes, yes, and no one is suggesting that your man was wrong to shoot him." De Silva chuckled. "If anything happened to you I am afraid that Roberta would never forgive me." Michael reddened. "Oh, come now, Lieutenant, we are both men of the world. But tell me, my men said you had to dash off somewhere?"

Michael felt deep water under him. "Ah, yes, General, I had an invitation to dinner. I sent a message saying not to wait for me, and that I would call later, if I could. The message was not delivered."

"Now that is awkward"', said de Silva. "Might I ask who you were dining with?"

"A Senhor Barros, I met him in Abrantes."

"The silk manufacturer?"

"Amongst other things, I believe, yes."

"And his delightful daughter, no doubt?"

"Err, yes, sir."

De Silva gave a small smile at Michael's discomfort. "Forgive me, Lieutenant, it is no great act of espionage. No, Roberta told me you had got to know them." The smile vanished and he became serious, "and she seems quite concerned about you. Be careful there, Lieutenant, for all our sakes." Michael wasn't sure if he meant the Barroses or Roberta. "Now," he changed the subject briskly, "what are you doing next?"

"Well, sir, now that I am up to date with events, I am going to call on the Ambassador and report to him."

"And then?"

"Ah, then I have to call on the Barroses and explain why I missed dinner last night."

"Hmm, good luck with that."

At the Embassy Michael was soon with the Ambassador, the Honourable John Villiers, and giving a full report on the events of the previous night, omitting his abortive call on the Barroses.

After listening attentively Villiers spoke, reflectively. "As you say, Mister Roberts, a shame that the man died, but I suppose it couldn't be helped. Well, it would seem that there is nothing now to detain you in Lisbon. With the shooting, and I expect half of Lisbon has heard about it by now, I doubt if Renard will come anywhere near us. So, you had better return to your Regiment. Wellington tells me that your Major Stanhope is not a happy man with you being absent on what he, apparently, calls extracurricular duties." Villiers smiled at Michael. "Do not let that worry you too much, your assistance in these matters is very much appreciated where it matters."

"Thank you, sir, that's good to know." Michael was also quite pleased to have his time in Lisbon curtailed, at least while the Barroses were there.

"Yes, but perhaps best to keep it to yourself. I suppose you can set off the day after tomorrow?" Michael nodded. "Then I shall write a note to Viscount Wellington. Take care of yourself. Mister Roberts, you are a useful young man." And with that the interview was over.

Michael's next call was at the Barroses' home. The same servant who had shut the door on him, opened it wide, and showed him into a cosy, comfortably furnished drawing room, saying that Senhor Barros would join him shortly. No sooner had he left than the door opened and Senhor Barros strode in, a stern look on his face.

"Lieutenant Roberts, I assume that you have come to apologise and explain?"

"Indeed, sir. I am afraid that I was unexpectedly required on official business. I sent a note, but it seems to have gone astray. I regret any inconvenience caused, and I beg your pardon."

"Ha! I can imagine the sort of official business that might detain a young cavalry officer in Lisbon."

Michael began to feel cross, and decided to put Barros in his place. "As it happens, Senhor Barros, I was called upon, by our Ambassador, to offer assistance to General de Silva. I would have called earlier this morning, but I first had to see both those gentlemen." Michael paused, enjoying the look of surprise on Barros' face. "However, if that is not an adequate cause for me to be absent from dinner last night, I shall bid you good day." Michael started to move towards the door.

"No, no, please," there was a sudden hint of panic in Barros' voice. "I did not know, forgive me, if the note had arrived, of course you had to do your duty, please, Lieutenant?"

Michael paused with his hand on the door handle. Barros continued. "Perhaps you would be kind enough to dine with us tonight? I am sure Maria would be delighted."

Michael felt torn between the demands of polite society, and the voice saying, "Go, get out, now, while you can." Polite society won. He turned away from the door. "Very well, Senhor."

Barros beamed at him, "Thank you Lieutenant Roberts, or may I call you Michael? I believe my daughter does?" He smiled effusively.

Michael gave a reluctant nod, "Of course, Senhor."

"And, please, let us say no more about last night. We shall consider it an unfortunate occurrence." Barros smiled ingratiatingly. "And, now, can I offer you some refreshment, some coffee?"

"Thank you, Senhor, a coffee would be most acceptable." Michael decided that he might as well make the best of things. He could afford to spend a little time, after all, he wasn't expected by Roberta until the afternoon, and in two days he would be returning to Abrantes and the Regiment..

"Splendid." Barros actually rubbed his hands together. "And I shall ask Maria to join us," he added, leaving the room.

As the door closed behind Barros Michael thought he heard some excited, female whispering. His guess was proven correct a few moments later when the door opened and Maria entered, alone. She stood just inside the room and frowned at him.

"Lieutenant Roberts, my father says that I am not to be angry with you for your behaviour last night."

"Senhorita," Michael felt a little formality was required, "I have explained to your father that I was unavoidably called away on urgent, official business for our Ambassador and General de Silva."

Maria flipped open her fan and waved it a couple of times before slapping it shut against her hand. "Then I suppose that I must forgive you," there was a very slight pause, "Michael. But I shall still expect you to make it up to me."

Michael gave a slight bow of acknowledgement, "Unfortunately, Senhorita," she raised her eyebrows, "Maria," he corrected himself, "I must return to my Regiment in Abrantes the day after tomorrow. I have accepted your father's invitation to dine tonight, but after that I shall not be free."

Maria got as far as "Oh, but," when the door opened and her father came in, followed by a servant with coffee. Half an hour of polite, but stilted conversation followed before Michael felt he could make his excuses and leave.

Back home Michael realised he was feeling hungry and wandered down to the kitchen to see if he could find something to eat. Senhora Santiago told him that her husband, Parra and Lloyd were all down at the stables, putting the finishing touches to them. He explained to Senhora Santiago that they would be leaving for Abrantes in two days, and that tonight he would be dining out.

"Somewhere nice, Senhor Michael?" she asked.

"Some people called Barros; I met them in Abrantes."

"That Senhor Barros and his daughter Maria?" The Senhora had a look on her face that Michael knew from his childhood, it used to precede a good telling off.

"Yes, Babá, why, do you know them?"

"I know of them," she replied, "And I remember Senhor Barros trying to use your father to get an introduction to

Baron Quintela. Ha! He was just a small silk producer then, but with ideas. Nothing but a social climber. You should be careful, Michael, they will use you, or try to marry that girl off to you."

"It's only dinner, Babá, and I have no intention of seeing them again."

"Well," she replied, busying with some food for Michael, and not looking at him, "you would do best to stick to the Senhorita Roberta."

"What!" Michael was taken completely by surprise. "Who?"

"Now, Michael," she faced him and wagged her finger at him, "you know very well who I mean. That Roberta de Silva. And don't look at me like that. It was a great relief to me and your poor mother when you took up with her. Better than some of the women you could have found."

"Mother knew?" Michael was completely astounded.

"Of course she did. A mother knows these things, and so does a Babá."

"And my father?"

"No, Michael, of course not."

"That's something I suppose."

"Yes, well, just be careful there, Michael. Their interest is money and society, believe me."

That afternoon Michael walked over to see Roberta, and tell her what had happened the night before. As it was she had just returned from seeing her cousin, General de Silva, and already knew about the incident at the inn, and also about the problems with the Barroses. Roberta was quite forthright in her views.

"Michael, you must be careful with that Maria Barros. I do not want to see you get hurt, and I think that you might. I do not think she is the sort of woman who could make you happy."

Consequently, when Michael went for dinner that night he was very much on his guard, although there was also a part of him that said, "To hell with everyone, telling me what I should do, if I want her, I'll have her," without quite knowing what he meant by it. Over dinner, however, he began to detect an interest, not so much in him, as in who he knew, and how wealthy he was. First, Senhor Barros knew about the house.

"Now, Michael," he began with a smile, "I think you have not been entirely honest with me."

"Senhor?"

"Yes, when I first invited you to dinner, taking pity on you as stuck in some poor billet, you did not tell me about your father's house?"

"Oh, that."

"Yes, Michael, and I gather it is now your house? It is indeed a very fine property."

Michael wondered how he had found out that. "Yes, Senhor Barros, and it is the house I grew up in."

"Of course, you were born here, in Lisbon. I suppose that, working for Quintela, your father knew many grand people, and now, clearly, you do?"

"'Father," Maria interrupted, "you should not ask Michael so many questions."

"No, of course not, forgive me Michael. I am simply curious. It is not every day that one meets such a well connected young man, the British Ambassador, our own General de Silva?"

"It's quite alright, Senhor," Michael reassured him, whilst desperately wanting to change the subject. He took comfort in knowing that he would shortly be leaving

Lisbon. He was beginning to suspect that he was being interviewed, and his prospects explored. Then Senhor Barros exploded the mine under Michaels fortifications.

"Maria tells me that are returning to Abrantes?"

"Yes, senhor, duty calls."

"As it happens, Michael, we find that we must also return to Abrantes, my sister is unwell, and we must go to her. I wonder, might it be possible to travel there with you? It would be a great comfort to me to travel in a group, and with soldiers."

Inwardly, Michael groaned in despair, outwardly, he smiled, and capitulated. Barros was delighted, Maria smiled at him, and tipped her head. "Thank you, Michael," she said, "I will feel so much safer travelling with you, and we will have much to talk about, I am sure."

It was arranged that Michael would call for them early on the day after tomorrow as they were not far off the road to Abrantes on the east side of Lisbon. That would give them a day to make all their preparations, and they assured him they would be ready for an early start. Eventually, Michael was able to make his escape, and took himself home, and to bed, feeling that he had been outmanoeuvred and, worst of all, that it was all his own fault for rising to Barros' criticism.

The following morning preparations began for the return to Abrantes. Francisco and Senhora Santiago managed all the packing while Lloyd and Parra readied the horses and mules. Michael had hoped to find a horse or pony for Parra, so he wouldn't have to ride whichever horse Michael wasn't, but there was a shortage in Lisbon, and that would have to wait. Once everything was in hand, Michael undertook his last outstanding chore in Lisbon, and went to see his lawyer Furtado.

It was the first time Michael had seen Furtado since he had turned twenty one. Furtado informed Michael that he had been in correspondence with Rutherford in London, and they had decided that it would be best to do nothing about Michael's inheritance until he came of age, which he now had, and until then to tell him nothing. That way Michael could plead all ignorance if his uncle, as his guardian, had tried to assert any control.

Furtado shrugged, "However, the caution was unnecessary, nothing has come to light that you are not aware of, although I can confirm that your father owned your home, which, of course, you know, and that he also acquired the small parcel of land and building behind the house." He smiled, "I think it is safe to tell you now that I have the deeds to both here, safe and secure."

"That's a relief, Senhor, but do you know of anything else?"

"No, Michael, I don't, but I only handled your father's private affairs. If there is anything outstanding from his business enterprises, I don't know of them. Perhaps the mysterious Augusto knows something, whoever he is. I have made some discreet enquiries, but found no one."

"I haven't had any luck either. I suppose I must just keep asking, he must be somewhere."

Furtado smiled sympathetically. "I have also completed arrangements for your banking in Lisbon. I have arranged for you simply to take over what was your father's arrangement. I have informed Mister Rutherford, so money can be transferred from Praed's."

"Thank you, that will make things easier."

"Ah, there is one other thing. It has bothered me a little."

"Oh, yes?"

"I had a visit yesterday, from a Senhor Barros."

"Oh!"

"I knew him because he did a little business with your father a few years ago, nothing I was directly involved in, but, more to the point, he knew I was your father's lawyer. He seemed to be rather interested in establishing how well off you are. Naturally, I refused to tell him anything. Unfortunately, as is often the way with some people, he seemed to take my professional discretion as hiding something. I rather got the impression that he gave himself the idea that I was hiding considerable wealth." Furtado shrugged. "Of course, I couldn't correct that view without breeching your confidentiality. I do hope that doesn't cause you any difficulties?"

"Senhor, you are not responsible for the self-delusions of others. But perhaps, if he calls again, you might manage to correct his impression?"

The meeting concluded after Michael and Furtado had settled arrangements for the house and the Santiagos. Furtado would continue to correspond with Rutherford as necessary. Michael's financial position was comfortable, the cost of his servants, horses, mules, the maintenance of the house, and his every day expenses were being met by his income. All that would change, of course, if Augusto could be found and the missing twenty five thousand pounds worth of diamonds recovered.

A thought occurred to Michael, and on his way home he took a small diversion, to the Palazio Quintela, to call on Senhor Rodrigues, Quintela's head clerk. Rodrigues was delighted to see Michael, and pleased to hear that they were very happy with Salvador Gomes and his mules. Gomes had been hired through Rodrigues to carry the baggage of the troop's officers. Then Michael broached the reason for his visit.

"Senhor Rodrigues, there is a small personal matter that you might be able to help me with." Rodrigues raised his eyebrows quizzically. "Do you know, or could you ask, if anyone has been asking questions about my father, or about me? Perhaps of your clerks? Forgive me, but someone has been trying to pry into my personal affairs, and I need to know what they might have learnt. I have no wish to get anyone into trouble, it is just a matter of knowing." He smiled at Rodrigues, disarmingly, he hoped.

"I am not aware of anything," replied Rodrigues, "but if you will allow me a few minutes?"

When Rodrigues returned he did not look pleased. "I am sorry, Michael, it would seem that someone has been asking questions. A Senhor Barros, do you know him?"

"Oh, yes, I do." Michael gave a thin grimace.

"We have occasionally bought silk from him, but nothing recently, other sources are a better quality and more reliable. The clerk he usually deals with was in a nearby coffee house yesterday when Barros joined him. He simply said he had met you in Abrantes, reminded the clerk that he knew your father, then asked if you had been in about your father's affairs." Rodrigues shrugged, "Of course, the clerk knew to be discreet about business matters, and told him nothing. Unfortunately, sometimes, that allows people to imagine all sorts of things. I hope that my clerk has not caused you any difficulties?"

"No, Senhor, it is just the imagination of others that is the problem."

Chapter 6

Michael's party rode up to the Barros's house at eight o'clock the following morning. To his surprise all was ready for an immediate departure. Senhor Barros, Maria, and their groom were on their horses, and in addition there was a bullock cart loaded with baggage and the footman and a maid perched on the back. The cart's driver, on foot with his long, spiked goad, completed the party. Michael's heart sank at the sight of the cart. Bullock carts were slow, and with a live axle fixed to the wheels, they were notorious for the dreadful squeaking and creaking noise they made. He realised that they would not reach Abrantes in the two days he had expected, it was going to be three days, with luck. He was not in a good mood, and it had just worsened. As he rode up, Senhor Barros greeted him with a warm smile.

"Good morning, Michael, as you see, we are all ready to go. Fortunately early starts are not unknown to us."

"Very good, Senhor. Then let us make a start!" Michael wheeled Johnny around to lead the procession. As he did so he muttered "With me, Lloyd," putting the two men at the front. With any luck the bullock cart would bring up the rear. Parra quickly pushed in behind them on Duke, followed by Francisco on Fred the pony, leading the two baggage mules.

By the time they got clear of Lisbon and out onto the open road, Michael was in a better humour. It lasted even when Senhor Barros pushed his horse to the front to join Michael. Lloyd unobtrusively dropped back to join his friend, Parra.

"Michael," began Barros, "I have done this trip many times, and I suggest that we stop tonight at an inn at Vila Franca. It is not as grand as perhaps you are used to, but hospitable, with good stables."

There it was, thought Michael, a little probe about his wealth. "That sounds good to me, Senhor. And better than bivouacking on the road side when it gets dark, which is what we usually do." That was, perhaps, something of an exaggeration for a trip like this, but Michael was keen to take any opportunity to counter any suggestion that he was somehow a man of substance.

Barros laughed at Michael's comment. "We could hardly ask Maria and her maid to sleep on the ground, under the stars."

Michael gave a small laugh in response, and thought about the wives following the army, including those with the Sixteenth. They put up with a lot more than the occasional night under the stars. Some had died during the long, hard retreat from Spain in the heat of the previous August, and then two of the Sixteenth's wives had died of fever at Vila Viçosa while another had lost her husband to it. She was still following the Regiment, helping the Surgeon, and everyone turning a blind eye to the fact that she should have been sent back to England. With any luck she'd soon find another dragoon to her liking and remarry.

At that moment Maria rode up alongside him. Perhaps a little uncharitably, Michael found himself wondering how she would manage on campaign. Senhor Barros reined back a little, leaving them riding side by side. They conversed as they rode, amiably enough, but somehow, for Michael, lacking the spark that had been there when they had ridden out from Abrantes together. The failed hunt for Renard had simply brought Elaine and everything she meant back to the forefront of his mind.

The inn was just as Barros had said, and the party passed a comfortable night. The next morning, as they were preparing to mount and leave, Lloyd approached Michael in the quiet of the stables. "Begging your pardon, sir."

"Yes, Lloyd, what is it?" Michael thought Lloyd was looking particularly uncomfortable.

"Err, well, sir," Lloyd paused.

"Spit it out, man, what is it?"

"Well, sir," he began again. Over Lloyd's shoulder Michael caught sight of Francisco peering nervously around a corner. "Begging your pardon, sir, but Francisco was telling me this morning, sir, and I thought you should probably know."

"For God's sake, Lloyd, know what?"

Lloyd shuffled uncomfortably and looked at his feet. "Well, err, begging your pardon, sir, but Francisco says that the Senhorita's maid has been asking him questions about you, sir." Then Lloyd suddenly burst out with, "And she told him that the Senhorita is going to marry you, sir. Sorry, sir."

"Oh, God dammit!" Michael was more then a little taken aback. He took a deep breath. "Alright, Lloyd, thank you for telling me. Francisco! Come here." Francisco shuffled over looking worried. "Francisco, don't worry, you were right that I should know." The boy's expression immediately lightened. "It would probably be best if you don't let on that you told me anything, and try not to tell the maid anything. Right, that's enough of that, let's get on."

The next two days seemed to drag on interminably, as Michael tried, mostly in vain, to keep to himself. Both Senhor Barros and Maria persisted in talking to him and probing with comments that were clearly designed to get Michael to reveal more about his circumstances, particularly his financial position. Michael found himself almost looking forward to the inevitable interview with Major Stanhope.

As soon as they arrived in Abrantes at Senhora Marquez' house, Michael pleaded the call of duty and took himself off to Regimental Headquarters, leaving everyone else to move back in. The adjutant, Lieutenant Barra seemed happy to see him, greeting him with a smile.

"Good to see you, Roberts, I trust all went well?"

"Yes, it did, thank you, Barra, Quite well. Is the Major in?"

"Oh, yes, and not happy with you, I fear. Nearly three weeks away, and he saw you arriving."

"Oh dear."

"Yes, best get it over with, eh, Mister Roberts? Oh, and Major Archer has arrived while you were away, so things are looking up a bit."

Michael knocked on Stanhope's door, and went in.

"Ah, Mister Roberts. Good of you to join us again. I gather you were able to conduct whatever business it was that the Ambassador needed you for. General Cotton tells me that the Ambassador wrote to Sir Arthur using the most glowing terms about you."

"Really, sir?"

"Yes, really! Dammit, Roberts," Stanhope snapped back, "d'ye think I'd invent something like that?"

"No, sir."

"No, sir. I would not." Stanhope paused. "And I don't suppose you can tell me what you were doing?"

"Err…"

"No, don't bother, I don't want to know. However, perhaps you can explain that caravan of civilians that you arrived with? It is not the job of His Majesty's army to play escort to damn civilians, Roberts."

"No, sir."

"Oh, damn it, Roberts. Just get out. You're supposed to be an officer of this Regiment, go and do some proper soldiering. Go and report to Captain Ashworth. I expect he will be glad to see you back."

Ashworth was indeed pleased to see Michael, and pointedly asked no questions about his trip to Lisbon. The squadron was beginning to recover from its casualties and illness, but there was a shortage of horses, so many had been lost at Talavera and after, others were simply not fit and were being nursed back to health. Poor Price hadn't had a horse since his had been shot with Farcy in Falmouth harbour, and he had spent all his time marching with the baggage. Each of the four squadrons was the same. All in all, the Regiment was short of about eighty horses. The men who had been ill with fever were gradually recovering in the healthier air of Abrantes. Duties were light, and the work mostly limited to the care of the horses.

Michael did his best to keep busy and avoid spending time in his billet. There was a lot to occupy him as the Regiment was preparing stabling to get all the horses under cover before the rains came in November. Senhora Marquez appeared to have made a remarkable recovery, if she had been ill at all. Michael had his doubts. He took dinner in the mess as often as possible, avoiding Senhora Marquez's invitations to dine with them for as long as possible. Eventually, he had to accept. Strangely, he thought, Senhor Barros was absent, away for two nights on some business towards Vila Velha, a long day's ride away. Dinner was pleasant enough, the conversation fairly easy as they had all got to know each other a little. Michael talked a little about his duties, and mentioned that in the morning he would be taking a small patrol out, across the river. Not that they expected to find any French, he hastily reassured the ladies, it was more for exercise and practice.

Then, with dinner finished, to his surprise, Senhora Marquez rose from the table and informed them "I am still a little fatigued after my illness, so I am going to retire. I am sure you two will find much to talk about." She smiled, and left them.

Michael sat silent, feeling rather awkward and uncomfortable. Maria looked at him across the table, the candlelight reflecting in her eyes and casting highlights on her glossy hair. She looked, thought Michael, quite beautiful. She smiled. "Michael". She paused. "We have not had much chance to talk alone, have we?"

"No, I am afraid there is much to do, we have a lot of work in hand, recovering from the effects of the last campaign."

"And dining with your fellow officers?"

"Ah…"

"You have been avoiding me, Michael, why?"

Michael took a mouthful of wine, while he thought desperately what to answer. In the time it took him to swallow he thought about how beautiful she was, what good company she was, about Elaine's letter, telling him he was free. And again it came back to that. He had her written words, but somehow that wasn't enough, He needed more in order to be free, but didn't see how he could, and, even if he was free, he was far from sure that Maria was right for him. Roberta's words, and his Babá's, ran through his mind. He put the glass down and stared at it, his hand still on it.

"Why, Michael." Maria asked again. He looked at her, helplessly.

"I…, I don't know what to say."

"Say what you think, Michael."

The recollection of their last parting came to him. He looked her in the eye, and lied. "I'm a soldier, Maria, I go where I am sent, when I am sent. I might be killed. Or maimed. And when the war is over, if I survive, I will go home to England. It would be neither fair nor proper to hold out anything to you." It was, so far as it went, true, but it was not the truth.

There was a long silence.

"And if I was prepared to take that chance, and follow you to war and to England?"

"No, Maria, I would not let you do that."

Maria stood abruptly and looked at him, anger in her eyes. "Isn't that rather for me to decide?" And before Michael could think of a suitable reply she left the room, leaving him alone. "That went well," thought Michael, but at least he had escaped any commitment.

Just after daybreak the next morning, Michael led his patrol down to the Tagus and across the bridge of boats. There were eighteen dragoons, including Lloyd, and Sergeant Evans. Once across the river Michael halted the patrol and ordered them to spring their carbines and load. The men unfastened their carbines from their saddles, fastened them to their carbine belts by the spring, swivel clips, and loaded. Michael loaded his pistol. He no longer carried a pair. In one holster was a telescope, which he found far more useful. Once all were ready he sent a corporal and three dragoons ahead by a few hundred yards as an advance guard, and while they rode ahead he detailed another corporal and three dragoons to act as a rear guard, a few hundred yards back. Then he ordered the patrol to march at the walk.

The weather was mild and dry, there was no real threat of bumping into the French, and Michael rode easily along on

Duke. He was mulling over the difficult conversation of last night, and wondering what to do about it, if anything. They had covered about five miles, and Michael was thinking that in another half hour he would call a halt. His train of thought was interrupted by Sergeant Evans.

"Rider, sir, coming from the rear guard."

Michael looked back for a moment, but didn't halt the patrol, the rider was coming at the trot and would soon be up with them, and he didn't want to have to send anyone to halt the advance guard, it was easier to keep moving steadily along.

The dragoon pulled up alongside him. It was Fletcher who had been with him on his patrol to the Alberche. "Begging your pardon, sir, but there's someone following us."

"What?" Michael was, frankly, surprised.

"Yes, sir, keeping a way behind, trying to stay out of sight, two riders, sir."

"Very good, Fletcher." Michael looked ahead, the advance guard was just rounding a curve in the road, with a low hill and wood to the side. "Wait here, for the rear guard, and tell them to just keep riding on. We will drop off into that wood, and see who it is when they come up."

"Right you are, sir," and Fletcher pulled over.

Michael called to a dragoon riding just behind him. "Riley, trot on, and tell the advance guard to get off the road somewhere out of sight."

"Yes, sir," and Riley pushed on at a fast trot.

As the patrol rounded the curve, Michael could see no sign of the advance guard. Once he was sure they were out of sight of the rear guard, he led the way off the road and into the trees. Quickly, and with no fuss, the patrol spread out into a skirmish line, parallel to the road and about twenty yards into the trees. In a few minutes they glimpsed the rear guard pass by, looking vey relaxed.

Michael quietly ordered the patrol to "Make ready", and with a series of gentle clicks the carbines were all brought to full cock, ready to fire. Michael drew and cocked his pistol. "On my word, push forward fast, and we will see who it is."

The patrol waited, there was not a sound save for some bird song. Then the faint thud of hooves was heard, and shortly after Michael could just make out two riders, walking along the road. As they came opposite the middle of the line of waiting dragoons, he called out, "Forward" and pushed Duke into a fast trot onto the road. At the sudden sound and appearance of the dragoons the two horses started and spun around.

Michael saw who it was, and in his astonishment shouted, "Maria, what the Hell are you doing here!"

Maria looked terrified as she fought to control her spinning horse, Raul, the Barros' groom steadied his and looked extremely unhappy. Michael realised that all the dragoons were gathered on the road, and grinning like idiots. All except Evans and Lloyd. Sergeant Evans looked cross, Lloyd looked shocked and horrified.

"Sergeant Evans, get these bloody grinning baboons formed up on the road properly. Jesus bloody Christ, Maria. What are you doing?"

Evans started shouting orders, getting the carbines made safe, forming the patrol up again, with their backs to Maria and Michael.

Maria looked as if she was about to burst into tears. "I am sorry, Michael," she gulped. "It was what you said last night, about not letting me follow you. I wanted to show you that I could, that I would." She started to sob.

"Oh, Maria, you could have got yourself shot. Those guns were loaded and cocked. And I suppose you made Raul come with you?"

Sobbing, Maria could only nod. Michael looked at Raul, who gave a shrug and a little nod.

Michael sat and stared at Maria for a moment, then raised his eyes to the sky and took a deep, calming breath. He turned in his saddle, "Sar'nt Evans, Lloyd, fall out and come here." He turned back to Maria who was wiping her face with a handkerchief, trying to still her sobs, and avoiding Michael's look.

Evans and Lloyd rode up next to him as he stared at Maria. "Sar'nt Evans, Lloyd, you will escort the Senhorita back to Abrantes." He looked at them. "I would also very much appreciate it if you can get the young lady back to her home without Major Stanhope seeing you. Raul might be able to help you there." Without another word, he wheeled Duke around, trotted to the front of the patrol, and marched it off.

Michael was out of luck. It was beginning to get dark as he led the patrol back across the Tagus. The rest of the day had passed uneventfully, and he had recovered some equilibrium. Then he saw Sergeant Evans waiting at the town gate. He came to attention and saluted Michael, who returned the salute, with a sinking feeling as he halted the patrol.

"I'm sorry, sir, but Major Stanhope rode down to the river just as we were crossing. He says you are to report to him as soon as you get here. I'm to take the patrol off your hands, sir."

"Very well, Sar'nt, not your fault. Where's Lloyd?"

"The Major told him to see the Senhorita home, sir."

"Thank you, Sar'nt. The patrol is yours." So saying Michael pushed Duke on towards the Regimental headquarters.

Stanhope was furious. "Ah, Mister Roberts. Tell me, sir, since when has it been Regulation for an officer on a patrol to be accompanied by a woman? Eh? Well, Roberts? D'ye have an answer, sir?"

"I beg your pardon, sir, but I did not invite Senhorita Barros to accompany me. She chose to follow me, sir."

"Then she damn well shouldn't have. I hold you responsible, Mister Roberts. You brought her here from Lisbon. It's unprofessional, it's unbecoming, it's damned improper behaviour, d'ye hear me Roberts? Improper."

"Yes, sir"

"Yes, sir, yes, sir. Is that all you have to say for yourself? God damn it, you're no gentleman and not fit to be an officer. I could have told Lord Harcourt that you'd be trouble. Just because your grandfather knew him, was the Regiment's chaplain in the American war, doesn't mean you are fit to be an officer. Do I make myself clear, Mister Roberts?"

"Yes, sir."

"If I could find a damned way I'd have you court martialled. Fortunately for you, Mister Barra tells me you haven't actually broken any Regulations, and Major Archer agrees. Which doesn't mean you are not a disgrace to the Regiment."

"No, sir."

"Now get out of my sight, and consider your future, Roberts, consider it."

Outside Stanhope's office Joseph Barra pulled a sympathetic face. "That was bad, and I can't say I agree with him, not at all."

"You heard him, then?"

"I'm afraid so, hard not to. Look, there's an order just come in, there's eighty horses being transferred to us from the Twenty-third, they're being sent home. I'll see if Archer will send you to collect them, I'll suggest that it might be a suitable way to get you away from Stanhope for a while. It would get you away from him and your lady friend for a couple of weeks, if you don't rush. They're at Vila Viçosa."

"Thank you, Mister Barra, I think that would suit me very well indeed."

The day after next Michael set off, accompanied by Lloyd, Francisco, Parra, Mister Peers, the Veterinary Surgeon, Sergeant Blood, Sergeant Flynn, and seventy two dismounted dragoons. In the meantime he had seen neither Major Stanhope nor Maria, which was alright with him. He had received his orders from Major Archer, now in command of the Regiment, and who had seemed more understanding. Michael had no intention of pushing the pace, some of the men were not long recovered from the fever, and they were further hindered by two bullock carts loaded with the men's valises, and saddlery and accoutrements for the horses. Late in the afternoon they arrived at a small village, that Michael decided would do nicely for the night. Quarters were quickly arranged and the men set about preparing a meal from their rations. Michael and John Peers got into the priest's house, and were well looked after by Lloyd, Francisco, and Peer's servant, a Portuguese from Lisbon.

After dinner, in the quiet of Michael's room, Francisco spoke quietly. "Senhor, may I speak?"

"Of course, Francisco, what is it?"

"It is about the Senhorita, Senhor."

Michael sighed. "It's alright, Francisco, what is it?"

"When Emyr, I mean Senhor Lloyd, brought her to the house the other day, she went straight to her room, and she hadn't come out when we left this morning." He paused, "But I heard her maid talking to one of the other servants. Senhor Barros went away so you could be left alone with the Senhorita by Senhora Marquez, Senhor. She was supposed to," he stopped and looked at the floor, red with embarrassment.

"It's alright Francisco, I understand."

"Thank you Senhor. And the maid said that Senhor Barros was cross with the Senhorita when he got back, because she had not, what did she say? Yes, she had not got you held fast, Senhor."

"Oh, really? Well, thank you Francisco."

"Senhor?"

"Yes?"

"The house in Lisbon, Senhor, it belongs to Senhora Marquez."

"Oh? Now that is interesting."

"Yes, Senhor, and Senhor Barros worked for Senhor Marquez, and now he works for the Senhora. The maid says they have no property of their own, Senhor."

"Well, well, well. That is interesting. Thank you, Francisco."

Two weeks later, Michael led the column of dragoons back over the Tagus and into Abrantes. Every one of them was now mounted, and a few extra horses were led along at the rear. They had taken it gently on the way back, and the new mounts had benefitted from the light exercise. Peers and Blood were particularly pleased with what they had acquired. It had also given the men a chance to get to know their new horses, and to regain some riding fitness. Lloyd told Michael that Price was very happy, but suffering a little after such a long break from riding. Michael had made a private purchase of a horse from an officer of the Twenty-third, a sound if unspectacular gelding for Parra. It was, he had been informed, called Harry.

The first person to greet Michael was Joseph Barra. "Hello, Roberts, two weeks to the day, eh?" He grinned at Michael. "I told Major Archer that you would probably be back today." Barra cast his eye over the new horses. "Not a bad looking lot, Roberts, he ought to be pleased."

Michael smiled back. "I hope so, Barra. And how is Stanhope?"

"Not too bad. He had a visit from Senhor Barros and his daughter just after you had gone. I gather that they came to apologise for the Senhorita's behaviour. Something about not wanting to get you into trouble. I couldn't quite catch every word, Barros' English is about as good as the Major's Portuguese, and the door was shut." They both laughed. "Anyway, he seemed to be somewhat mollified after that. And talk of the devil, I'll see you later." And Barra slipped away.

"Back on time, I see, Roberts."

Michael saluted Stanhope. "Yes, sir. It went well."

"Right, then let's have a look at what we've got."

Accompanied by Michael, Peers, Blood, and RSM Williams, Stanhope proceeded to inspect every horse. At the end of it he addressed the little group. "Well, those all seem to be acceptable, well done, Mister Roberts, Mister Peers, Blood." And that was that.

Michael made his way to his quarters, not sure whether he was relieved or disgruntled with Stanhope's off handedness. He was also wondering what was in store for him at his billet. Lloyd, Parra and Francisco had got there ahead of him with the baggage, and only Parra was in the yard, looking over Harry, and waiting to take care of Duke. Inside everything was quiet, and he made his way up to his room. Lloyd and Francisco were busy sorting everything out and Michael collapsed into a chair, answering the odd question about this and that piece of uniform or kit. In response to a tap at the door, he called out, "Come in." It was the Senhora's servant, who asked him if would be so good as to join Senhora Marquez in the parlour.

In the parlour Senhora Marquez was seated on a chaise, Maria next to her, Senhor Barros was standing with his back to the fireplace. The weather was still mild and there was no fire. Michael closed the door, and Barros launched straight into what he had to say.

"Senhor Roberts, thank you for coming down. This is very awkward, but I am confident that you will act like the gentleman you are." Michael wondered where this was going. "I have heard all about what happened in my absence, and I can assure that I am not happy." No, thought Michael, I don't suppose you are. "I am very disappointed with my daughter's behaviour." I'll wager that you are, thought Michael, but for what she didn't do, not what she did. "And she has something that she would like to say to you. Maria?"

Maria looked at him and spoke so quietly that Michael could barely make out what she was saying. "Senhor Roberts, I am very, very sorry for my thoughtless and foolish behaviour in trying to follow your patrol. It was impetuous and dangerous. I beg your forgiveness."

Michael could feel the tension in the room as they waited for him to respond. He frowned at her, it seemed appropriate, and Maria's gaze dropped to the floor. He wondered how long he could drag it out. Obviously they didn't realise that he was perfectly aware they saw him as a wealthy young man who would make a very suitable husband for Maria. They realised that a huge blunder had been made, and were desperately trying to rescue the situation. He was cross, very cross, with all of them, what sort of fool did they take him for?

He tried to look stern. "Thank you, Maria. Will you promise me never to interfere with my duties again?" Not that he was going to give her the chance.

Maria looked up, hope mixed with relief clear on her face. "Of course I do, I promise," she paused, "Michael."

"Then I forgive you."

"Oh, thank you, Michael, thank you." She beamed at him, and her head tipped. Michael saw it, and was unmoved, this was no Elaine.

"Thank you, Senhor," Barros spoke, "my sister and I are grateful." He made a small bow, which Michael returned. "And now, Senhor, I believe dinner is almost ready, will you do us the honour of joining us?"

"Of course, Senhor."

Over the next few days Michael maintained a cool, distant formality, which, he hoped, said I may have forgiven, but I have not forgotten, and there is ground to be made up. His demeanour was reinforced by the passing of the anniversary of Elaine's death. The recollection of that awful night and everything that she had meant to him, the recollection of their all too little time together, all served to drive the thought of any other woman from his mind. His melancholy was mixed with a flaring up of the absolute hatred he had for the man who had killed her. For a few days he was barely worth knowing.

Still, Barros and Senhora Marquez did their best to restore things between Michael and Maria, culminating in a suggestion a few weeks later, that, perhaps, the Lieutenant would care to escort Maria to a ball that the garrison officers were holding? The eighth of December would be the Feast of the Immaculate Conception, one of the most important religious festivals in Portugal. Michael was well aware of the significance. As a boy he had crept into the Cathedral in Lisbon to watch the mass being celebrated. Here, there would be a mass and then the garrison was holding a ball in the evening. Michael hesitated, he didn't want to give them any encouragement, then Barros said that both he and his sister were also invited. Why not thought, Michael, a couple of dances and his duty would be done. Then he could leave her to the attentions of the garrison's officers. That should send a clear message that he really wasn't interested in the senhorita. A message to everyone, to Stanhope, the Regiment, the garrison, and, particularly, the Barroses. Her father and aunt could escort her home, if necessary. It was, perhaps, cruel, but he didn't feel kindly. He agreed.

The ball was in the Palacete dos Albuquerques, which had served as headquarters for both the French Marshal Junot and Sir Arthur Wellesley, or Viscount Wellington as he now was. It was a grand affair, with many of the Sixteenth's officers present, along with those of the two Portuguese infantry regiments that made up the garrison. It was a short walk from Senhora Marquez' house, and they went with Maria on Michael's arm, followed by Senhor Barros and his sister. Two servants with lanterns lit their way. Maria looked her very best, with a magnificent dark green gown, and her dark hair piled high, with drop pearl earrings and a matching necklace. For the walk she wore a deep crimson cloak. Michael was in his dress uniform, with a bicorn instead of the usual Tarleton, and breeches with silk stockings and silver buckled shoes. Slung over his left shoulder was a pelisse edged with brown fur, something that the light dragoon officers had adopted from the hussars. Both his jacket and pelisse were covered with yards and yards of silver braid and dozens of silver buttons. They made a fine picture.

The Palace was richly decorated, lit by scores of candles, and full of the cream of Abrantes society, civil and military. Senhor Barros and Senhora Marquez contented themselves with observing the dancing, and chatting with friends and acquaintances. Michael danced twice with Maria, then, gladly, stepped aside for one of the Portuguese officers. As Maria danced Michael noticed that she kept glancing across to where he was standing, idly chatting with George Keating. The dance ended and she was promptly swept up by another Portuguese officer. George leant in close to Michael. "I rather think Senhorita Barros only has eyes for you, Michael."

Michael grunted. "Perhaps, George, perhaps, but I think I need a drink." With that, followed by George, he set off around the ballroom for the refreshment room. There they found Captain Patton of the Royal Engineers who was responsible for fortifying Abrantes. Soon they were deep in conversation with him about his work. As they talked Michael became aware of a small group of Portuguese officers that was standing near them. They were not from the garrison, and Michael assumed from their brown uniforms that they were from one of the regiments of Caçadores at Tomar, a few hours ride away. He remembered that Maria's brother was an officer in one of them. They returned to the ballroom just in time to see Maria dancing with another Portuguese officer.

As he watched the dancing he felt George give him a nudge. "Those Portuguese over there seem damned interested in you."

George nodded towards the group of officers that Michael had noticed in the refreshment room. They were talking to an officer that Michael recognised as a member of the garrison. They were throwing glances across the room at him, and seemed to be having an animated conversation. George noticed Henry van Hagen nearby, and gestured for him to join them.

"George, Michael, what's afoot?"

George answered, "'Not sure, Henry, but those Portuguese fellows are taking an uncommon interest in Michael."

"Ah," said Henry, "I wonder if that's anything to do with the rumours?"

"Alright, Henry, tell me," said Michael.

"Well, err, while you were away, one of the garrison officers was talking to me, and he asked me if it was true about you, that you were an infamous swordsman and had killed three men in duels, and that's how you got your scar."

"Iesu Mawr," exclaimed Michael, using an expression picked up from Lloyd. "Where the Hell did they get that from?" He looked at Henry, who looked embarrassed. Michael thought for a moment. "No, not Maria?" Henry shrugged apologetically.

George was watching the Portuguese. "You don't think that one of them is going to try to provoke you, do you? Pick a fight, take down the great English swordsman?"

"Oh, bloody Hell," said Henry, "one of them is coming over."

A tall officer of Caçadores with a long droopy moustache approached them. He addressed Michael in Portuguese, "Lieutenant, I believe that you are the escort of Senhorita Barros, the sister of my friend Captain Barros?"

Michael had been standing with his back slightly turned to the room. Now he turned to face the Portuguese officer, a slight smile on his face, the scar clearly visible. "Indeed, I am, Senhor."

Michael's anger had been growing slowly, now he was furious, and with it came the coldness and calm he had known before. He had had enough of this damned game playing with Maria. It was time to put an end to it.

"Then I must observe that your neglect of the lady is not the behaviour of a gentleman."

"I say…" George began. Michael stayed him with a hand on his arm.

Michael's slight smile broadened. "In that case, Lieutenant, it is Lieutenant, is it?" The man nodded. "In that case," Michael went on, "perhaps you had better offer her your services instead. I assume you are a gentleman?" The Portuguese officer looked taken aback at this unexpected response. Michael went on, but now the smile vanished, and he leant in, close to the man, and spoke softly. "You see, the thing is, Lieutenant, that, apparently, I am not a gentleman, and that I am, in fact, Lieutenant, a killer. Now, I am sure that you don't want to die at the hands of a mere killer who isn't a gentleman? So, I suggest that you go back to your friends, explain that it has all been a misunderstanding, and then go and dance with Senhorita Barros. Twice at least. I would consider it a favour if you took over my responsibilities as her escort. I am sure that you will find her excellent company." He paused a moment as if struck by a thought. "Tell me, Lieutenant, are you a wealthy man?"

The Portuguese Lieutenant stammered, "Yes, I suppose so."

"In that case, you should get on famously. I am sure her brother will be delighted, as will her father and her aunt. Now, go away."

The officer stood for a moment, a look of bewilderment on his face. Then he gave a slight bow, turned and made his way back to his friends. Michael turned his back on the room. George and Henry stood with looks of utter amazement on their faces. "Bloody Hell" exclaimed George.

"George, Henry, watch them, tell me what they do."

"He's talking to them," observed Henry, "they're laughing, one's clapped him on the shoulder, he's walking over to Senhorita Barros, asking her to dance, they're taking the floor."

Michael relaxed, and smiled at his friends. "I think that went rather well. But, do you think one of you could find room for me in your billet, tonight?"

Chapter 7

The following morning came the inevitable summons from Major Stanhope. Michael had stayed with George Keating, having been escorted there by him and Henry. George's batman had been dispatched to Senhora Marquez' house and roused out Lloyd and Francisco, who had swiftly packed the bare necessities for Michael. The rest would follow once Michael had a new billet. Thus it was that Michael, properly dressed, arrived at the Regimental headquarters.

Barra greeted him with a broad grin. "Well, Roberts, you've put the cat amongst the pigeons. Best go straight in."

To Michael's surprise Stanhope wasn't alone, with him was Major Archer and Colonel Lobo, the Portuguese garrison commander. Stanhope was staring out of the window, Lobo sat relaxed in an armchair, Archer was leaning against the wall, and to Michael's surprise not only gave him a smile, but winked!

"Mister Roberts," began Stanhope, turning to face him. "Major Archer and I have heard all about last night, from Colonel Lobo. We are not entirely sure what happened, but I understand from the Colonel that you are to be congratulated on diffusing a potentially difficult situation, one that could have had severe repercussions for relations between ourselves and the Portuguese army."

Michael was stunned, this was not what he had been expecting. Stanhope continued, "However, Major Archer feels, and I agree with him, that it would be a good move for you to leave Abrantes." Michael glanced at Archer, who had a slight smile on his face and gave Michael a brief nod. "Lieutenant Bence has been looking after our affairs in Lisbon while he recovered from his wound, and he is now fit. We have been advised that the Regiment should be receiving a supply of men and horses in the next few weeks. Bence can bring them up to the Regiment, and you can replace him. I believe you have a house in Lisbon where you may stay with no charge to the Regiment or the army, so, pack your baggage, I want you away from here as soon as possible. Take yourself off to Lisbon, and stay there. Is that clear?"

Winter in Lisbon was mild and wet. Michael went first to his home, surprising the Santiagos, who started rushing around preparing his room, and rooms for Lloyd and Francisco. Parra would stay in the rooms in the stables. Once all that was in hand, he rode on his own out to Belem, reported to the officer in charge in Lisbon, and then went in search of Henry Bence. He found him in a dingy coffee shop near the main depot at Belem. He was sitting alone by the fire, and looking very miserable, but his face lit up when he saw Michael.

"Michael, Good Lord, what are you doing here?"

"Looking for you, Henry. I come bearing your freedom."

For the next hour they sat and talked while Michael brought Henry up to date with all that had happened in the Regiment, including the reasons for his exile to Lisbon. Henry told Michael that he was completely recovered from his wound, save for a very slight limp. Michael asked him where he was billeted, and on learning that he was in a hotel, and paying for himself, he immediately invited him to stay with him until the new men and horses arrived and he went back to the Regiment. Henry accepted without hesitation. There was a general awareness that Michael had a house in Lisbon, but little was known about it. Lloyd had kept quiet about it, resisting the temptation to tell Sergeant Taylor.

It didn't take long to move Henry into Michael's home, along with his batman, baggage and horses. Henry was impressed, and Michael took great pleasure in having his first guest for dinner. Senhora Santiago provided them with a traditional Portuguese fish stew, and there was a fine wine from the cellar. After dinner there was a good bottle of port, and they relaxed by the light of the fire and a couple of candelabra.

"Now that," said Henry, "was a quite excellent dinner. Thank you, Michael. And you have a splendid house, far better than that hotel. I knew you were from Lisbon, and that you had a house here, but that's about all anyone knows. You are a bit of a mystery in the Regiment."

"Really? Well, there's not a lot to tell." Over the rest of the port Michael gave Henry his, edited, autobiography. He left out the difficulties with his uncle, but spoke of his grandfather's connection to Earl Harcourt. He said not a word about Musgrave or Elaine.

Henry listened, but when Michael fell silent, he asked, "But what about all these special duties that Stanhope complains about?"

Michael laughed. "Nothing very special, I'm afraid Henry. It's the price of being fluent in Portuguese and knowing my way around Lisbon." Fortunately, Henry seemed satisfied.

They idled away a week or so, purchased some new clothing for themselves, found a shirt maker recommended by Senhora Santiago, bought half a dozen each, and arranged for the maker to supply the other officers on demand. Michael treated himself to a new pair of ankle boots to wear under his overalls. Then the new men and horses arrived, and they were kept busy for another week, preparing them to march to join the Regiment. Henry departed with them on New Year's Day.

After that, there was little for Michael to do. He attended at headquarters out at Belem in the morning, conducted whatever business was necessary for the Regiment, and then his afternoons were free. With Henry gone, Francisco took a note to Roberta for him, and in return he was told to call as soon as possible. He needed no urging. They made love urgently, passionately, comfortable with each other.

Roberta propped herself up on one arm. "So, tell me, Michael, how was Abrantes? And what are you doing in Lisbon?"

Michael groaned, and started to tell her all that had passed. When he told her about the patrol incident Roberta stuffed the sheet into her mouth to stop her laughter. "It wasn't funny, Roberta. Stanhope was livid, and I got sent away for a fortnight to collect horses from Vila Viçosa."

"Oh, Michael, sometimes you are just so English. It is funny."

He smiled, "Well, yes, I suppose it is. You should have seen Maria's face when we burst out from the trees." He chuckled at the thought. "And you were right about her. She was just after a rich husband. And I might have found her one."

"What?" exclaimed Roberta. "Tell me, tell me!"

So Michael did, about the ball, the Portuguese officer, and calling himself a killer.

"Oh, Michael, that was so dangerous. What if he had called you out?"

"I expect it would have been stopped. I am sure Stanhope, Archer and Colonel Lobo wouldn't have let a duel go ahead. At least, I am fairly sure. Anyway, they thought it would be better if I got out of Abrantes for a while, and sent me here."

"And I am glad they did," said Roberta. "And I am glad that you are done with Maria Barros."

"Which reminds me" said Michael, "Senhora Santiago was also quite pleased to learn that things were over with Maria." He smiled mischievously. "I didn't tell you, did I? She also told me, before I went back to Abrantes in October, that she and my mother were well aware of you and me and our affair."

Roberta looked surprised. "Oh! Oh dear."

"Yes, apparently they decided that you were a lot better than some women I might have ended up involved with. I suppose that counts as approval."

"Better than some? Ha!" She poked Michael in the ribs. "However, she was right about Maria Barros. She was not right for you, and you let yourself get entangled just because she was there." Michael tried to protest. "No, Michael, listen to me. You can't expect to find true love with the next woman to come along after Elaine. Have you decided that you really are free of any ties to her?" Michael said nothing. "No, I thought not. And until that happens you will not find anyone." She paused. "Well, not your true love, anyway. You will just have to make do with friends." She poked him in the ribs again. "That's a hint, Michael."

Together they want to see General de Silva. Michael wanted to know if anything had been discovered about the man who had shot at him, and had been shot down by Lloyd. Roberta hadn't seen de Silva for a few weeks, and she was as keen as Michael to learn the latest news, if there was any. De Silva greeted them warmly, and they were soon settled comfortably in his office with a supply of coffee.

"It has taken some time," began de Silva, "but we have found out who he was. Something of a solitary individual, who worked as a very minor clerk for Sampaio."

"Good Lord," exclaimed Michael. "I assume you mean Henrique de Samapaio? His business is huge, on a par with Quintela."

"Yes, him, and it is." replied de Silva. "You will know as well as I do that Sampaio's business has been supplying a very large proportion of the army's supplies, as well as importing huge quantities of flour and other goods from the Americans."

Roberta spoke up. "But surely that's fairly common knowledge? What did he do? Sampaio's business is very large."

"So far as we can discover he seems to have been some sort of glorified messenger. He carried documents between various offices, warehouses, and so on. And not just in Lisbon. He went as far afield as Oporto."

"That would make him a useful courier for Renard," said Michael. "But if he had never met Renard, I don't see what he was doing?"

"Perhaps Renard wanted a courier, and this man was sent to him by someone?" suggested Roberta.

"A messenger for Sampaio could go pretty much anywhere," said Michael. "He could have been approached and recruited for that alone, and nothing to do with Sampaio's business."

"Still, Renard isn't in Lisbon now," objected de Silva, "well, not so far as we know, but we will keep investigating. Someone told him where to go to meet Renard, and they are, presumably, still here." De Silva gave a shrug. "The only real answer is to find and eliminate Renard."

"I'm all in favour of that," stated Michael.

Michael also took advantage of his free time to visit his lawyer, Senhor Furtado. He had him draw up a will.

Michael wanted to make sure that those who looked after him now, would be looked after if the worst should happen. Furtado said he would send a copy to Michael's London lawyer, Rutherford.

In mid-January Michael heard that Villiers had been replaced as Ambassador by Charles Stuart, who had been the Ambassador to Spain, and he was not entirely surprised during one of his daily visits to headquarters to be told that the new ambassador wanted to see him. Arriving at the embassy he was shown quickly into the presence of Stuart.

"Lieutenant Roberts, it's a pleasure to meet you." Stuart stepped forward, offering his hand to Michael, his handshake was brief, but firm. He was a well built man of about thirty, with an oval face, a small mouth, and a high forehead topped by short brown hair. His grey eyes had a slightly melancholic look. "I heard from Villiers about your activities in counter intelligence, very useful, I must say. When I heard that you were in Lisbon I thought I would take the opportunity to meet you. I have heard good things, Mister Roberts, good things." He gestured to a chair at a side table, "Now sit you down, and we shall have a little talk." He turned to a clerk who had been hovering. "That's all, thank you, Rodgers, and see to it that we are not disturbed." He took a seat opposite Michael, and poured tea for them both. As he handed a cup to Michael he said, "First, I should very much like to hear how you know this fellow Renard? I believe you grew up with him, here in Lisbon?"

Michael was surprised at Stuart's knowledge. "Yes, sir, until his father was recalled, he was a minor French diplomat." Michael went on, telling Stuart briefly about his life in Lisbon, and how he had come to be an officer in the Sixteenth.

"So, by good fortune we have someone who can identify Renard? That must make you unique outside the French Army?"

"Almost, sir, de Silva has an agent who also knows him."

"Ah, another boy from your youth?"

"Err, something like that, sir."

"Ah, discretion," Stuart chuckled, "I like that. And you get on well with de Silva and his agent?"

"Yes, sir." Michael supressed a smile.

"Excellent. As you know, the Spanish guerrillas prevent most French agents getting into Portugal. They also provide us with much useful intelligence about the French Army. They cause all sorts of difficulties on the French lines of communication. Single couriers are dead men. This Renard, however, is a very different matter. From what I gather he seems to be able pass himself off with complete conviction as a Portuguese and get in and out of Lisbon without difficulty. That makes him a very dangerous man, Mister Roberts, very dangerous. And it doesn't help that there are only two people who can readily identify him. So, take care Mister Roberts, we need that knowledge. If Renard returns he must be stopped, the defence of Portugal is delicately balanced. At the moment French ignorance of our situation is in our favour, it would be good to keep it that way."

"I see, sir."

"Good. So you may well be called upon again to help with the intelligence war. Do not underestimate the importance of that war."

"No, sir." And Michael thought to himself, if it gets me close to Renard I shall be a happy man.

"And now," said Stuart, "can you recommend a good shirt maker?"

A few days later Michael's exile in Lisbon was ended when he received orders to march immediately to Coimbra and prepare quarters there for the Sixteenth. They were expected to arrive at the beginning of February, as the whole army gradually concentrated and moved north to oppose the French gathering around Salamanca.

The familiar route took Michael's party along the north bank of the Tagus, the weather was cold, with light rain blowing in the wind. He and Lloyd were wrapped in their dark blue cloaks, with water dripping off their Tarletons, while Parra and Francisco wore heavy, wool capotes with several capes, and broad brimmed hats. Huddled up against the weather Michael was taken by surprise as they neared Castanheira. Hundreds of local peasants and militia were labouring at what looked like extensive field fortifications on the hills overlooking the road. Further on a dam was being constructed across a river. It looked as if the intention was to flood the plain between the hills and the Tagus. Michael shook his head in disbelief. If the French got this far, all the army would be able to do would be to board the transports and sail for England. A few field fortifications might delay the French, but not stop them. No one really believed that the British Army and its untried Portuguese allies would be able to defeat the overwhelming numbers of French that were rumoured to be gathering. It had even been said that Buonaparte himself would lead the French, bringing with him his famous Imperial Guard.

As they rode north, and the altitude increased, it got colder, and Coimbra was a lot colder than Lisbon, situated as it was, where the narrow valley of the Mondego came out of the mountains and turned into the wide valley that took it to the sea. There was going to be a lot to organise, as all the horses had to be stabled against the winter cold and rain. They were still recovering condition after the Talavera campaign. Johnny, Duke, Harry and Edward had all benefitted from their stay in stables in Lisbon, with

Parra and Lloyd lavishing care and attention on them. It was Lloyd's considered opinion that the Regiment's horses wouldn't fully recover until there was fresh grazing in the spring.

They approached Coimbra across the long bridge over the Mondego, the town rising above the river and capped by the huge buildings of the university, white with red roofs. Coimbra was a grand city, a university city through and through, but the university was closed, and instead it was housing troops and horses, including the Sixteenth. Michael managed to find each Squadron a house for its officers adjacent to the billets for the men and the stables. The large quadrangles of the University would be used to exercise the horses, the tall buildings giving shelter from the cold winter winds. When the regiment arrived, Major Archer expressed his satisfaction with the arrangements made by Michael. The greatest problem, as ever, was getting sufficient fodder for the Regiment's six hundred or so horses.

While Michael was in Lisbon there had been changes to the organisation of all the cavalry regiments. Troop Quartermasters, who were senior NCOs, were to be replaced with Troop Sergeant Majors. In Michael's troop poor Redmain, who had died at Vila Viçosa, had been replaced by Flynn as the Troop Sergeant Major. Others would be replaced as opportunity arose. There was now a Regimental Quartermaster, a commissioned rank, and Troop Quartermaster John Harrison had been appointed, giving Blood the step up to Troop Sergeant Major. The make-up of the Squadrons was unchanged and Michael, in addition to Cornet George Keating of Ashworth's Troop, would once again be working with his friend Henry van Hagen of Lygon's Troop.

One evening Michael was invited to a small soiree at the home of Commissary Gordon, in charge of the stores at Coimbra. The evening was presided over by Mrs Gordon, an attractive and vivacious lady, noted for her hospitality and sense of fun. Michael went with the Sixteenth's Commissary, Mister McNab. There was a good number of people present, and many had brought musical instruments, while some demonstrated no little ability to sing. Michael, whose voice was more suited for the parade ground and the hunting field than it was for the drawing room, kept out of the way and settled down to play a few hands of cards. He found himself partnered with a woman of about his own age, Portuguese, dark haired, brown eyed, handsome rather than pretty, and with a liveliness about her. A local merchant and his wife were their opponents. The stakes were a few Vintins, allowing for a fairly light hearted game. Sitting opposite his partner, Senhora Monteiro, it was natural that they should look at each other a lot, but Michael realised that they were also smiling a lot at each other as they enjoyed the game.

The game broke up and Michael went in search of refreshments, accompanied by his whist partner. They had a glass of wine each, and then Michael asked her to dance. The company were enjoying some English country dances, and Michael led Senhora Monteiro through two of them, with much laughter as she was guided by all through the intricacies of a hay for the first time. At the end she held Michael's hand, laughing with the pleasure of the dancing. Then their eyes met, he smiled at her, gave her hand a slight squeeze, and both were returned.

Supper followed, and Michael escorted her in and sat next to her. There was loud chatter all around, and he leant close to hear what she was saying. As he did so he smelt her perfume, and felt the pressure of her leg against his. He learnt her name was Sofia. He pressed back with his leg. They talked about inconsequential things, to each other and those of the company nearest. Mrs Gordon, sitting across from him, caught his eye. She raised her eyebrows, shrugged, smiled, and turned to talk to another guest. Michael looked at Sofia, and it was clear she had seen Mrs

Gordon's actions. She looked at Michael, and laughed, her eyes bright. Their hands found each other below the table.

Henry van Hagen was also present, and as Michael left to escort Senhora Monteiro home, he agreed to cover Michael's duty in the morning if Michael was delayed. He was.

Sofia was a widow. Her husband had been in Oporto when the French arrived, and, as far as she knew, he had died on the bridge of boats across the Douro when it collapsed. He had vanished without trace. That had been almost a year before. Now she lived simply, in a single room, high in a building near the university, the sort of accommodation usually occupied by students. She had no servants, eking out the little money she had, accepting invitations to anywhere she would be fed. As an educated, attractive, single woman with the army in town, she was in demand at soirees, and had become a frequent attendee at the Gordons'. But she was lonely. Michael enjoyed her company, her conversation, their love making, but he was under no illusion. They both understood that they were supplying a need that each other had, and that one day, soon, Michael would leave. In the meantime, he was happy to dine with her, and to share her bed when he was not on duty. It was an arrangement that suited both of them.

Naturally, he came in for some ribbing from his closer friends in the Regiment. He and Henry van Hagen were supervising the Squadron exercising their horses on fields outside the city. Henry called him a lucky dog, and said he was envious. Then Henry bluntly expressed his view of Maria.

"I tell you, Michael, you did well to get away from Abrantes, and Senhorita Barros. I grant that she was a very attractive young woman, but I think that whoever she manages to marry will find her very expensive. It was pretty clear to Alexander and myself that she was just after your money, and your house in Lisbon. I heard about your house from Bence."

"Yes, I think you are right, Henry." He paused. "You are not the only one to tell me." He paused, and wondered how much he could tell Henry. "Perhaps, one day, I'll tell you and Will all about it. And what came before, in London, and this." He pointed to his scar. "There's more than I told Bence. Perhaps after dinner in my house, over a bottle or two of port, but not now, but one day. And for now, I shall take comfort with the lovely Sofia."

Henry looked at Michael, he knew as well as anyone about the accident that had resulted in the ferocious looking scar, or at least he thought he did. Now he wasn't sure. He didn't press his friend, that would be poor form, and by the next day he had forgotten.

In February the new clothing for the men finally caught up with the Regiment. Due on the twenty fifth of December the bundles of uniforms had been delayed in transportation to Lisbon, then sent to Abrantes, and finally to Coimbra. The next two weeks were busy with every tailor in the Regiment, and in the city that could be engaged, employed in fitting the uniforms to the men. The regiment's tarleton helmets had suffered in the rain and heat, the leather warped, the metal trim fell off, but they were expected to last three years, and cobblers were employed to do what they could by way of repairs. Slowly, but surely, the Regiment was recovering from the effects of the Talavera campaign.

In early March the townspeople of Coimbra celebrated Shrove Tuesday, as usual with a mass, a religious procession, and then a grand ball. The religious observations were diplomatically avoided by the army, but many officers, save those with duty, turned out for the ball, including a good number from the Sixteenth. Michael escorted Sofia. She already knew Henry van Hagen, but now she met more of Michael's fellow officers. Stanhope avoided them, but Major Archer was perfectly pleasant, and even danced with her, as did Captains Ashworth and Lygon. Lygon was a particularly accomplished dancer, and returned a slightly flushed Sofia to Michael.

Later Michael and Sofia sat close together in her room near the University. A small fire warmed the room, while a little extra light came from two candles on the table. After the fun and exhilaration of the ball, they were enjoying a relaxing glass of wine. Sofia's head rested comfortably on Michael's shoulder.

"Sofia?"

"Yes?"

"You know that one day I will be leaving Coimbra?"

"Yes."

"What will you do?"

"I don't know." She paused. Staring at the fire. "I might go to Lisbon. I might go to Oporto. I don't know." She took a sip of her wine. "I suppose I could just stay here!" She laughed quietly.

"Perhaps you should go to Oporto, see if you can discover what happened to your husband?"

"I don't know, Michael. I can't really think about it now. Now I am happy just being here with you." Another sip. "I know it won't last. You will ride off, and I shall never see you again." Michael sat still, said nothing. "That's just the way it is. You need a woman's company; I need a man's. We get on well, we don't love each other. I still love my husband, although I believe him to be dead. I think you love someone else as well, and while you are bound to someone by the bonds of love, you cannot love another." She shrugged, finished her wine, and stretched. "For now, though, we have each other's company, let's not waste it, Michael." She stood. "Now, help me out of this dress."

The next day Michael took a party out, down the side of Mondego valley, towards the coast, which was a mere thirty miles away, they were looking for forage. McNab the commissary was with them. In a small village they found a quantity of last years straw. While McNab haggled over a price, and the men loaded up horses and mules, Michael rode Johnny to the edge of the village, and looked out across the broad valley, covered here and there with flood waters. He sat deep in thought. He thought about what Sofia had said. Roberta had told him the same. Even Maria seemed to recognise that, so far as love was concerned, he wasn't a free man. Although, of course, he was, he had it in writing, so why couldn't he be free? He now accepted what Roberta had said, that love could come again, but not to be in a rush to look for it. But, somehow, he would have to turn the words in Elaine's letter into a reality. How to do that eluded him completely. He wasn't even sure if he wanted to. He still deeply and desperately loved her. He shook his head, and rode slowly back to the foraging party.

Chapter 8

Towards the end of March Michael was called to the Adjutant's office. With Barra was Major Archer, who addressed him first. "Well, Mister Roberts, it looks like you are off on another of your jaunts on special duties."

"Sir?" Michael wasn't sure of where he stood with Archer, but he noticed that Barra looked cheerful enough.

"Yes, you are to take yourself off to Lisbon and see the Ambassador, no less. I have orders here from Colonel Murray himself." He waved a sheet of paper at Michael. "You can set off in the morning, it will give you time to, err, settle things here before you go." He smiled briefly. "I suspect we will be moving north before long. I am afraid that you can't count on coming back here." He shrugged. "That's the way it is. Make the best of it. Mister Barra here will see you have no duties tonight." Barra nodded in agreement. "We will see you when the Ambassador has finished with you. Now, off you go." Michael headed for the door, but Archer hadn't quite finished. "And, Roberts, be careful."

Once he had informed Lloyd, Parra and Francisco of what was happening there was little for him to do, and he left them packing and preparing the baggage and horses. He went to see Ashworth, who already knew. Henry van Hagen and George Keating expressed their views colourfully, but cheerfully, Henry offering, only half in jest, to look after Sofia for him. Then Michael walked around a corner and almost into Major Stanhope.

"Beg your pardon, sir," said Michael, saluting.

Stanhope gave his usual languid wave in return. "I gather you're off to Lisbon, Roberts," he paused for a split second, "again," he added with a slight sneer.

"Yes, sir."

"I can't say that I like it, Roberts, but you know that. Major Archer is of a different view." Stanhope shrugged, and looked away from Michael towards the distant mountains. He continued, almost speaking to himself. "But perhaps that won't matter much longer."

"Sir?"

"Nothing, Roberts, nothing." Stanhope turned abruptly and strode off. Michael watched him go, shook his head, and went on his way to see Sofia.

Sofia was philosophical about the news. "Oh, so soon? Well, it was going to happen." She held him tight.

"Have you thought what you might do?" asked Michael, gently stroking her hair, his other arm holding her close around her waist.

"No, but I suppose that now I will have to."

"Look, if you get to Lisbon, find my lawyer, Senhor Furtado, he's well known, easy enough to find. He will know where I am, and will help you."

"Thank you, Michael, but you don't owe me anything, I must work things out for myself."

"If you need anything, I am sure Henry would help you."

She thumped him playfully on the arm. "Michael Roberts, what do you take me for?" She laughed. "Henry is lovely, but not really my type of man." She placed her hand on his chest and looked up at him. "No, once you have gone, I shall decide what to do, but for now, kiss me."

Michael left Sofia's early the next morning, while it was still dark. He had no idea if he would ever see her again.

The journey to Lisbon took three days, on the last day they travelled from Alenquer and dropped down onto the familiar road alongside the Tagus. As they rode beyond

Castenheira Michael was surprised to see that the fortifications that were being constructed there had been filled in. Approaching Alhandra, however, he found new works under way, running from the Tagus and up into the hills above the road. He shook his head at the labour being expended on what appeared to be no more than field works. They arrived, tired and weary, at Michael's house as it was getting dark. Quickly and efficiently Lloyd and Francisco unpacked the baggage and Parra took care of the horses and mules. By the time all was done, Senhora Santiago had prepared hot food for all. She seemed to be getting used to his sudden appearances. There was no fire in the dining room, so Michael ate with everyone in the kitchen. Michael soon retired to his room for the night, leaving the others to relax without his presence. As he sat on his bed to pull his boots off, he took a long look at the miniature of Elaine that stood on his bedside table. The old dilemma still held him fast and went around and round in his mind. He knew Elaine had set him free to love again, had told him that he might, but he didn't feel free.

The following morning Michael sent Francisco to tell Roberta he was back in Lisbon, and to see his sister. "Tell Senhorita Roberta that I am going to see the British Ambassador, then go and let Juan Moreno know that the boys are well. After that, you can help Senhora Santiago clean up my uniform." Michael had dressed in his civilian clothes for his meeting with the Ambassador.

The Ambassador, Charles Stuart, was brisk and business-like. "Lieutenant Roberts, thank you for coming so promptly. Sit you down, sit you down. Now, we have received information, reliable information, the source need not concern you, that part of Renard's network is still active in Lisbon. By the way, it might interest you to know that Renard was seen in Paris last month." Michael raised his eyebrows at that, but said nothing. "This information could tie in with the fellow killed back in, err," he consulted a sheet of paper, "in October, I believe?" He looked at Michael for confirmation.

"Yes, sir, that's correct."

"I understand from de Silva that the fellow was employed by Sampaio as some sort of clerk cum messenger, and was obviously working for Renard. But that doesn't really get us anywhere, does it, with anyone else?"

"No, sir, it doesn't."

"The thing is, Roberts, that we have no other information to go on. Nothing at all, beyond the report from Paris about an agent still active in Lisbon." He paused. "It's a reliable report, if our source says there is an active agent, then there very probably is. Every time our source sends us information they are taking a huge risk. Consequently they only send what they consider important and reliable. All of which leaves us with a considerable problem."

"Yes, sir."

"And we can't ignore it. So, what I want you to do is see to it that this network is finally shut down, for once and for all. You are to go and see de Silva, he is expecting you, and between you, find what remains of this network and destroy it."

"Yes, sir."

It came as no surprise to Michael to find Roberta waiting for him with de Silva. De Silva was as ebullient as ever, greeting him warmly. Roberta gave him a warm smile. Stuart had already shared with de Silva the same information he had given Michael. It didn't take long to review it, and soon the three were sitting in silence, sipping their coffee, at a complete loss.

Roberta was the first to speak. "Lucas," she addressed her cousin, "do you have a list of all those agents of Renard who were caught last October?"

"Yes, of course, it's here somewhere." De Silva sifted through papers on his desk. "Yes, here you are." He handed Roberta a single sheet of paper. Michael knew there were about a dozen names on it. He and de Silva watched Roberta intently as she studied the paper with a furrowed brow. Eventually, she looked up at them both, her eyes alight with excitement.

"Merchants," she said, "all these people were connected one way or another with merchants, Renard was, or is, using the merchant networks for his own network."

"What!" De Silva shot out of his chair to look over her shoulder.

"Yes, look. The man killed at the inn was an employee of Sampaio, here's some one who worked for a flour merchant, and we know how much flour is being imported for the army. This one was a muleteer, this one a carrier, and here, this one worked for Quintela."

"Quintela?" asked Michael, surprised. "What as?"

"Some sort of messenger, apparently, hmm, another messenger," Roberta observed thoughtfully. She went on, "This one worked in a chandlers, a big one, this one in the customs house, and this one was another merchant's clerk. This woman was mistress to one of Sampaio's chief clerks, amongst others, and this one worked at a coffee house on Black Horse Square where a lot of merchants meet. All of them are connected to merchants and trade."

De Silva sat down heavily. "That," he said slowly, "makes a considerable amount of sense. They had access to all sorts of information, much concerning the supply and movements of the army, and they would have had the means to travel almost anywhere to communicate their information. That was bad enough last year, but if some of the network is still active, if the French get to know numbers and locations now, it would greatly aid any French invasion."

"I'm curious about the one who worked for Quintela," said Michael. "When I arrived here last April I went to see Quintela's head clerk, Rodrigues, I knew him from when my father worked for Quintela, which gave me a reason to call, but I also went because Musgrave asked me to." De Silva raised his eyebrows. "Yes, well, it was before I knew you, Senhor. Anyway, Musgrave was curious to know if any of the staff had stayed on there while it was Junot's Headquarters. Rodrigues said that no one had, so far as he knew, he had taken his family south of the Tagus while the French were here. However, I did mention Renard to him and the possibility he had set up a spy network."

"Ah," was de Silva's comment.

"Yes, sir, I would know better now. Anyway, he said he would make enquiries among the clerks, to see if anyone had heard anything of Renard. He told me later that no one had, although I realise now that no one would admit to knowing Renard, rather it would have caused alarm. And now I come to think about it, he volunteered that information, on a later visit, without me asking him about it. It is just possible that he wanted to make sure I believed there was no connection between Renard and Quintela's."

"So you don't know if he did actually make any enquiries?" asked Roberta.

"No, I don't," Michael replied. "I called on him again in October, after the shooting, and the subject didn't come up. I was there on a personal matter," Michael saw the unasked question on de Silva's face, "about Senhor Barros, he had been asking questions about me."

"Ah, yes," de Silva actually looked slightly embarrassed. "I gather that has, err, resolved itself?"

"Yes, sir," Michael glanced at Roberta who was trying hard not to smile, "it has."

"Good, good. Now, let us see. We have two messengers, one worked for Quintela, one for Sampaio, so we are faced with the possibility that there might be an agent in either Quintela's or Sampaio's business, or even both, who is probably well connected in order to gather useful information. In the case of Quintela's, there is just a slight chance that it might be Rodrigues. The question is, how to find him and catch him?"

"It needs," began Roberta, slowly, "to be something that will tempt the spy to act, whoever it is, but what? If he is in Quintela's and has heard from Rodrigues that Michael was asking about Renard he will be very careful, particularly as he probably has no easy way of communicating with Renard."

"Look," said Michael, "why don't I just call in on Rodrigues, there's still plenty of time today, and see what happens? If he tells me anything useful about Renard, all well and good, and we will know we can trust him, if not, we haven't lost anything."

De Silva and Roberta looked at each other, then de Silva shrugged. "I can't say I have a better idea, and it would be a start. If there is a spy in Quintela's, Rodrigues' help would be useful. Yes, do that, and can we meet again tomorrow morning? One of us might have had an idea."

"Then, Lucas," said Roberta" might I suggest that you send some men to watch Rodrigues now. Just in case?"

"Yes, yes, of course, a good idea, excuse me for a moment and I will see to it." De Silva rose and left the room.

"Michael, after you have seen Rodrigues, will you come and have dinner with me?"

"Yes, of course I will," and they smiled at each other.

As Michael strolled down the hill and came to the square overlooked by the Palacio Quintela, his eye was caught by the sight of a flower seller sitting opposite the main entrance to the Palacio. He walked across to have a look at what she had, he thought he might buy some for Roberta. The woman was elderly, dressed in black, her face dark and wrinkled, but with eyes that looked sharp and bright.

"Ah, back again, eh?"

Michael was startled. "What do you mean, Senhora?"

"Ooh! You speak Portuguese! You were here last October, and before that in the spring, but you were in uniform. You are a British officer."

"Yes, Senhora, I am, and you have a very good memory."

"There's not much else to do except watch people when I am sitting here all day, every day."

A thought occurred to Michael. "Tell me, do you know my friend, Senhor Rodrigues, he works in there?" Michael gestured at the Palacio.

"Oh, yes, a very nice man. He buys flowers for his wife from time to time, and always on her birthday."

"How do you know it's for her birthday?"

The old woman laughed. "Because it's the same day every year!"

"You've been selling flowers here for a long time?"

"Oh, yes, since I was a young and beautiful woman."

"Oh, Senhora, you still are!"

She laughed and flapped her hand at Michael. "Ha, then you need spectacles, young man."

Michael laughed in turn, then asked, "Tell me, did you sell many flowers to the French when they were here?"

"Oh, yes, and I always charged them double," she laughed.

"And did Senhor Rodrigues buy flowers for his wife then?"

"No, I didn't see him from the time the French arrived until after they had gone."

Michael thought very carefully about his next question. "Senhora, I will buy that that bunch of roses, please." While the old lady was tying up the roses, and taking his money, he asked, casually, "So, if Senhor Rodrigues was away, who looked after the Palacio while the French were here?"

"Why, young Senhor Serrano. He was in and out all the time. I think he must have worked very hard, because no one else came, just him."

"Thank you for the roses, Senhora, they are very beautiful, as you are." The old woman laughed and waved a dismissive hand at him.

Michael turned to walk slowly towards the Palacio. Could it really be that straightforward, that easy? He walked into the gloomy lobby of the Palacio, looking for the porter, instead he saw a pile of baggage and a cavalry officer with his back to him. The officer turned around and called out, "Roberts, good to see you. Are those roses for me?" He laughed loudly.

"Good Lord, Tomkinson, what on earth are you doing here?" Michael strode forward and shook the hand of William Tomkinson firmly. "It's good to see you so well."

Tomkinson laughed, "Yes, it was a bit touch and go, but I am perfectly well, and fully recovered, thank you. I'm here with Sir Stapleton, Lord Tweeddale, his Quartermaster, and Sam Dudley who's come out as his aide again." General Cotton, now Sir Stapleton, had been in England following the death of his father, and having succeeded to his father's Baronetcy, had returned to take command of all the British cavalry under Viscount Wellington. Tomkinson continued, "We've been billeted here, and they're just off looking at rooms while I do baggage guard duty. And what are you doing here, carrying a bunch of roses, and out of uniform as well?"

"All of that, Tomkinson, is a long story. How long are you here for?"

"A couple of weeks, I expect. We've the usual to sort out, I need a horse until I can get to the regiment and find out how Bob is, and a couple of baggage animals wouldn't go amiss. I hope Owen has looked after Bob."

"I saw him in Coimbra, but you must remember things have been hard for the horses. Feed hasn't exactly been plentiful."

At that moment Sir Stapleton Cotton appeared with Tweeddale, and Lieutenant Dudley, also of the Sixteenth.

"Hello, Roberts, what are you doing here?" asked Sir Stapleton.

Michael thought quickly, "Just calling in on Senhor Rodrigues, sir, the head clerk, he's an old family friend."

"Yes, of course," Sir Stapleton looked sombre for a moment, knowing Michael's history, "but come up to our rooms when you've finished, you can tell me how things are with the Regiment."

"Yes, sir, I will."

The porter appeared with some help to carry the baggage, and he took Michael along to Rodrigues' office. The greeting he got did not strike him as one from a man with a guilty secret. "Michael! What a pleasant surprise, come in, come in. Tomas," he called out to the porter, "have some coffee sent in to us. Sit down Michael, we have one of your Generals and two others staying here, just arrived."

"Yes," replied Michael, "I saw them as I came in. The General is an important man, Senhor, he commands all our cavalry."

"Really? Then I must see that he is taken great care of. The Baron would want it no other way. Nothing is too good for you British who have freed Portugal from the French."

If Rodrigues is a spy, he's a damn good actor, thought Michael. "You are too kind, Senhor. I am just in Lisbon for a few days on leave, so I thought I would just say hello."

"And buy some flowers, I see. From old Priscila in the square?"

"Yes."

"She has been selling flowers there for as long as I can remember."

"There is one thing, Senhor."

"If I can help, Michael, I will."

"It is nothing new, just the question of the identity of Augusto."

"Ah, no, I'm sorry, Michael, I have asked around. Of course, Augusto is not an unknown name, but I cannot find any with a connection to your father."

"Thank you for trying."

The conversation continued with generalities. Then Michael mentioned the weather was much better than when he had last been in Lisbon. He asked Rodrigues if he remembered how wet it had been the previous October.

"Ah," said Rodrigues, his memory prompted, "a strange thing happened last October. One of our messengers disappeared, vanished, not a trace!"

"Really," answered Michael, knowing full well the truth of the matter, "that must have been disturbing?"

"Indeed. One of our clerks was very upset, he had got him the messenger's job."

"Poor fellow. Perhaps he felt some responsibility?"

"Perhaps, but young Serrano will learn that nothing in life is certain."

Michael supressed his delight at hearing that name. "Indeed, Senhor, indeed. But I have taken up enough of your time, and the General, Sir Stapleton, wishes to speak to me before I leave."

"Then you must go to him, Michael. But call again, it is always a pleasure to see you."

Michael found Sir Stapleton and the others settling into a suite of rooms on the top floor of the Palacio. "There you are, Roberts, how are you and the Regiment?"

"Very well, sir, but I wonder, may I have a word with you in private?"

"What?" Sir Stapleton looked around in surprise, but the others were busy and appeared not to have heard. "Yes, of course, through here, I think." He led the way into a small sitting room and closed the door. "What's this about?"

Briefly Michael explained to Sir Stapleton what he was doing in Lisbon, and, without saying how he knew, that there was probably a French spy in the Palacio. As he talked Sir Stapleton had looked first of all surprised, and then concerned.

"Damn it, Roberts, that is not good. D'ye think we should move our billet? There are some sensitive papers in my baggage."

"You could, sir, but we need to catch this fellow, and if you suddenly move it could drive him into cover."

"What d'ye suggest then?"

"Obviously we need to keep your papers secure, sir, and we can do that by making sure that they are always under guard, but without making it obvious. While you are all in residence they should be safe enough. There are the four of you and your two servants. I shall speak to General de Silva and see what we can do about catching this fellow. It helps that I think I know who it is."

"Do you, bigod? Very well, do that now, and come back later."

"Yes, sir."

De Silva was surprised to see Michael again that day, but was delighted by his news. "Well done, Michael, very well done. Now, what shall we do about it? We have a name, but no proof."

"No, sir, but with Sir Stapleton in the Palacio we could set a trap. The possibility of access to the General's papers would be a great temptation. If the spy stole them, and was caught with them…" Michael left the rest unsaid.

"It's a great risk, Michael. What if we didn't catch him, and he got away with them?"

"I've thought about that, sir. We can get false papers prepared in the next few days, then arrange for the rooms to be left unattended, and you can have men watching for our man. I think we can assume our spy isn't Rodrigues, if you can identify Serrano, have him followed from now on, find out where lives, and take him there."

"I can arrange that, I have already sent men to watch Rodrigues, they can easily change to this Serrano, but how do you propose to get Sir Stapleton and his party out in a realistic manner?"

"That's easy, sir, I shall invite them to dinner, and perhaps you and your wife would also like to attend, Roberta as well. The more it looks like a convivial party, the more convincing it will be."

"And the real papers?"

"I have a safe."

"I like it, Michael, I like it very much. Do you think Sir Stapleton will agree?"

"I think so, sir, I can promise him some good wine. I just need a few days to organise everything at my house."

"And that would give me enough time to make my arrangements."

Sir Stapleton did agree. Roberta thought it was a splendid plan. Senhora Santiago was both pleased, at the thought of Michael entertaining in his home for the first time, and horrified at the prospect of putting on a dinner for such a distinguished company.

Three days later all was ready. Senhora Santiago had been helped by Roberta's maid, Constanca, and had called in the help of two of her friends. Senhor Santiago was to deal with the wine, Francisco and Parra acting as footmen. Lloyd had his uniform cleaned and put into good order, and was on duty at the entrance. Sir Stapleton and Tweeddale had made sure that everyone in the Palacio Quintela knew about the dinner, while Tomkinson and Dudley had both been hard at work producing false returns and locations of all the British cavalry in Portugal.

General and Senhora De Silva arrived first, accompanied by Roberta, who was to act as hostess for the evening. Moments later the four officers arrived, accompanied by their two servants, who were there, ostensibly, to light their way home with lanterns. Sir Stapleton's papers were quickly locked away, and then the evening passed sociably. Michael had finally taken the chair at the head of the table, with Roberta to his left, Sir Stapleton to his right. As he glanced at Roberta, delighted though he was at her presence, he could not but help feel a little sadness. It would have been perfect if Elaine could have taken that place. Roberta caught the look, saw the sadness, and squeezed his hand under the table. De Silva and Sir Stapleton were both complimentary about the wine served, and Senhora de Silva sang the praises of the lamb. The conversation flowed as well as could be expected with Michael the only person fluent in both languages, but everyone tried, to the accompaniment of much laughter. No one mentioned the reason for the gathering.

The table was being cleared, and the two ladies were about to retire to refresh themselves, and leave the men to a glass of port, when Lloyd appeared at the dining room door. Silence fell as everyone looked at him. "Begging you pardon, sir, there's a gentleman at the front door asking for General de Silva."

De Silva rose from the table immediately, and, with an "Excuse me, Ladies, Gentlemen," followed Lloyd out. Senhor Santiago served the port, Roberta decreeing that she and Senhora de Silva would stay until the General returned. A few minutes passed with barely a word spoken, then the General reappeared, and smiled. "We have him!"

The sense of relief around the table was palpable. The General and Michael were both congratulated, Senhora de Silva looked very proud of her husband, and Roberta smiled at Michael, and squeezed his hand again, where it lay on the table. The General resumed his place at the table, and held his hand up for quiet. "We have arrested a Senhor Serrano attempting to steal confidential papers from your quarters, Sir Stapleton. His rooms are being searched as I speak. There is nothing else we can do tonight, my men are taking care of everything, so I suggest we continue to enjoy the excellent hospitality and wines of Lieutenant Roberts."

It was late when the dinner party finally broke up. De Silva and his wife left first, followed by the party from the Palacio. As he left, Sir Stapleton shook Michael's hand firmly, and said "Thank you Roberts, for a splendid evening, and well done, very well done."

Michael returned to the dining room where Roberta was still sitting in her chair. "Roberta, I'll get Lloyd and Parra to escort you home." He looked around. "I'll just go and find them."

"No, Michael." She smiled shyly. "Constanca and I are staying here tonight. It's all arranged with Senhora Santiago."

"Oh? Yes, of course. She's prepared a room for you?"

"No, Michael." She rose from her chair and walked towards him. "That isn't necessary."

"What? Oh!" Realisation dawned. "But I thought you didn't want any man to see you in the morning?"

"Michael, you're not any man."

Michael took a candelabra in one hand, Roberta's hand in the other, and led the way upstairs. In Michael's room Roberta saw the diptych, with the miniature of Elaine, on the table next to the bed. Before Michael could do or say anything, she had picked it up and looked at it by the light of the candles, the lock of copper red hair shining. "She was very beautiful."

"Yes, she was." Michael gently took it from Roberta, closed it, and placed it carefully in a drawer. He turned back. "But she's not here, you are, Roberta."

Roberta raised her eyebrows in surprise. "Thank you, Michael, I know what that took, and I love you for it." She held out her hands to him. "My friend, my very, very best of friends."

In the morning they breakfasted together in the dining room. Senhora Santiago brought them coffee, cold meats, and bread rolls. When she thought Roberta wasn't looking she gave Michael's shoulder a squeeze. She was pleased to see Michael sitting at the head of the table, at last where he belonged. She couldn't claim to understand the relationship between Michael and Roberta, but it seemed to make him happy, and that was enough for her. And better than that Barros girl.

Michael and Roberta walked across Lisbon to de Silva's headquarters. It was a glorious, spring day, warm, still, the sky blue and cloudless. By comparison the expression on de Silva's face was gloomy. When they were shown into his office, he was sitting at his desk, going through a pile of papers.

"Good morning, Lieutenant, Roberta, please take a seat." He called out to his clerk for more coffee and cups. He passed his hand over the papers. "These are what were seized at Serrano's rooms. There is no doubt that he is our spy. These are his uncyphered letters, the fool kept them. Fortunately, most of them seem to be from last year, and the information is now out of date. In fact he seems to have done nothing since last October, when we know Renard left Lisbon, until last night. They are not addressed to anyone, but there is little doubt they were for Renard. There's one in particular…" The door opened and the clerk brought in the coffee. De Silva waited while he poured cups for Michael and Roberta, and left, closing the door behind him. "This one, it's dated last April, and we have to assume that it was sent, or given to Renard. I will read part of it to you. 'A British officer visited Rodrigues yesterday. After he had gone Rodrigues asked all the clerks if they knew anything of you. The officer's name is Michael Roberts'." De Silva threw the paper down. "I am afraid, Michael, that we must assume that Renard knows about you."

"Oh!" was all Michael could say.

"Lucas," Roberta asked, "has Serrano given you any idea where Renard is?"

"No, only that he isn't in Lisbon."

"And has he said anything about other agents still active?"

"No, not yet, but he is still being questioned. We can't be sure that there isn't also an agent in Sampaio's, but we will see what we can do about that, I have some ideas."

Michael hardly heard. Renard knew about him. If he knew one thing about Renard, it was that he didn't like being crossed. He thought back to when they had been boys together in Lisbon, the cause of their fight had come back to him. Renard had caught a stray dog, and was beating it with a stick. Michael had stopped him, they had argued, Renard had pushed him, Michael had punched him, and then knives had been drawn. Fortunately, or not, other boys had intervened. He doubted Renard knew his connection to Elaine, or that Michael was determined to see her avenged, in person if possible, but he had no doubt that Renard would kill him, if he had the chance. Renard was, always had been, a bad loser, and Michael had done him a lot of harm.

"Lieutenant?" De Silva spoke to him.

"Sorry, yes?"

"I was saying, I will have copies of all these made, and sent to Mister Stuart, and I think copies should also go to Viscount Wellington. Perhaps Sir Stapleton could take them? They should be ready in a few days."

"Yes, I'll speak to Sir Stapleton and Mister Stuart about it."

Both Sir Stapleton and Stuart were happy with de Silva's suggestion. Stuart was also happy that Michael should return to his Regiment, and Sir Stapleton said Michael could accompany him as far as Santa Comba Dao, where the Regiment had moved in the last week. He would then go on to Viseu where Wellington's headquarters had been established. Rodrigues was horrified by the news about Serrano. In his remorse he offered to give any help he could. Tomkinson reaped the benefit in the form of the acquisition of a nice mare and a couple of baggage ponies at a very fair price.

While all the preparations were going on Michael found himself dining with just Sir Stapleton one evening. The conversation, inevitably, turned to the Sixteenth, as Sir Stapleton was an officer in the Regiment as well as now commanding all the cavalry. Suddenly, in the middle of the conversation, Sir Stapleton said "The Ambassador has spoken to me about the help you have been in intelligence matters, and I must say, for myself, that I was impressed by your part in this latest business. Stuart told me that, according to de Silva, it was entirely your doing that the spy was caught. I realise that this business has taken you away from the Regiment, but you should know that you are well thought of where it matters. I hope it hasn't caused you difficulties in the Regiment?"

"Err, well…" Michael hesitated.

"I will take that as a yes, and that can't be allowed. You appear to have a skill, Mister Roberts, and one not granted to many, let alone young cavalry subalterns. Let me see, Major Stanhope has been in command until recently, and now it's Major Archer. Clement Archer is a good man; I'll make sure he is aware of circumstances." He looked intently at Michael. "No need to worry about anyone else, d'ye understand me?"

"I believe so, sir, thank you."

Chapter 9

It was a large party that set off northwards a few days later. For Michael it was a pleasure to ride with his two fellow subalterns from the Sixteenth, neither of whom he had seen for some time, Tomkinson since he had gone home the previous May to recover from his wounds, and Dudley since he had gone to England with Sir Stapleton in December. Lord Tweedale was a Lieutenant in the First Guards, and Michael only knew him by sight. Major General Sir Stapleton Cotton, as its Lieutenant Colonel, had trained the Sixteenth before he left for the Peninsular, and was well known to all the party. Trailing along behind them came Lloyd, Francisco, Parra, Sir Stapleton's two English servants, and two Portuguese hired in Lisbon to manage the baggage.

Their destination, the small village of Santa Comba Dao, was thirty miles to the north of Coimbra, which was now occupied by the Sixth Portuguese Line Regiment, under the command of Colonel Ashworth, the brother of Captain Ashworth, and well known to Sir Stapleton. The General decided they should break their journey there, he wanted to take a good look at the Portuguese infantry. There was a lot of speculation about how well they might perform in battle. It was a convivial visit, and the Portuguese infantry looked fine and steady. The policy of using British officers to train and command the Portuguese army was promising to pay dividends.

Michael took the opportunity to slip away from the party to go and see Sofia. Her room was empty, she had gone. He enquired of her neighbours, but got no more than a vague suggestion that she had gone to Oporto, someone thought she had gone in search of relations of her late husband. No one was really sure. Michael walked slowly through the narrow streets, back to his billet. He was disappointed not to see her, but wasn't entirely surprised. What had been between them had been born of necessity, of need, there had been affection, but never love. It had helped him to realise that it hadn't been love that had driven him towards Maria. Love was what he and Elaine had had, even if they had only admitted it when it was too late. He missed her desperately, but seeking to replace her with other women was not the answer. He now knew that he wouldn't be able to find true love again until he decided for himself that he really was free of the bonds that still held him to her.

They arrived at the headquarters of the Sixteenth two days later. Michael's squadron was also there, the other three being in outlying villages. Everyone was delighted to see the fully recovered Tomkinson back, and Michael was able to slip away and find Ashworth. He found him in one of the buildings being used for stables. He and Troop Sergeant Major Flynn were looking over the horses with their dragoons, discussing condition and fitness. Just a quick glance was enough to tell Michael that things were looking up. The horses were not back to their condition before the demands and hardships of the Talavera campaign, but they were now well on the way. Another month and they would be ready for anything.

Ashworth spotted him. "Roberts, it's good to see you back." He let down the hoof he had been examining and straightened up. "I think we will leave the shoes off for another week, Sar'nt Major, should be alright by then. Is that the last of them?"

"Yes, sir, just the half dozen not fit now."

"Excellent, carry on Flynn. Now, Mister Roberts, come and have a coffee and we will catch up on things."

Ashworth's billet was providing a home for all the squadron officers, and Lloyd, Parra and Francisco were already sorting out Michael's baggage and the horses and mules.

"I'm afraid that you are going to have to double up with young George for the moment." Ashworth informed Michael as they made themselves comfortable with a cup of coffee. "And it seems that old George won't be returning. He's not enjoying the best of health. Still not recovered from the fever. So we are going to need you, Michael, particularly with Alexander still in England for little longer. Wheeler is supposedly coming out to join us shortly, but I don't know who will get him. I know Cocks is hoping to get Tomkinson."

Ashworth continued to bring Michael up to date with the state of the squadron, and then Sir Stapleton came in. Both men jumped to their feet, but were waved back into their chairs. "Hello, Ashworth. Good to see you. I thought I would just let you know that young Roberts here did very well in Lisbon. Saved us all a lot of embarrassment and pleased the Ambassador no end."

Ashworth beamed. "That's very good to know, sir."

Sir Stapleton turned to Michael. "D'ye think you could give the Captain and myself a few minutes?"

"Yes, sir, certainly." Michael took himself off to see how Francisco was getting on.

Once Michael had gone, Sir Stapleton settled himself in an armchair, and accepted Ashworth's offer of coffee. "Yes," the General continued to Ashworth, "Roberts did very well, and I have just been telling Stanhope and Archer the same, but I fear that Major Stanhope doesn't quite like the idea of Lieutenant Roberts and his, err, other activities. Doesn't like 'em at all. I hope I haven't made things worse for Roberts. I saw Anson while I was in London. He told me all about the business in Hythe. I don't think there is any doubt that Stanhope set Roberts up to fail. The fact the Roberts didn't will have annoyed Stanhope. I don't like it,

Ashworth. Don't like it at all. And, of course, I haven't said any of that. Not right, discussing a senior officer with his junior. Still, I shall plead unusual circumstances."

"You can rely on me, Sir Stapleton."

"Excellent, thank you, but, tell me, how is Roberts as a Regimental officer?"

"He's very good, efficient, competent, conscientious. Takes a genuine interest in the men and they like him for it." He paused, thoughtful for a moment. "He is developing a bit of an edge, not sure if that's good or bad, yet. You know about the business at the ball in Abrantes, of course? Van Hagen told me that when Roberts faced down that Portuguese officer he was shocked by it. Said that when Roberts called himself a killer, he believed it, absolutely." Ashworth shook his head. "On the other hand, he does seem to have straightened out Lloyd."

"Ah, yes, Lloyd. He seems to be a reformed character. Might he make corporal again?"

"From what I can gather, sir, mostly from Sar'nt Major Flynn, Lloyd isn't interested, prefers being with Mister Roberts."

"Does he, now? I know he's a useful man with a sabre, good to know he's backing up young Roberts. As for his edge, as you put it, I think I know what you mean. It will all depend on how he chooses to use it. Now, will you dine with me tonight?"

Despite Sir Stapleton Cotton's best efforts, and his assurances that Michael had the approbation of himself, Viscount Wellington, Ambassador Stuart and Earl Harcourt, Major Stanhope seemed more determined than ever to make Michael's life a misery and drive him out of the Regiment. Indeed, as Sir Stapleton had feared, the latest news of Michael's success had merely served to antagonise Stanhope further. Major Archer was aware of it, and tried to mitigate it without undermining Stanhope. The whole Regiment was aware that Stanhope had a down on Michael, the constant criticism was impossible to miss, or justify. No one shared Stanhope's view of Michael as an officer, he was well regarded. Matters were not helped when, inevitably, word got out about Michael's home in Lisbon. Stanhope heard, but knew little more than there was a house.

All the officers of the Squadron and the Regimental headquarters had formed a mess in the headquarters building. There, Stanhope chose to be particularly cutting after dinner one evening, taking advantage of Archer's absence at the army's headquarters.

"Roberts." Usually, Stanhope ignored Michael in the mess, and at his addressing Michael, the conversation around the dining table died away.

"Sir?"

"I hear you have a house in Lisbon, Roberts?"

"Yes, sir."

"What is it? Some sort of shop? Dry goods and the like?" The convivial atmosphere of the mess froze. Everyone knew about Michael's house from Bence and Tomkinson. Sitting next to Michael, Ashworth slowly put his wine glass down, resting his hand on the table.

Michael took a deep breath, and decided he had little to lose. "Not at all, sir, it's a rather fine house, built after the earthquake of '55. Four floors, apart from the cellars, and there's stabling for a dozen horses on land at the back. Apart from the dining room, there are three other reception rooms. The ballroom is a little on the small side, but it has a splendid view across the Tagus."

Stanhope glared at him, he felt he had been made to look foolish. In his anger he lashed out. "I also hear you've a Portuguese baggage keeping table for you."

Ashworth's hand shot out, gripping Michael's arm tightly, and he spoke quietly, barely a whisper, but full of warning, "Roberts." It earned him a hostile glance from Stanhope.

William Tomkinson had gone pale, a horrified expression on his face, and he spoke quickly, before Michael could say anything. "No, sir, not at all. She is a lady, sir, cousin to General Lucas Seabra de Silva, the head of the Portuguese police. I met her when we dined at Roberts' home, sir, with Sir Stapleton and General de Silva."

Stanhope turned his gaze on Tomkinson. His expression was impassive, but his eyes blazed with fury. After a moment he rose from the table and left the room. A collective sigh of relief went around the room.

Captain Lygon was the first to speak, and he addressed Ashworth. "Well done, Ashworth." He nodded at Ashworth's hand, still restraining Michael. "I think perhaps you and I might have a word?" He rose slowly from the table, looking to Ashworth for an answer.

"Yes, yes, of course, I think that's a very good idea." Ashworth released Michael's arm. "Mister van Hagen, you will keep Mister Roberts company. You too, I think, Mister Tomkinson." He rose, nodded at the assembled officers, and left with Lygon.

Michael looked slowly around at those left, Henry van Hagen and William Tomkinson, John Harrison, Joseph Barra, John Peers, Isaac Robinson, and 'young' George Keating. The silence was palpable. Then Michael spoke. "Will Alexander is going to be furious he missed that." There was a pause, and then everyone burst out laughing, releasing the tension. Michael smiled across at William Tomkinson, "Thank you."

With the atmosphere somewhat restored, both Michael and Tomkinson were pressed for information about Michael's home, but mostly about the cousin of General de Silva. It was good humoured, and Michael answered modestly, while Tomkinson answered with gross exaggeration, leading to more laughter.

The following day the consequences of the incident began to make themselves felt. At midday Archer arrived back from Viseu, and according to Lloyd, who told Michael, having heard it from Sar'nt Major Flynn, who got it from Archer's orderly, first he had been visited by Ashworth and Lygon, and then there had been a stand up blazing row between Archer and Stanhope. Then Tomkinson was summoned to see Archer. He returned with a grin to where Michael and Henry van Hagen were waiting. "It seems that as I am not yet posted to a troop, Archer wants me to go and supervise the horses grazing out at Frieshada. I'm to stay there until I'm posted. I hope some of you will come and see me in my exile?"

"Why you, and not me?" asked Michael.

"That," replied Tomkinson, "is something that Major Archer chose not to share with me. If you will excuse me, gentlemen," he gave a mock bow, "I must be on my way. 'At once', the Major said, and I don't think he's in the mood to be argued with." He hurried off to his quarters.

"Hell's teeth," exclaimed Henry. "What is going to happen about you?"

"Thank you for those words of comfort. We shall just have to wait and see."

The next event was Joseph Barra riding off in the direction of Viseu, twenty five miles away. Michael stayed around the stables, talking to the dragoons as they cared for their horses, aware that every man knew something was going on. He also knew, from Lloyd, who had got it from Flynn, that RSM Williams had told the mess servants and others who had witnessed the incident the night before, to "keep your damned mouths shut, or I'll have the skin off your backs." The Sixteenth was not a flogging Regiment, that was reserved for the very worst crimes, but no one was going to call the RSM's bluff.

It was late mid- morning the next day when a tired looking Barra returned. He handed his horse to an orderly and disappeared inside the Regiment's headquarters. A quarter of an hour later an orderly came out with a summons for Ashworth. Michael was summoned half an hour later. Making his way into headquarters he was relieved to see no sign of Stanhope. With Archer in his office were Ashworth and Barra. Their expressions gave nothing away as Michael came to attention and saluted. Archer was behind his desk, Ashworth in an armchair in the corner, while Barra leant against the empty fireplace.

"At ease, Mister Roberts." Archer placed some papers on the desk. "I cannot say that I am happy, nor is Captain Ashworth. However, we do not hold you responsible for the, ah, incident the night before last. You were, without doubt, provoked. That said, Major Stanhope is a field officer of this Regiment, and has commanded it with some distinction, including at Talavera. He is a fine officer. The whole circumstances are extremely unfortunate, and quite unprecedented in my experience. Consequently I took it upon myself to ask for advice and assistance from the senior officer of the Regiment here in Portugal, namely Sir Stapleton Cotton. That is where Mister Barra has been. He was, as a witness, able to give Sir Stapleton a full account of what passed. He was also able to inform Sir Stapleton that Mister Alexander is due to return within the next week or two, he will be accompanied by Cornet Wheeler, and, of course, Mister Tomkinson has returned already." Archer paused for a moment." As a result it has been decided that we can manage without you."

No, thought Michael, no, don't send me home!

"These," Archer gestured at the papers, "are your orders. You are to pack immediately, and report to Colonel Murray at army headquarters. He will give your new duties to you. Headquarters is moving from Viseu to Celorico tomorrow, you should catch up with them in a couple of days." Michael's heart sank, not home, but a job pushing paper in headquarters, he'd had enough of that during two weeks in Oporto. "At the request of Sir Stapleton, you may take Lloyd with you. Your other servants are, of course, your own business."

Archer paused and looked at Ashworth and Barra. "Anything else, gentlemen? No? Then off you go Mister Roberts. You can leave first thing in the morning."

A slightly stunned Michael found Henry van Hagen nearby, looking out for him. "Well, Michael? What's happened?"

"Exile, Henry, I've been exiled to the Quartermaster General's Department."

The weather had been wet, and it continued to rain throughout the two long days it took to get to Celorico. The weather suited Michael's mood, and Lloyd, Parra and Francisco shared the misery of the ride in silence.

Celorico was a long, thin town, built on a spur of the Serra da Estrela, with the river Mondego just to the north. It was less than sixty miles from the Spanish frontier fortress town of Ciudad Rodrigo, with its Spanish garrison commanded by General Herrasti, which effectively blocked any advance by the French, and which they would have to capture before they could enter Portugal. The British Light Division under General Crauford lay between Ciudad Rodrigo and the Portuguese border, watching the fortress, while the bulk of the combined British and Portuguese army was just in Portugal. When Michael arrived at Headquarters in Celorico, the French under Marshal Ney were around Ciudad, which sat on the north bank of the Agueda, but with the atrocious weather, the river in flood, and limited numbers they were only able to manage a partial blockade on the northern side. Nothing more would be possible until the arrival of the bulk of the French army and the siege guns. There was still free access into the town across the river from the south, through a suburb on the south bank, and across a long bridge. The old castle, which acted as the town's citadel, stood on a circular knoll overlooking the bridge.

Celorico was strangely quiet, considering it held the Army's headquarters, and it took Michael a while to find Quartermaster General Murray's quarters. He was relieved to find a familiar face in Lieutenant Colonel De Lancey, Murray's deputy, hard at work in a gloomy room.

"Hello, there, Roberts, isn't it?" De Lancey sounded cheerful as he returned Michael's salute. "I've been expecting you, but you're not joining us, you are off to Sir Stapleton, Dudley has fallen from his horse and broken his arm, so Sir Stapleton asked for you." He smiled. "A narrow escape from scribbling, eh?"

"No, sir, not at all…"

"Ha, don't give me that," De Lancey laughed. "Although in this damned wet weather you might prefer it to riding around the countryside. Still, it isn't helping the French. Sutcliffe!" A redcoated infantry private appeared in response to De Lancey's shout. "Take Mister Roberts here over to Sir Stapleton's quarters." He addressed Michael. "I'm afraid that you'll find everything a bit rough and cramped. But needs must, eh? Right, off you go." He waved dismissively and went back to the documents on the table.

Sir Stapleton's quarters were in a moderate sized house, which was similarly deserted, save for a handful of servants. One of these showed him to the room, which, he was informed, he would be sharing with Sam Dudley, while another took Lloyd, Parra, Francisco and the horses around to the back of the house. Within an hour he had moved in, Francisco improvised a bed for him, his trunk making do for a dressing table. Lloyd found him and reported that the horses were all under cover, and that he and Parra would bed down over the stables with the other grooms and batmen. Francisco was to share a room with four other servants. It was, indeed, a bit cramped, but better than a bivouac.

The first officer to appear was Dudley, looking pale with his arm in a sling. "Hello Roberts, I see you've found us?"

"Dudley! How are you, what the devil did you do?"

Dudley gave an embarrassed laugh. "Too much of the local wine, just fell off and landed badly. Sir Stapleton was furious, threatened to send me home. Fortunately Barra turned up, and here you are, filling in for me for a month or so until the doctor allows me to ride."

"So you have all heard what happened'.

"I'm afraid so, Roberts. Frankly, I think Stanhope is a fool, and this business has made him no friends, but then I have visited your house and met the Senhorita Roberta." He grinned. "Sir Stapleton was a bit struck, I think."

At that moment there was a clatter of hooves from outside. "Speak of the devil," said Dudley, "that will be him and Tweedale. You'd best come down and report to him. We will be dining shortly."

Sir Stapleton and Tweedale were peeling off sodden cloaks in the narrow hallway. The General seemed pleased enough to see Michael. "Roberts! Good to see you. Have you made yourself comfortable? We are a bit strapped for space, but never mind, at least we've a roof. We will be dining in ten minutes, then we can have a talk about what I want you to do. I'm afraid we can't match the dinner you gave us in Lisbon, but we will do what we can." He laughed and the others all smiled.

Michael thought that the dinner was as good as any in the Sixteenth's mess, and afterwards he and Sir Stapleton retired to a small parlour that was serving as the General's office. They were no sooner seated in a couple of armchairs than Sir Stapleton launched straight in. "I am glad to have you here, Roberts, it's timely with Dudley breaking his arm, but it is also extremely unfortunate with regard to how it has come about. Usually such circumstances would result in one officer or the other exchanging into a different regiment, and usually the junior officer. Frankly, I don't want that, and neither does Viscount Wellington. It would mean sending you home, and you are too useful here, as you demonstrated in Lisbon." Michael couldn't help but looked surprised. Sir Stapleton went on, "Yes, Wellington knows all about what happened in Lisbon, he's seen the spy's letters, and he knows your role in it all. He heard all about it from Stuart, the Ambassador. He also knows about the business with Stanhope. He's not so happy about that." Sir Stapleton paused to sip his wine.

"I think, however," he continued, "that we can forget about that problem for a while. As you know, the French already have some forces blockading Ciudad Rodrigo on the far bank of the Agueda, and we expect the main body of their army shortly. Wellington wants me to go and see some Spanish guerrilla leader, fellow calls himself Don Julian Sanchez. He's got a band of lancers down in Nave d'Aver. I want you to help with the language. We will leave early the day after tomorrow. I've a few things to do here first, and it will give you a chance to find your way around."

Two days later, the small party was on the road an hour before dawn. It was a fifty mile ride that took them around the northern end of the mountains and then south, through Guarda. Michael had chosen to ride Duke, who was younger than Johnny, with a little more stamina. At Guarda, with stunning views to the west and the mountains behind it, they found the British 4th Division, and Sir Stapleton called briefly on its commander, General Cole, while Michael and Tweedale took some food and drink with Cole's staff. For once the weather was fine and dry, and they pushed on and made good time, arriving at Nave d'Aver in the mid-afternoon.

Nave d'Aver turned out to be a small village set in a rolling countryside, half way between the Coa and Azaba rivers, and it was full of Don Julian's lancers. Somewhat to Michael's surprise they were uniformly dressed in blue jackets with red facings and yellow lace on the chest. They gave an impression of competence and efficiency, not the hotch potch band of brigands Michael had been expecting. Don Julian himself was a thick set man, in his mid-thirties, a little shorter than Michael, and with a long, black moustache and black curly hair. His uniform was also in blue, although with more gold lace, and he wore a French cavalry shako, with the Imperial Eagle turned upside down. When he removed it, it revealed that his hair had receded off his forehead. Fortunately he spoke a very passable English and introductions were quickly made, including the officer with Sanchez, Lieutenant Strenuwitz, who it transpired was from Bohemia, his English having a strong Germanic accent to it.

"General Cotton, it is a pleasure to meet you!" Sanchez welcomed them warmly and waved them into a large house in the centre of the village. "I am afraid that we cannot offer very much in the way of hospitality, but what we have is yours."

Inside a lavish meal with plenty of wine awaited them, and the occasion became very sociable. While they were eating the conversation remained general, but after the table was cleared, Sir Stapleton made a suggestion. "Don Julian, might I suggest that you and I, and Lord Tweedale, discuss our future cooperation and how best to employ you and your men? And, perhaps, Lieutenant Strenuwitz could show Lieutenant Roberts something of your men?"

"Of course, General, you wish to know if my men are an effective force." He smiled as Sir Stapleton tried to object. "No, General, it is quite acceptable, I would do the same. Strenuwitz, please show the Lieutenant around."

Michael and Strenuwitz walked through the village, strolling from building to building in the late afternoon sunlight.. All the horses were under cover, and the Bohemian took the opportunity to inspect billets and horses. Michael was impressed by the condition of the horses and remarked on it to Strenuwitz. "Thank you, Lieutenant", he replied, "but, you see, these men grew up riding and caring for their horses. Around Salamanca the main farming is cattle, and the herding is done by these charro, as they are called, who use a long pole like a lance to manage the cattle. They are skilled horsemen and lancers by upbringing. Indeed, Don Julian is sometimes called El Charro. And now, perhaps we can ride out and visit our pickets? I would be interested to know how the English cavalry arrange such things."

As they rode along Michael asked Strenuwitz how he came to be with Don Julian's lancers. He explained that he had been in an Austrian Uhlan regiment in Italy, had been wounded, got separated from his regiment, and in trying to avoid the French had found himself driven further and further south, until he took a ship and found himself in Spain. By sheer chance he had finally ended up in Salamanca, heard about Don Julian's lancers, and sought them out. His background and knowledge as an Uhlan officer had made him very welcome. He had helped Don Julian turn the cattle herders into soldiers.

The story took as long to tell as it took to reach the outlying pickets, and both men were pleased to find that there was little difference in the way they were organised and conducted compared to British cavalry. By the time they returned to the village they were well on the way to becoming friends. Later that day Michael was sitting in the warmth of the setting sun, along with Sir Stapleton and Tweedale, for once the rain had stopped, and the sky had cleared.

"Now then, Roberts, what do you make of these fellows?" asked Sir Stapleton. "You've been out and about with that Strenuwitz, all we have heard is Don Julian telling us how wonderful they all are. He's certainly an enthusiastic fellow, clearly doesn't like the French at all."

'Well, sir, they are all through and through horsemen, their horses well cared for. Strenuwitz tells me that around here they are raised to it. We went out to their pickets and they seemed to be as good as anything we do. They know the country around here very well, that's clear, and being all local men they are well supported by the Spanish peasants. Frankly, sir, I was surprised to see how well organised they are, and I think that is down to Strenuwitz, he was an officer with an Austrian Uhlan regiment in Italy, sir."

"Is that so? That would account for quite a lot."

"Yes sir, of course, I have no idea how they might perform in a fight, but for scouting and picket work they seem more than adequate, sir."

"Good, because that is exactly what we want them to do. They are going to be the southern end of our picket line watching the French at Ciudad Rodrigo, and also keeping a watch on movements on the road to Salamanca. Sanchez reckons they can make a damn nuisance of themselves into the bargain." He stubbed out the cigar he was smoking. "Right, gentlemen, an early start in the morning, I am turning in, Roberts, be good enough to check on the horses, will you? Ask these fellows to have them ready for five o'clock."

As Michael returned from the stables to the house where they were accommodated, dusk was falling, and a voice came from the shadows. "Lieutenant Roberts, how was your day, and what do you think of my men." Don Sanchez emerged into the last of the daylight.

Sanchez had spoken English, but Michael replied in Spanish, "It was most enjoyable, Senor, and I think your men are fine horsemen."

"Thank you, and your Spanish is excellent, but I think I detect a Portuguese accent? How is that?"

"I was born and grew up in Lisbon, Senor, speaking Spanish just seemed to happen, I suppose my father working for Baron Quintela and being involved in trade helped."

"And where are your parents now, safe in England?"

"No, Senor, they were lost at sea escaping from the French."

"Ah! My pardon, lieutenant." Sanchez was silent for a moment. "So, you are fighting the French for personal reasons, for revenge?"

"Yes, Senor, I suppose I am."

"I am also fighting them for revenge." Sanchez went on, very softly, Michael straining to catch his words. "The French have done me great wrong." In the growing dark Michael could barely make out Sanchez' face. "They killed my parents; they raped and killed my sister. For that I must kill all that I can." He paused, looking without seeing for a moment. When he spoke again it was simply to say, "Good night, Lieutenant." With that, Sanchez turned and walked into the darkness.

Michael stood alone in the dark. He thought of his own loss and his hatred for one particular Frenchman. For a moment he felt pity for Sanchez, who would never know if he was revenged on the men who had killed the ones he loved, but Michael would know, and he would not rest until he knew.

Chapter 10

There was only one cavalry regiment immediately supporting the Light Division, the First King's German Legion Hussars, the rest of the cavalry were further back into Portugal where the fodder was better. It was helping Sir Stapleton get those ready for the coming campaign that occupied much of Michael's time. When not riding to and from one regiment or another Michael was occasionally sent into Ciudad Rodrigo. Don Sanchez had moved his lancers into the town to harass the French, but also to watch the road from Salamanca for the rest of the French and, most importantly, the advance of their siege guns. On these visits he usually stayed overnight and got to know Sanchez and Strenuwitz better.

Strenuwitz was a very professional cavalry officer, and he instilled in the lancers a discipline and effectiveness, but it was Sanchez who had the charisma and the flair to hold together his men, and lead them against the French. Lloyd was a frequent companion on these trips and the two men were soon able to help Sanchez and his men. They had been issued with British light cavalry sabres in addition to their traditional lances, but had little idea how to use them properly. Michael and Lloyd were able to address that shortcoming whenever they could find the time. When Michael had told Sir Stapleton about this, he had encouraged Michael to give all the help he could. "It would be no bad thing," he had said, "if Sanchez and his men feel a little gratitude towards us."

Gradually the French forces facing Ciudad Rodrigo grew in number. On the first of June they began to build a bridge across the Agueda a few miles upstream of the fortress. In two days it was finished and they started to push cavalry patrols across, but made no attempt to establish a permanent presence on the south side of the river. Sir Stapleton decided that he wanted to have a look at it, and with Michael and Tweedale, rode out in the torrential rain, first to Gallegos, where he found General Crauford, commander of the Light Division, who decided that he would join their reconnaissance. Gathering up some two hundred of the Hussars as an escort, they set out towards Ciudad Rodrigo.

Once they had gone two or three miles, Sir Stapleton ordered Michael to ride into Ciudad Rodrigo and see if Don Sanchez was available to join them, with his men. Michael pushed on with Lloyd, and was soon clattering over the long bridge over the Agueda and into Ciudad Rodrigo. As luck would have it he found Sanchez in the large square in the centre of the town, with his lancers already mounted.

"Don Julian, your pardon!" Michael rode up, saluted, and greeted him.

"Lieutenant Roberts, what can we do for you? This is an unexpected pleasure!"

"Generals Cotton and Crauford are going to have a look at the bridge at La Caridad, and General Cotton has requested that you and your lancers join him."

"But of course! Perhaps the French will come across and we can kill a few of them." He smiled at Michael. "Please ride with me. Strenuwitz! Bring the men on!"

An hour later the lancers and hussars were concealed behind a hill overlooking La Caridad and the new bridge. Sir Stapleton, Crauford, Michael, and Sanchez cautiously made their way over the brow of the hill and down through the scrubby trees and undergrowth towards the river. Around them a dozen of the Spanish lancers were spread out in a protective cordon. Ahead, Strenuwitz and two lancers reined in some fifty yards in front, just visible through the thin scattering of trees, and waved them forward. Despite the rain, from where Strenuwitz sat quietly on his horse, it was possible to see the bridge below, about half a mile away. The bridge was built on wooden trestles, and troops could be seen building a fortification on the near side. On the opposite bank the bridge was overlooked by high ground where artillery was visible. On the near bank, a line of French light cavalry vedettes was visible, and a guard of about a squadron of dragoons.

Despite the rain, the small group of horsemen soon caught the eye of the French, and a patrol of a dozen and more dragoons started slowly towards them. "Well, gentlemen," said Sir Stapleton, "I think we've seen all we need. Time to go, I think."

On their return to Celorico, they found General Anson waiting to see Sir Stapleton. He had returned from England to take command of the brigade, the Sixteenth Light Dragoons, and the highly respected First Hussars of the King's German Legion. Inevitably, he came across Michael.

"Hello, Roberts, how are you finding staff work?" he asked Michael.

"Well enough, sir," Michael replied, "but it would be good to be back with the Regiment."

"Yes, and I know that Captain Ashworth would like you back. It's all a bit unfortunate, the business with Stanhope." He paused for a moment. "Still, I am sure matters will resolve themselves in due course. And I hear that you did good work in Lisbon over that spy."

"Thank you, sir."

"Well, you just carry on, and, remember, you have friends, Roberts, good friends."

The following day the French began to build another bridge, this time downstream from Ciudad Rodrigo. They also started to push more cavalry across the finished bridge, and skirmishing between them and Beresford's pickets became increasingly frequent. Finally, an advance in strength by the French pushed the pickets back until the most advanced of them was at Marialva, some ten miles beyond Ciudad Rodrigo. Beresford and Sir Stapleton decided to try to get a convoy of mules carrying corn into the fortress. Despite the French advance it was still possible, just, to get messages in and out, and Herrasti had been warned. There were a hundred mules, and Sir Stapleton sent two squadrons of the German Hussars with them. Michael and Lloyd went along to liaise with Sanchez if he became involved. Herrasti played his part to the full, several large sallies were made from the fortress, which occupied the attention of the French on the north bank of the Agueda. Sanchez met the convoy a few miles out, and together lancers and the Hussars escorted the convoy to the end of the long bridge into Ciudad Rodrigo. There followed a nervous wait of over an hour until the mules reappeared, relieved of their burdens. The lancers rode back with the Hussars and mules to where they had met them, and then returned to Ciudad while the Hussars got the mules back to Gallegos and safety. It was a fraught few hours. Michael had managed a few quick words with Sanchez, and then they set off through the interminable rain to return to Gallegos and then on to Celorico.

A few days later Captain Scovell, now commanding the Corps of Guides, arrived at Celorico with serious news from Ambassador Stuart. A conference was quickly convened, with him, Michael, Sir Stapleton and Murray. Scovell brought them up to date with developments in Lisbon. Although the spy in Quintela's business had been caught, de Silva had thought it worthwhile to put a man into Sampaio's organisation to check on the staff. He had detected nothing unusual until three weeks ago. There had been a clerk who always worked late, but de Silva's agent thought nothing of it, it seemed to be a normal, habitual thing. Then the man hadn't appeared for a few days. The agent reported it to de Silva, who made his own enquiries direct with Sampaio. Sampaio had expressed surprise when he heard about the clerk who worked late, he didn't know of any reason why that should be. The man was identified from his description, and Sampaio informed de Silva that the man had no business being where he was seen. He was a cattle buyer, the office he had been in was involved with dispatching supplies, rations, tools and equipment in particular, to the army. De Silva had sent men to the clerk's address, there they found that he hadn't been seen for several days. Further enquiries had established that the man had regularly visited the Salamanca area in the past to buy cattle. The suspicion was that he had information that he believed would be useful to the French, and had made his way north hoping to get to the French, who were known to now be at Salamanca. De Silva had informed Stuart, who had asked Scovell to take the news to Murray.

"Do we have any idea exactly what information he might have?" asked Michael.

"No, the dispatch department dealt with anything and everything sent out to the army", replied Scovell.

"So it might not matter at all if he gets to the French." Murray made a statement, rather than posing a question. "It's not as if they don't know where we are, and he might also have already got to them."

Scovell spoke, "I'm not sure that we can take the chance, sir. He had a few days start, but I came as quickly as I could, he might still be trying to get across to the French, and he'd have to be cautious about that, so as not to arouse suspicion."

"Do we at least have a name?" Murray asked, looking to Scovell.

"Yes, sir, Soares, Raul Soares."

"Very well," replied Murray, "I shall see to it that the name is given out to all the Commissaries, some of them may have come across him before, and also send it out to Beresford. His pickets and outposts can keep a watch out. There can't be many civilians trying to move towards the French. I don't see there is much else that we can do."

"I beg your pardon, sir," Michael spoke.

"Yes, Roberts?"

"We should also let Sanchez know, sir. His lancers are out and about all around Ciudad and the French army."

"Good idea." Murray paused. "We are going to try to get another convoy into Ciudad tomorrow. You seem to have a knack for this, you can go with it, see Sanchez yourself, I believe you are getting to know him quite well? If that's acceptable to you, Sir Stapleton?"

"I expect I can manage without him for a few days," Sir Stapleton replied, "Dudley can just about manage a horse again." He looked at Michael. "Just be careful, Roberts, see your man and get out."

An hour before dawn Michael and Lloyd joined the expedition to resupply Ciudad Rodrigo. The supplies were three hundred thousand rounds of musket ammunition carried on almost a hundred mules. As before, the escort was two squadrons of German Hussars, but this time there was uncertainty about whether or not they would get help from Sanchez and his lancers. A message had been sent, but there had been no reply. Captain Bergmann commanded the Hussars and sent out patrols to the front and flanks as they cautiously moved towards Ciudad. Fortunately they knew where the French outposts were, and managed to work around them, moving to the south before swinging back towards the fortress. Sanchez had managed to maintain an outpost on a hill south of the fortress, and they were seen coming. As they reached the top of the hill he was waiting for them with a party of lancers.

Without losing any time, the lancers led the way down the hill towards the bridge into the fortress. Michael pushed forward and got alongside Sanchez. "Don Julian!"

"Hola, Lieutenant Roberts. What can I do for you?"

"Simply look out for a man, a Portuguese spying for the French."

"Ha, with pleasure, do you have a description, a name? How might we know this man?"

"He is travelling as an employee of Henrique de Sampaio, his name is Raul Soares. We think he is probably using his real name, as that will match the documents he has."

Sanchez looked thoughtful for a moment. "We can certainly keep a lookout for him, but it is getting more difficult to patrol this side of the river now that the French have completed their two bridges. I'll get Strenuwitz to instruct the patrols." He turned in his saddle and called out, "Strenuwitz!"

Strenuwitz rode up alongside Sanchez who explained what Michael wanted. Strenuwitz looked thoughtful for a moment. "One of our patrols brought in a civilian the day before yesterday. I seem to remember he was supposed to be an employee of Sampaio, trying to buy cattle." Michael started in his saddle, and Strenuwitz went on, "I didn't see him myself, but I will ask the sergeant who led the patrol." He wheeled his horse away and rode off towards a distant group of lancers. A few minutes later and he was back. "Yes," he addressed Michael, "your man was picked up by a patrol, claimed he was trying to buy cattle for Sampaio, had documents backing that up. He was escorted in Ciudad Rodrigo for his own safety."

"Do you mean he's still there?" Michael asked, astonished.

Strenuwitz shrugged, "I don't see why not."

"I think," said Sanchez, "that you had better come into Ciudad with us, and speak to General Herrasti."

"Yes, I think I better had, I'll let Captain Bergmann know."

As Michael was explaining the situation to Bergmann one of the hussars galloped up and spoke rapidly, pointing away to the south east. Bergmann called out orders to one of his officers, and then spoke to Michael. "Come with me, I need to speak to Sanchez, there is a large body of French dragoons approaching."

Bergmann and Sanchez quickly agreed that the Hussars would try to distract the French, while Sanchez's Lancers got the convoy into Ciudad Rodrigo, now only a mile or so away. As Bergmann turned to rejoin his Hussars, Sanchez was already calling out orders, urging his men to push the mules on quickly. Michael turned to Lloyd, "Come on, Lloyd, we are going with the convoy."

Michael and Lloyd followed the mass of braying and complaining mules, the lancers prodding them onwards with their lances, the muleteers swearing and cursing. The persistent rain had eased, but the ground was saturated and muddy, in their haste mules slipped and fell under the weight of their loads, to be hauled back to their feet by swearing and cursing muleteers and then prodded onwards by the lancers. The convoy dropped down behind a spur, concealing them from any French eyes to the south east. Glancing back Michael saw the Hussars forming along the top of the spur, creating a screen. Then he turned to concentrate on getting into Ciudad Rodrigo. Ten minutes or so later they had passed through the fortified suburb of Santa Marina, on the southern bank of the Agueda, and were clattering over the long bridge into the fortress. Sanchez was sitting calmly on his horse on the far side. Michael pulled Johnny over and joined him, looking back.

The Hussars had vanished, and in their place was what looked like a full regiment of French Dragoons. Sanchez spat. "I do not think you will be going back to Gallegos today, Lieutenant."

Sanchez invited Michael to put up at his billet, and they left Lloyd to take the horses there while the two men walked to the castle to see Herrasti. Herrasti was not a happy man. He had hoped, expected even, that Wellington would march to the relief of the fortress, but as the days passed this seemed less and less likely. Consequently he was not inclined to be helpful.

"Lieutenant, I understand your eagerness to apprehend this man, but I have to defend this town before all else, and it seems that your Viscount Wellington will not come to our aid after all." Michael started to protest, but Herrasti cut him short. "No, Lieutenant, I have to hold out against the French for as long as possible, it is a question of honour. All I can do is let Don Sanchez give you what help he can, his lancers are little use inside the town. If the man came into the town, he is still here, no one can leave, and I assure you that no one will be leaving. Catch him if you can, do with him what you will."

Michael was disappointed, but saw there was nothing to be gained by arguing. He thanked the General, and left with Sanchez. Back at Sanchez's quarters they made a frugal meal of bread and cheese, washed down with a little wine. Sanchez said little until they had finished.

"So, Lieutenant, what will you do now? You have a name, but you don't know what this man looks like. There are thousands in the town, he could be hiding anywhere, he is probably with some afrancesados." He referred to those who supported the French.

Michael sat thinking, while Don Sanchez poured more wine. Gradually an idea formed in his mind. "Don

Sanchez, you have some men who saw Soares, will you let them help me search?"

Sanchez shrugged, "Of course. They might recognise him, but it is not certain."

"And do you think anyone might know who the afrancesados are? We could search their houses."

"I don't know, Lieutenant, the known ones are fled, or arrested, others are keeping very quiet, but we can ask questions." He smiled. "My men can be very inquisitive, particularly where traitors are concerned." The smile vanished. "But listen, I have to tell you, I have no intention of being taken by the French. When the time comes we will try to escape, to cut our way to the British lines. Will you ride with us?"

"Yes, of course, but when will that be?"

Sanchez shrugged again. "I don't know, a few days, perhaps a week. General Herrasti likes us being here, it gives him a force that can move quickly against the French, but as the siege tightens we will be less and less able to do anything, then we will leave. I will tell you when we are leaving."

The next day Strenuwitz took Michael to meet the Lancers who had escorted Soares into Ciudad Rodrigo. The sergeant who had commanded the patrol was eager to help, and he and his men said they remembered Soares well. They had been surprised to come across him, and he had been the subject of no little curiosity. They were also unhappy that he had fooled them, and wanted to make amends. Michael suggested that they make a start by simply walking around the town, and in the meantime he would visit the town's Junta and make enquiries about possible afrancesados.

Four days later and Michael was still looking for Soares. Accompanied by the lancer sergeant, Hernandez, and his five men, he had been scouring the streets of Rodrigo, looking in taverns and hotels, all without any success at all. He had got no useful information about afrancesados, the Spanish seemed reluctant to discuss the topic, simply claiming they had all been dealt with. The man seemed to have simply disappeared in the narrow streets and crowded houses of Ciudad Rodrigo.

The four days passed slowly, with every daylight hour spent walking the streets with Hernandez and his men. It was frustrating, tiring, and the incessant rain was thoroughly dispiriting. Still, as Sanchez pointed out, it was a lot worse for the French, bivouacking out in the countryside. Sanchez and his lancers could do little, bottled up as they now were, but their presence seemed to be good for the garrison's morale, with their record of success against the French and their confident, swaggering ways. Sanchez understood why Herrasti wanted him in Rodrigo, but he found it difficult, passing the days in idleness when he wanted to be out in the open, harassing the French. Michael found himself warming to both Sanchez and Strenuwitz, both driven by a hatred of the French that matched Michael's for one particular Frenchman. He would have liked to tell them about Elaine, but that would have meant telling them too much.

Lloyd spent his time either out with Michael or caring for Johnny and Edward. One evening Michael strolled around to where the horses were stabled. As he approached he could hear Lloyd singing quietly in his pleasant tenor voice. He was grooming Edward, and didn't hear Michael approach and stand in the doorway, listening. He couldn't understand a word of the Welsh, but the tone was soothing and the sounds soft. The horses certainly seemed to like it. Lloyd fell silent, still brushing away.

"That was rather good, Lloyd, what was it?"

Lloyd straightened and saluted. "Oh, beg your pardon, Mister Roberts, I didn't hear you coming, sir."

Michael returned the salute. "That's alright, Lloyd, I enjoyed listening."

"Thank you, sir. It's called Suo Gan, sir, it's an old lullaby", he paused, thoughtfully, for a moment. "My Mam used to sing it to me and my brother and sister."

"I didn't know you had family, Lloyd?"

Lloyd hesitated. "I don't know as I do, sir. My sister died of the measles when she was two, and I haven't heard anything of them since I left home, best part of six years now, sir." Michael, waited without speaking to see if Lloyd would volunteer more, he didn't want to press him if didn't want to tell Michael. Lloyd started brushing Edward again, absently, his thoughts elsewhere. He glanced at Michael, and then spoke again, haltingly. "My father was Chapel, you see, sir, didn't hold with drinking at all." He gave Michael a wry grin. "But as you know, sir, I'm partial to a drink." Lloyd stopped brushing and stroked Edward's neck, looking at the horse. "We argued, he struck me, I nearly struck him back." He shrugged. "It seemed like a good idea to leave."

"I'm sorry to hear that, Lloyd, but how did you end up in the Sixteenth?"

"I walked to Hereford, sir, and there was a Lieutenant Richardson there, sir, with a recruiting party, he left the regiment in '05. I knew horses, so it seemed like a good idea."

"You certainly do know horses, Lloyd, even the Vet'n'ry says so."

"Yes, sir," he smiled, "that's one thing I got from my Da. He was head horseman at a big house near Brecon. I was working with him since I was four or five."

"He taught you well."

"Yes, sir."

An awkward silence fell. "They look well." Michael nodded towards the horses, and the conversation turned to rest, fodder, and the need for exercise.

Raul Soares was a frightened man. The last place he wanted to be was Ciudad Rodrigo. It had seemed so simple, take the papers, ride north, find the French, take any rewards going. The French were supposed to be besieging the place, they should have had it surrounded, but, no, they hadn't crossed the Agueda, and those damned Spanish lancers had found him, and escorted him into Rodrigo, telling him how lucky he was that they had found him and not a French patrol. He hated the Spanish, only a little less than he hated the English. He hated any monarchy, he was a republican, and proud of it. He wanted the French to sweep away the corrupt Crown and Government of Portugal, and they had, until the English came. The bastard English with their arrogance, their drunkenness, their whoring, their money. They were buying Portugal, but no one could see it. He wanted to see them driven into the sea like they had been at Corunna, but he knew how they planned to stop that happening, and he needed, desperately needed to tell the French. And the French represented safety. He knew exactly what happened to spies, but at least there was no possibility that anyone in Rodrigo suspected he was other than an employee of Sampaio, unfortunately in the wrong place at the wrong time. He had no doubt that the city would fall to the French, and then he could pass on what he knew, safely. Until then he just had to keep himself safe from all the hazards of the siege. He shuddered at the thought of bombardment that everyone said was coming, when the big French guns would arrive, and start to pulverise the city and its defences.

His friend, a Spanish commissary called out to him, and he returned to the work of helping with the garrison's supplies. At least that meant he wasn't required to help with the defence of the city, the stores were in as safe a place as anywhere, and the man had shared his billet with him. Soares despised him for his conscientiousness in opposing the French, and looked forward to the inevitable fall of the city.

The crash of artillery brought Michael awake with a jerk. It was just getting light. There had been some sporadic cannon fire during the preceding days, but nothing like this. From the sound of it dozens of Spanish guns were in action. He dressed quickly, and was buckling on his sword belt when Lloyd appeared. "Bore da, sir"

"And good day to you too, Lloyd. Any idea what's going on?"

"No, sir, but I can have the horses ready in ten minutes if you give the word, sir."

"Very good, you stay here, I shall see what I can learn."

Outside the billet Sanchez was talking to Strenuwitz and a handful of his officers and NCOs. The group broke up and Sanchez saw Michael. "A rude awakening, eh Lieutenant?" He smiled at Michael.

"It was, Don Julian, do you know what is happening?"

The smile disappeared from Sanchez's face. "The French have broken ground for their trenches and batteries. I think that in a very few days they will begin to bombard the city and its fortifications, and then we shall leave."

"Then I had better get on with looking for Soares."

"Indeed, you had. Your time is running out, Lieutenant."

"Do you know where Hernandez is?"

"I have sent him on an errand, but he shouldn't be very long. I want every horse reshod before we leave, and I sent him to speak to the commissary about shoes and nails. I have farriers, but without nails and shoes…" He shrugged.

Michael nodded, and was about to speak when one of Hernandez's men came running up.

"Lieutenant Roberts, Senhor, we have found him!"

"What? Where?" Michael and Sanchez spoke together.

The man beamed at them. "At the commissary, he is helping them there."

Michael turned and bellowed "Lloyd!" He turned back to the man, "What is Hernandez doing?"

The man's smile broadened. "He is talking to him, Senhor, he did not recognise us."

Soares was getting irritated. The sergeant was going on and on about nails and horseshoes, asking questions about them, their quality, how many there were, could he help him count them. Spanish imbecile, he thought. Then another one strolled in and joined the Sergeant, giving him a nod. The sergeant turned back to Soares, "My man here has spoken to our commander, and he wants as many as you have."

Soares had already told him to help himself. "Sergeant," he began. Over his shoulder he saw two English cavalrymen walk in. Now what did they want? Did everyone want horseshoes. The two Spaniards saw him look, and they turned towards the Englishmen, moving casually, to stand one on each side of Soares. The one who looked like an officer looked him in the eye and spoke.

"Raul Soares, you are under arrest." The two Spaniards seized his arms, and his heart sank.

Half an hour later Michael was going through the papers found in Soares' billet. At first they made no sense to him. There was nothing to do with buying cattle. There were lists of tools, pickaxes, shovels, crowbars, and wheelbarrows, orders for timber and fascines, along with the places they were sent to. There were also records of rations, thousands and thousands of them, going back months, and where they had been sent. Michael did not see what use this information could be to the French. Then a place name caught his eye, Alhandra, where he had seen field works being constructed. There was a list of material sent there, and thousands of rations. Well, he thought, there had been a lot of workers there. He looked again at the other names, they were places he knew from his youth, Alverca, Montachique, Mafra, Sobral, and others. All places in the hills to the north of Lisbon. If the same was happening at all those locations as he had seen at Alhandra... Suddenly he realised the significance of the lists. He gathered up all the papers and went down to the kitchen of the commissary's billet. A cheerful fire was burning and a Spanish woman was busy cooking. Ignoring her and her protestations, Michael removed a large pot from the fire, and, one by one, fed all the documents into the flames.

Soares was taken to the castle, and Michael set about interrogating him. He couldn't explain what he was doing in Ciudad Rodrigo, vehemently denied being a spy for the French, and demanded to be freed. After an hour Michael took a break, with Sanchez, who had been a silent spectator.

"Lieutenant, do you believe he is a spy?"

Michael thought for a moment, he had no proof that Soares was going to pass on the documents, but then Soares had no reason to have papers not concerned with cattle. "Yes, I do."

"He is not going to admit it." Sanchez looked hard at Michael. "And you might have destroyed the papers, but he knows what he knows. What will happen if he falls into French hands?"

"I suppose he will tell them what he knows, the papers were just proof."

"And if the French learn what he knows?"

"I don't know, but I think it could be a disaster for Wellington's plans."

"Then he must not fall into French hands, must he?"

"No, he mustn't."

"Then there is only one thing we can do, isn't there?"

Michael paused for a long moment, and then took a deep breath, "Yes, there is, but first there are some more questions I want to ask." He was silent for a moment. "And, please forgive me, but I want no one else in there other than Lloyd."

Sanchez looked askance, shrugged, and said "Very well, Lieutenant, he's your spy."

Michael explained to Lloyd what he wanted, and what he was going to do. Grim faced, Lloyd nodded, and went in search of a length of good, strong rope.

Sanchez entered the room where Soares was, followed by Michael and Lloyd. He ordered the two Lancers watching Soares out of the room, following them out himself, and firmly closing the door. Soares watched, concern written on his face. Michael nodded to Lloyd, and without a word the dragoon walked around behind the chair Soares was sitting on. Quickly and efficiently he secured Soares to the chair, and then dragged away the table in front of him. He walked back behind Soares and grabbed him by the hair, pulling his head back and up.

Soares cried out as his hair was pulled, "Stop it, please, don't hurt me."

Michael ignored him. Slowly, and with deliberation, he removed his sword and belt and laid them on the table, followed by his Tarleton. Then he sat on the edge of the table, one leg swinging. Still without looking at Soares he put his hand into his sash, and pulled out his knife. He opened it, locked the blade, and began to trim his finger nails. "I'm going to tell you a story," he began, "about a beautiful English woman, an English woman who was brave, intelligent, and who I loved more than I can tell you." He paused, not a sound could be heard in the room, from outside distant cannon fire was faintly audible. "She was killed by a French spy. A man who I am going to kill, along with anyone who gets in my way. I think you know him." He finally looked Soares full in the face. "His name is Raposa." The look that flashed across Soares' face told Michael all he need to know.

"What I want to know is how you met him, where he stays when he is Lisbon." Michael tested the edge of the knife with his thumb. "Tell me, and you might get out of here alive." He stood and walked slowly towards Soares, and Lloyd pulled his head further back, exposing his throat. Michael gently laid the blade on the spy's neck, and looked into his scared eyes. "I do hope you are not going to be stupid and lie to me."

"No, senhor," Soares stammered and gulped, a sharp smell filled the room and over his shoulder Lloyd could see Soares had emptied his bladder. Michael's gaze didn't flicker, he just increased the pressure of the blade. "Raposa found me, senhor, he got talking to me in a coffee house near where I worked. I told him I admired the French Republic. He offered me a lot of money, he would just turn up from time to time to see if I had any information for him, then he stopped coming, senhor, I never knew how to find him, I swear it, senhor."

"So why did you come here?"

"There are a lot of supplies and rations suddenly going out, but not to the Army, senhor, it was so unusual, and I thought I knew what it was all for, I thought it might be important, so I thought I would travel north until I found the French, then ask for Raposa. I hoped I would be well rewarded."

Michael took the blade off Soares' neck, and closed the knife, putting it back in his sash. "Oh, I think you are going to be very well rewarded, Senhor."

Soares was summarily hanged that evening.

Chapter 11

Michael and Lloyd spent another six, long days in Ciudad Rodrigo, as the French trenches crept closer, and the siege gun batteries were constructed. Daily, they went up to the ramparts to see what progress the French had made under cover of darkness, and to watch the Spanish guns trying to destroy the advancing trenches. There was little response from the French, although that would change as soon as the siege batteries were completed and the big guns put in place. Sanchez and Herrasti had made it clear that as soon as that looked likely, it would be time for lancers to try to get away. So far the French presence on the far side of the Agueda was more of a watch than an attempt to completely seal off the city. That would take infantry and guns that were needed on the city side of the river. A night time break out through the suburb of Santa Marina, across the bridge, was the plan.

It was a difficult time. There was little to do, except try to keep the horses fit and ready. Sanchez and Strenuwitz had indeed ensured that all were newly shod, including Johnny and Edward. Fortunately there was a narrow strip of land along the river, under the walls of the city, where parties took turns to exercise for an hour, twice a day, secure from French interference. Michael and Lloyd took the opportunity to work with the lancers on their sword exercise, and in return were given instruction in how to use a lance. They also practiced against the lancers, knowing the French had lancers. They were not aware of any in Spain, but that could change.

Through it all the Spanish guns kept up a steady fire, inflicting casualties, destroying the siege works, but not as fast as they were built. Finally the siege batteries appeared to be complete, and waiting for the guns to be installed.

On the morning of the 21st of June, Sanchez spoke to Michael. "Lieutenant Roberts, we will be leaving tonight. I assume you are coming with us?"

"Of course we are, Don Julian."

"Good. I think you have some passable French?"

"Some, enough to get by."

"Then perhaps you will help by riding at the head of the column? If we are challenged you can respond in French, it might just give them pause and give us a chance to act." He grinned. "One of our sergeants will also ride with you, with his wife. A woman's voice should add to their confusion." Sanchez saw the look of surprise on Michael's face. "You should not be concerned, she is an excellent rider, and a very good shot. She has already killed three Frenchmen." Sanchez went on, "We will ride south at first, and then swing west. I do not know where the pickets are, or if we will meet Spanish or English, if it's English troops that is another good reason to have you in front. Be ready by ten o'clock. I suggest you get some sleep if you can. It will be a long, hard night."

Michael had become accustomed to getting sleep whenever he could, and managed a couple of hours during the early afternoon. After a hearty dinner with Don Julian and Strenuwitz, he and Lloyd began to prepare for the breakout. It didn't take long, but every strap, buckle and fastening was double checked. Their cloaks were left unpacked, they would be wearing them to cover the silver and white of the lacing on their jackets and the white of their pouch belts. Finally, they checked the flints in their pistols and Lloyd's carbine, and carefully loaded them. By half past nine they were in the plaza where Sanchez's Lancers were gathering. The mood was tense, little was being said. Picking up on the atmosphere the horses were restless, heads tossing and hooves stamping while their riders stood at their heads, trying to settle them.

With a clatter of hooves Sanchez and Strenuwitz appeared, and dismounted. Strenuwitz busied himself giving last minute instructions, and Sanchez led his horse over to where Michael and Lloyd were waiting.

"Good evening, Lieutenant, it should be dark enough shortly. We will lead the horses across the bridge to Santa Marina and mount there. I hope that will make us harder to spot. We will go slowly, and as quietly as possible." He gave Michael a slight smile. "If you and your man," he nodded at Lloyd, "will be kind enough to lead, as we discussed, Sergeant Fraile and his wife will ride with you. I shall lead my Lancers, we will stay a little behind you, but not far."

There were about two hundred of the Lancers gathered in the central plaza, from which a long street led to a gate out of the fortress, and then down to the river and the bridge. Michael and Lloyd made their way to the head of the column and found Sergeant Fraile, reins of his horse in one hand, the other arm around his wife. She smiled at Michael as her husband released her and saluted Michael.

Michael returned the salute. "Sergeant, Senora." He was a little lost for words. "I understand the senora is no stranger to action?"

They both laughed. "No, Lieutenant," it was Senora Fraile who spoke, "I have ridden with my husband for over a year now, and killed Frenchmen." Sergeant Fraile just smiled and shrugged.

At that moment Sanchez called out from behind them. "Lieutenant Roberts, will you lead on?"

The narrow street echoed to the sound of hooves as they made their way towards the gate. There was barely room for two horses abreast, and the towering buildings made the dark of the early night almost impenetrable. The street sloped steadily downwards, and then widened out, allowing a little more light to ease their way. Then they were passing between two high walls and ahead the bulk of the gatehouse loomed out of the night. Reaching it they suddenly plunged into the tunnel leading under it. A few dim lanterns lit the way. They emerged in a small outwork and within seconds were outside the walls, turning left towards the river.

Inside the city they had been sheltered from the weather by the high buildings, but out here the full force of the wind hit them, carrying a little rain with it. The moon and stars were hidden by clouds. Michael was glad of his cloak, even if it was mid-June. The incline got steeper, and as they neared the end of the bridge Sanchez called out quietly.

"Lieutenant, halt there!"

Sanchez came forward and joined them. "We will just wait a moment for the column to close up. Then, slowly and quietly across the bridge, Lieutenant. There will be a guide at the other end waiting for us." A few minutes passed and then came a long low whistle from the darkness. "Very well, Lieutenant, off you go."

Michael knew well that the bridge was some two hundred yards long, but in the dark it seemed a lot more, and it was impossible to see how far they had come, he could see little more than the white stonework parapet of the bridge. Intermittent cannon fire from behind them effectively drowned out any sounds they made. Then he felt the bridge stop rising, and begin to drop towards the far bank. Half way, he thought. Soon he could make out the buildings of Santa Marina, silhouetted against the dark night sky. At the far side a group of dark figures waited. One came forward, and spoke. "Follow me." The shadowy figure led the way immediately to the left, and along the riverside, until they reached a small area of open ground. Here they halted. Michael could just make out a street leaving the open area in the direction away from the city.

Sanchez appeared by his side and pointed at the street. "Lieutenant, that leads directly to the bridge out of Santa Marina. Once across it we must push on, we must pass the French pickets before dawn, we have about five hours." He turned away from Michael and called out, softly, "Mount!" Once they were all on their horses, Sanchez spoke again, "Good luck, Lieutenant, ride on."

They rode down the dark street four abreast, Lloyd on the right, then Michael, next Senora Fraile, and Sergeant Fraile on the left. After a few hundred yards they came to a breastwork at the head of the bridge, a cannon and its crew were just visible. A narrow opening, dimly lit by a lantern allowed them to pass through, and then they were on the short bridge. Another few yards and they were out in open country, walking steadily along the rough road.

The countryside immediately out of Santa Marina was flat and open, much of it cultivated, but as they approached the high ground where they had met Sanchez with the convoy, it became rougher, with scattered, sparse, scrubby undergrowth. Now they were clear of the city there was a little more light, and it was possible to see the road, paler than the farm land, stretching ahead, and the darker shadows of clumps of bushes and trees around them. Cautiously they pushed on, senses straining for any sign of danger. They were nearing the crest of the hills overlooking Ciudad Rodrigo, when, suddenly, a voice rang out in French from somewhere in front of them.

"Halt! Who goes there?"

Michael had given some thought on how to respond, and he shouted out, "Don't fire, I am Lieutenant Janvier of the Twenty Second Chasseurs. I have escaped from the English with my Senorita!"

Senora Fraile added her voice, crying out "Please don't shoot us, please!"

Michael sensed movement out to his right coming from behind him, and shouted again. "Don't fire, damn you, I am a French officer."

Senora Fraile kept up a beseeching wail of anguish, "Messieurs, messieurs, please don't shoot us, I am just a poor woman."

He saw movement as Lloyd drew his sabre, he did the same, and was aware of Senora Fraile drawing a pistol. Then there was a flash from the front, a shot rang out, he never knew who from, or where it went, he just shouted "Charge!", and clapped his spurs on Johnny, who shot forward to a flat out gallop in a few strides. A French dragoon suddenly loomed out of the dark, distinguished by the shape of his helmet and white crossbelts, and Michael caught him a savage cut across his face. A pistol cracked to his left, a man screamed in agony, and he heard Sergeant Fraile cry out, "Thank you, Maria!" Lloyd had disappeared in the darkness, but he could hear horsemen thundering in from his right and Sanchez shouting, "Get them all, don't let any escape!"

Michael reined up and peered around, trying to grasp what was happening. A horseman came towards him and he took guard with his sabre, and then saw the distinctive outline of a tarleton helmet. "Lloyd? Is that you, are you alright?"

"Yes, sir, diolch yn fawr. I think I've killed a French officer, but I lost his horse, look you, sir. I think one of the Lancers got it."

"Well, done Lloyd, but bad luck with the horse, that would have made you some prize money."

Sergeant and Senora Fraile reappeared with Sanchez who addressed Michael. "Well done, Lieutenant, I think we have taken the entire picket, all dead, but we need to push on fast in case those shots bring more dragoons down on us."

Riding as before they pushed on south. Over the next hour the weather improved and occasional breaks in the cloud cover allowed the waning moon to give them some illumination so they could push the pace a bit, even to the odd trot where the road was in reasonable condition, trusting the horses' superior night vision.

Somehow they managed not to meet any more French pickets, and once they were over the hills immediately south of Ciudad Rodrigo they turned west, towards the Azaba and the allied pickets. After the excitement of the fight with the French dragoons, the tension ebbed away, and tiredness began to set in. Sanchez decided they were probably clear of the French, and relieved Michael and his companions of the role of advanced guard. He sent Strenuwitz forward with a few men, and rode along with Michael.

"Thank you, Lieutenant, you did very well back there."

"Thank you, Don Julian, but I think Senora Fraile also did very well. I think she may have shot someone."

"Indeed she did, it seems a dragoon was taking a cut at her husband. She shot him out of his saddle, and then the Sergeant finished him with his lance."

It was nearing dawn when they approached the Azaba. Strenuwitz and his party were challenged by a Spanish picket, and quickly established who they were. Half an hour later they were all across the river, dismounted with the horses picketed, and fires being lit to produce something warming. As Michael and Lloyd sat together on a fallen tree, sipping hot coffee, Sanchez walked over to them, followed by one of his Lancers leading a fine looking dark bay gelding, with what looked like a French dragoon officer's saddle and equipage on it.

"Lieutenant Roberts, I believe this is yours," he smiled broadly, "it was taken from the officer your man here killed, so it belongs to your unit, and as there are just the two of you…" He shrugged.

"Oh! Ah! Thank you, Don Julian."

"No, thank you, Lieutenant." Sanchez gestured at the Lancer who handed the reins to a bemused Lloyd. "And now, we must move on. I believe you will need to get to Celorico to see Viscount Wellington, that's another sixty miles if not more from here, and I must report to General Carrera at Gallegos. But at least we are out of Ciudad Rodrigo, and not a man lost."

Ten minutes later the column was mounted and riding on, the going much easier in the daylight. Michael rode deep in thought, Lloyd beside him, leading the French horse. After a quarter hour or more had passed, Michael spoke. "Lloyd?"

"Yes, sir?"

"Look, I think you should have that horse."

"What? Begging your pardon, sir, and diolch yn fawr, but that's not possible, sir. I've Edward, and I've never heard of a dragoon who had his own horse, sir."

"No, Lloyd, you're right, but while Edward is a good mount for a dragoon with the Regiment, it wouldn't hurt if you also had something with a bit more about it, like that animal there, if it is a good as it looks. Something for when we are out and about on our own, and might need a turn of speed and stamina."

"That's very true, sir."

"So what I suggest Lloyd, is that I add it to my horses, so far as anyone is concerned, but so far as I am concerned, Lloyd, he's yours."

"Well, diolch yn fawr, sir, diolch yn fawr, that's a wonderful thing, sir." Lloyd grinned happily.

"And we will see if we can sell that fancy equipage, eh, Lloyd?"

"Oh, yes, sir. But the horse, sir, what are we going to call him?"

Michael thought for a while. "How does Rodrigo sound?"

Lloyd chuckled. "Very good, indeed, sir. Rodrigo it is."

It was still early in the morning when the weary column rode into Gallegos, where they found General Crauford with the Spanish general, Carrera. They listened to what Sanchez had to tell them, while Michael saw a relieved Captain Bergmann.

"Lieutenant Roberts! This is a pleasant surprise, I thought you were stuck in Ciudad Rodrigo waiting to be taken by the French."

"No, sir, we got out with Don Julian and his Lancers last night."

"Are you stopping here?"

"No, sir, I have to get to headquarters with some important information."

"Ach, I was looking forward to hearing about the siege, but did you get your spy?"

"Oh, yes, sir, all taken care of."

"Good news, and we will dine another time."

It was a further fifty mile ride to Army Headquarters at Celorico, and by the time they arrived in the late afternoon men and horses were all tired. They halted first at Sir Stapleton's quarters, Parra and Francisco came rushing out, delighted and relieved to see Michael and Lloyd. Michael dismounted and left Parra and Lloyd to deal with the horses. Wearily he went in in search of Sir Stapleton, and found him with Dudley and Tweedale enjoying a supper. Food and wine were quickly supplied to him and he told them what had passed.

Sir Stapleton asked him, "Did you get your man?"

"Yes, sir, and I gathered some intelligence that I must pass on to Colonel Murray."

"Very good, I shall walk over with you."

At the Headquarters building they quickly gained admission to Murray, and found him in conference with Wellington.

Sir Stapleton broke in on them, "Evening, My Lord, Murray," they turned at the sound of his voice, "I've Mister Roberts here, fresh from chasin' a spy into Ciudad Rodrigo. Says he has something to tell you."

Wellington replied, "Well, Sir Stapleton, let's hear what he has to say. Thought we'd lost you Mister Roberts, so, what news, sir, what news?"

"My Lord, I learnt that some of Don Julian's men had escorted the spy into Rodrigo, thinking he was genuinely an employee of Sampaio. I went in after him, and with the help of some of Don Julian's men I managed to capture him. There is no doubt sir, that he was working for Renard, and he had information and papers that would have been of great interest to the French, My Lord."

"And just what did he have?"

"My Lord, papers detailing with the supply of very large numbers of tools and rations to places such as Sobral and Torres Vedras."

"Ah," Wellington shared a look with Murray, "and what did you do with those papers?"

"I burned them, My Lord."

"Did anyone else see them?"

"No, My Lord."

"And the spy?"

"Hanged, My Lord."

"Excellent, Mister Roberts, that news is a great relief. I am sure we can count on your discretion not to mention this to anyone?"

"Certainly, My Lord."

"Good, good, then we leave Sir Stapleton to dispose of you as he sees fit. Good day, Mister Roberts, Sir Stapleton."

Michael and Sir Stapleton left headquarters and started to walk back to the General's quarters. "Wellington seems happy with your actions, Roberts, I must admit I was beginning to think we'd lost you. Bergmann reported that you and Lloyd had gone haring off into Ciudad Rodrigo after a spy. Can't say I knew what was going on, but I mentioned it to Murray and he was quite pleased. Anyway, glad you're back."

"Thank you, sir."

"Now, since you've been away things have moved on a bit. The regiment is still around here, but tomorrow it's moving forward and two squadrons will go on to Gallegos to join Crauford and reinforce the hussars. You know the country, so I want you to guide them."

"Yes, sir."

"One more thing." Sir Stapleton paused at the door to his quarters. "You should know that the two squadrons will be commanded by Major Stanhope."

Michael's heart sank.

"However, remember that you are a member of my staff." Sir Stapleton hesitated again. "You should also know, and I'll thank you to keep this to yourself for the moment, Stanhope has asked to return to England, and that request has been granted. He will be leaving about the middle of

July." Sir Stapleton smiled, and continued, "Also, hopefully, Dudley will soon be fully fit, and you can return to the Regiment. And now, let us see what we have for supper."

That evening, tired as he was, Michael was kept up telling Sir Stapleton, Dudley and Tweedale all that had passed while he had been away. It was not until the following day, as he set off to rendezvous with the Sixteenth, accompanied by Lloyd, that he had a chance to speak to him about Rodrigo.

"Tell me, Lloyd, how is Rodrigo, and what did Parra make of him?"

"Well, now, sir, he's not in the best of condition, look you, he has some nasty saddle sores, but that's the French for you, and he needs to put a bit of weight on, sir. But Parra and I agree that he has the makings of a fine animal, sir, given a bit of time."

"So poor old Edward is going to be carrying you around for a while yet?"

"Yes, sir, a couple of weeks, most like, and we are keeping Rodrigo away from the others until we know he isn't carrying anything." Michael nodded, Farcy, Strangles or Glanders could sweep through a squadron and destroy it. "Anyway, sir, I could just imagine Major Stanhope's face if I rode up to the Regiment on a horse as good as his, sir."

Michael roared with laughter at the thought, cheered by the knowledge that Stanhope would soon cease to be a problem, at least here, in Portugal and Spain.

They found the Regiment's headquarters billeted in the same village as their squadron, Ashworth's and Lygon's troops. Fortunately Stanhope was not there, he was with the other squadron bound for Gallegos, the one made up of the troops of Captains Belli and Cocks. As it was Michael received a warm welcome from Major Archer, and Captain

Ashworth and the other officers. That evening dinner was a very relaxed and jolly affair, with Michael being asked a lot of questions about Ciudad Rodrigo and the ongoing siege. There were also questions about Sanchez's Lancers, everyone keen to know about a unit they might well be working with, and a weapon they had no experience of. He enjoyed it. Once again he had a feeling of belonging, a feeling he had missed.

The next day's march was a comfortable eighteen miles or so to Valverde, and the two squadrons met on the road after only the first hour. Stanhope was as cool towards Michael as ever.

"Ah, Mister Roberts, good of you to join us. I believe you are to guide us to Valverde and then on to Gallegos. Perhaps you would care to join Mister Alexander, he has the advance guard, and I would hate him to get lost."

With a "Yes, sir," Michael rode off with Lloyd to catch up with the advance guard. He got a warmer welcome from Alexander.

"Hello, Michael, damn glad to see you."

"Hello, Will, how was England?"

They rode along together exchanging news and renewing their friendship. Alexander had heard all about the infamous incident over Michael's house and Roberta. Van Hagen had told him everything, and he was indeed disappointed to have missed it.

That evening the atmosphere was subdued, Stanhope's presence, with that of Michael, made for a careful, strained gathering for dinner. There was little conversation. Happily, the early start ordered for the next day gave everyone an excuse to turn in soon after dinner.

As they rode out in the cool of the early morning, Michael felt cheerful. He was up with the advanced guard again, this time with William Tomkinson, who had joined Cocks' troop, and he was happy to be back with the Regiment. Stanhope was well behind with the two squadrons, and Michael knew that he would soon be free of the Major's constant sneering. He was possibly a better officer in the field than Major Archer, but he lacked the latter's way with the men and junior officers.

Less than an hour after setting off they came to the river Coa. Michael had been on this road before, but the rugged splendour of the deep, rocky valley and the high bridge was not lost on William. It crossed high above the water of the river, swollen by all the recent rain, its three arches leaping from one rocky outcrop to another, and carrying the road in a curve, wide enough for the men to ride comfortably across in threes.

"I say, Roberts," said Tomkinson, "you could hold this bridge for days with a battalion and a couple of guns."

The countryside was rough, with scattered boulders, covered with grass, green after the rains, and scrub and spindly trees. They passed the fortress of Almeida to their left as they pressed on. From their road they could make out the low lying earthworks and the roofs of the town's buildings.

It was midday and just beginning to get hot, when they rode into La Alameda, where they were due to spend the night before joining the German Hussars at Gallegos early the next day. Everyone was looking forward to getting out of the saddle, getting a drink, and caring for the horses. It was not to be. As they were about to dismount, a German Hussar came galloping into the village, his horse lathered in sweat. He rode to Major Stanhope, and spoke briefly. The Major turned, and his orders came quickly.

"Roberts, lead on to Gallegos, at the trot. Ashworth, Cocks, the French are advancing, move your squadrons on at the trot."

It was about three and a half miles to Gallegos, and they went all the way at the trot, arriving some twenty minutes later. As they approached the village, Stanhope cantered up to the advance guard and took the lead. Drawn up behind the village were several battalions of infantry, and as they continued down the road, an officer, who Michael recognised as General Crauford, galloped across to Stanhope, and spoke a few words to him, before riding back. Stanhope led them straight through the village and out onto the plain beyond, sloping gradually up and away from them. Ashworth's Squadron was leading, and he turned to call out to Ashworth. "Ashworth, I am going on, follow on." He put his spurs to his horse and cantered away, up the slope, and disappearing over the top.

As they neared the crest of the slope, Stanhope reappeared, and shouted to Ashworth, "Form line to the right of the road. Tomkinson, Roberts, rejoin your squadrons."

Ashworth turned the squadron off the road, and into the wheat that covered the plain all around Gallegos, sending a pale yellow cloud of grain into the air around them. He ordered "Squadron, Walk! Rear rank, right incline and double your front!" the squadron changed from a column three wide, all the road could take, to one six wide. "Squadron, halt! Threes, left, wheel!" In a moment the squadron was in a two deep line facing the way they had been advancing. To their left Stanhope had placed Cocks' on the other side of the road. Michael had taken post on the extreme left of the squadron, with Lloyd behind him. Twenty yards away he could see Tomkinson on the flank of his squadron. Men and horses were sweating profusely as they got their breath back and looked to their front.

Four hundred yards or so ahead, Michael could see the two squadrons of German Hussars similarly drawn up. All seemed quiet, there was no sign of any French, and no sounds of gunfire, save the distant sounds of the heavy French siege artillery at Ciudad Rodrigo. Stanhope cantered his horse across to the Germans, every eye on him. Two or three minutes passed, then he started back towards them, walking his horse slowly.

He rode up to Ashworth. "The French have driven all the outposts across the Azava. However, they seem to have contented themselves with just that. You may dismount your squadron and take water." He rode off to repeat it all to Cocks.

The squadrons spent the rest of the day on the same ground. Eventually they saw the German Hussars all dismount. It was an interminably long, hot afternoon. Flies gathered, attracted by the sweating horses, nag tails swished ineffectively, hooves thumped, dragoons muttered to their horses and grumbled to each other. Half a dozen dragoons at a time were allowed to walk their horses around for five minutes. It helped, a little.

They watched, curiously, as General Crauford rode up and past them, a couple of staff officers with him. The sun was beginning to sink when he returned. He spoke briefly to Stanhope and rode slowly on his way. Stanhope led his horse over to Ashworth, waving at Cocks to join them. They spoke for a minute or two, then mounted their horses. Wearily, dragoons were climbing to their feet, expecting orders. They were ordered to mount, wheel by threes, and they were soon on their way back through Gallegos, and then La Almeda and their billets.

Chapter 12

It was almost dark by the time the weary men and horses reached La Almeda. There would be little rest, and the billets went unoccupied. The horses were all untacked, groomed, fed, and watered. Then they were tacked up again, ready to ride back to Gallegos instantly, if the French attacked. Equipment was checked and cleaned, the men ate, hard biscuit and hard cheese, then got what sleep they could, lying in the streets by their horses, fully clothed and accoutred. The officers' horses were looked after by grooms and batmen, among them Pedro and Rafael, who looked after Johnny for Michael. Parra and Francisco were with his personal baggage, at headquarters in Celorico. As a staff officer, Michael had no specific regimental role, but he set to, and helped the short-handed Ashworth and young Keating with ensuring all was well with the Troop. Arguably he had no business staying, he had done his job, but he enjoyed being back amongst familiar faces. He hoped Sir Stapleton would understand. It was midnight before everything was complete, and Michael fell quickly asleep, like all the men, still fully dressed.

Two hours later everyone was roused form their slumbers, and the squadrons began to prepare to return to Gallegos. They arrived a little before dawn, passing through the battalions of infantry forming behind the village, and riding on to join the Hussars out in front again. There they formed their squadrons into line, dismounted, and waited. There was an expectation that the French would make a further advance, trying to push the allied pickets further away from Ciudad Rodrigo.

The French didn't come.

Two hours after sunrise Crauford decided that they weren't coming, at least not today. The tired Dragoons rode to Gallegos, and sought out their new billets. One of the German hussar squadrons moved off, to watch the bridge at Barba de Puerca, further to the north. With the possibility of the French suddenly appearing at any moment, the horses were kept fully tacked up, and the men sat or lay around with the reins in their hands.

The day grew hot, a small stream flowed by the village, and parties of Dragoons took turns to water their horses, and fill their canteens. Michael dozed, from time to time Johnny shifted his weight from one leg to another. He was vaguely aware of the sound of approaching horses, and then Lloyd muttered, "Major Stanhope, sir, and General Crauford."

Michael scrambled to his feet and saluted, just as the small party of mounted officers came to a halt. Stanhope spoke, "General Crauford, this is Lieutenant Roberts."

Crauford was a slight, dark visaged man, in his mid-forties, and he addressed Michael in a soft Scottish brogue. "Mister Roberts, Major Stanhope tells me that you know your way to Ciudad Rodrigo?"

"Yes, sir." Michael wondered what on earth this was about.

"Major Napier here," Crauford gestured at another of the riders, an infantry officer, "has a need to pay a visit to Marshal Ney. I'll be pleased if you will show him the road."

"Yes, sir," was all a stunned Michael could manage.

Crauford pulled out his watch and glanced at it. "Napier, I suggest you leave at dawn, give yourself all the daylight you can. We don't want you getting shot in the dark by nervous pickets, do we, eh?"

Napier smiled, "No, General, we do not."

"Then I suggest we get ourselves some dinner." He looked at Michael. "Will you join us, Roberts, I am sure Major Stanhope can spare you. You're one of Sir Stapleton's staff anyway."

Stanhope glared, clearly it was an invitation that he had wanted for himself. "Yes, sir. Thank you," was all Michael could say.

"In an hour then." Crauford and his party rode off, Stanhope with them.

Michael turned and caught a grin on Lloyd's face that immediately vanished. "Well, Lloyd?"

"Sir?"

Michael laughed. "Never mind, Lloyd, never mind."

Dinner was a simple affair, they were too close to the French for any elaborate arrangements, and it was Crauford's delight that the whole of his command, the Light Division, could be ready to march in a quarter of an hour. Present were Crauford and Napier, along with his other ADC, Captain Shaw-Kennedy, and half a dozen of the Division's headquarters staff. Michael found himself seated between Napier, and a Chaplain, who said little, apart from Grace, and whose name Michael did not catch.

"I expect you are wondering why I need to see Marshal Ney?" Napier asked Michael.

"Yes, sir, it does seem a little unusual," Michael replied.

Napier laughed. "Oh, it is, but the Marshal and I are old acquaintances. Ye see, Roberts, I was with my Regiment, the Fiftieth, at Corunna, when I was wounded and taken prisoner. Eventually Ney came and replaced Soult, and he allowed me to live quite comfortably in Oporto, with the French consul, even gave me money. Then a Royal Navy frigate came in under a flag of truce, and Ney put me aboard on my parole that I wouldn't serve again until I was exchanged. And now I have been, but my Regiment is in England, so I have come out to serve as a volunteer. The problem is that Ney has questioned my exchange, and has cast doubt on my word of honour." He frowned. "The only thing I can do is go and see him, and show him the papers for my exchange." He shrugged. "Your job is to come back and tell Crauford if Ney doesn't accept them, and keeps me."

"Oh, I see, sir," was all Michael could manage in response.

The evening ended early, as Crauford had ordered the Division to turn out and stand to at two in the morning. He still expected a French attack. Michael thanked the General, and made his way back to the squadron. Like all the horses, Johnny was standing fully tacked up. Once again the horses had been briefly untacked, groomed, fed and watered, and then tacked up again to be immediately ready. All around were Dragoons, asleep next their horses, reins in hand. Lloyd was snoring gently between Johnny, who was asleep standing, and Edward, who opened one eye briefly. Michael sat down quietly against a stone wall, and closed his eyes.

In no time at all Michael felt a hand gently shaking his shoulder, and a voice saying, "Come on now, Mister Roberts, sir, time be mounting." He peered groggily into the dark, and recognised Sergeant Wilson.

The sound of activity woke Lloyd, who climbed slowly to his feet, and then saw Michael. "Bore da, sir."

"Mornin", Lloyd.' Michael took Johnny's reins, they both tightened their girths and surcingles, and then mounted. "Lloyd, you had best stay with the Troop today, and hopefully I will be back before dark, if the French stay quiet."

"Yes, sir. And good luck, sir."

"Thank you, Lloyd." Michael rode off to find Napier.

Napier was with Crauford, watching the infantry fall in and take their positions behind Gallegos. Napier greeted Michael with a brief "Mornin, Roberts", while Crauford merely threw a fleeting glance at him.

Apparently satisfied with what he saw, Crauford turned his horse. "Well, Gentlemen, let us go and see if Monsieur is stirring." They rode back through Gallegos, and then cantered past the three squadrons, up to the top of the slope overlooking the Azaba. There they waited for the dawn. As the sun rose, Crauford, Napier and Shaw-Kennedy pulled out their telescopes and scanned the countryside across the river. The early morning sun was casting long shadows towards them, and making it difficult to see anything. Michael heard horses behind him, and turned to see Henry van Hagen leading up the replacement for the dragoon picket watching the bridge below. Behind a was a small body of infantry, toiling their way up the slope to relieve their comrades on the picket.

Van Hagen halted his picket near Michael. "Mornin' Michael."

"Mornin' Henry."

Crauford looked over at the sound of the exchange. "Carry on, relieve the picket, there's no sign of movement. Napier, Roberts, off you go, and good luck."

Michael and Napier pushed ahead of the relief picket and headed for a small rise overlooking the bridge, half a mile away, and where the old picket was waiting. The dragoons were commanded by Will Alexander, who had been on the picket for twenty-four hours, and did not know about Napier's mission. The infantry officer was a young ensign. Alexander saluted Napier, "Good morning, sir." His puzzlement was clear.

"Good morning. Nothing to concern you," Napier replied. "Mister Roberts and I are just going to pay the French a little visit. Do you have the flag Mister Roberts?"

Michael lifted a short pole, with a large napkin tied to it, from his saddle. "Yes, sir."

'Then be so good as to display it, and we shall be off."

Leaving a bemused Alexander, the two men put their horses into a steady walk down the slope, towards the bridge, Michael holding the white flag of truce well above his head. On the far side of the river the rough road snaked into a shallow valley amongst scrubby trees. Napier said, "I would imagine they have a cavalry picket in those trees."

"Yes, sir, it's where I would put one."

There was little sound as they walked down towards the bridge, just the occasional click of a horse shoe against a stone. The napkin fluttered fitfully in the light breeze. At the end of the stone bridge they reined in. The bridge was about fifty yards long, and partially blocked on the far side by two wagons, local farm carts, with just enough room for a horse to get through. Michael glanced down, the water in the river had fallen since the rains had stopped, that would expose more fords, making it harder to watch for French crossings. He looked up to see two French dragoons emerge from the trees, and begin to ride towards them, muskets cradled across their bridle arms.

"Here we go,' said Napier, 'how's your French, Roberts?"

"Passable, sir."

"Might be an idea to make out you don't speak it." He glanced sideways at Michael, a slight smile on his lips. "You never know what you might hear."

"Yes, sir."

The two French dragoons halted at the other end of the bridge, one was a sergeant, who called out. "What can we do for you, gentlemen?"

"I need to see Marshal Ney!" Napier's reply clearly came as a surprise to the two dragoons.

"Marshal Ney?" the sergeant shouted back.

"Yes! We are old friends, and I need to see him on a personal matter."

The two Frenchmen conversed for a moment, and then the sergeant called out, "Very well, monsieur, come across."

With Napier leading they cautiously walked across the bridge, letting the horses find their way past the carts. Once across the sergeant asked, "What are your names, monsieur?"

"I am Major Napier, and this is Lieutenant Roberts, I am afraid the Lieutenant doesn't speak French."

"Very well," he gestured behind him, "if you would ride on along the road?"

Followed by the two Frenchmen Michael and Napier walked their horses on along the road from the bridge. As they neared the trees they could make out more dragoons in the shadows, staring at them, curiously. The road wound on up a shallow valley, and at the top was a small farm where more dragoons, with an officer, and a handful of infantry looked at them with unabashed curiosity as they approached. It was, thought Michael, the very mirror of their picket back across the river. The sergeant said, "Halt here", and rode past them to the officer. After a few moments conversation, the officer walked over to them.

"My sergeant tells me that wish to see Marshal Ney?"

"Indeed, I do." Answered Napier. "Lieutenant?"

"Forgive me, I am Lieutenant Colbert, and my sergeant tells me you are Major Napier and Lieutenant Roberts. And why do you think Marshall Ney will want to see you?"

Napier paused for a moment before he replied. "Lieutenant, the Marshal knows me. I was his, err, guest in Oporto before he sent me home under parole." The Frenchman's expression changed to one of surprise. "A question has arisen over my exchange, and as I gave my parole to the Marshal, I wish to see him, straighten the matter out, and for him to release me from that parole. It is a matter of honour; I am sure you understand?"

"Major, of course I understand. Please, allow me to escort you to our headquarters. It's not far, and I am sure my Colonel will be only too glad to help you." He glanced at Michael, and continued, "But the Lieutenant must remain here, I am afraid. One pair of eyes in our lines is quite enough." He shrugged. "My apologies."

Napier turned to Michael with a rueful smile. "Mister Roberts, I am afraid the Lieutenant insists that you wait for me here. I shall be as quick as I can."

Napier and the French Lieutenant rode off together, a couple of dragoons as escort. Michael dismounted and looked around. The French dragoon sergeant asked, "Monsieur, can I get you something to drink, or perhaps to eat?"

Michael looked at him blankly, shrugged and smiled. The sergeant mimed drinking, and Michael nodded. One of the dragoons offered him a wineskin. Cautiously, Michael raised it to his lips and drank. It was surprisingly good. He took a good few mouthfuls, and offered it back with a "Thank you." A few yards away were a couple of stunted trees, Michael looked at the sergeant, pointed at himself and Johnny, and then at the trees. The sergeant nodded. Michael tied Johnny to one tree in the shade, removed his tarleton, sword belt and sabre, and settled himself down in the shade of the other. A couple of the French dragoons stationed themselves nearby. Michael glanced at them, catching the eye of one of them, who smiled and shrugged.

Michael knew how far it was to Ciudad Rodrigo, and the French headquarters were even further. He was in for a long wait. He settled back against the tree, and for a while amused himself watching the French picket. The dragoons looked reasonably competent, although their horses were not in the best condition. As for the infantry, their sergeant aside, he thought they looked a lot younger than the average redcoat. It was quiet, warm, he was tired, very tired, he closed his eyes, and slept.

He was rudely awakened by someone kicking his foot. A Portuguese voice from above him said, "Well, well, my old friend Michael Roberts!"

Michael opened his eyes and squinted, standing over him was an officer in the green uniform of the French Chasseurs. With a shock he realised it was Jean-Paul Renard. Even after the intervening years he knew him at once. He tried to scramble to his feet, but another vicious kick caught him in the ribs and he sprawled, gasping, on the ground.

"You have caused me immense trouble, Michael, and look, here you are!" He laughed. "And now I can pay you back!"

Michael rolled away, and managed to sit up, hugging his ribs. "You bastard, Renard, what are you talking about?"

"Oh, come now, Michael, don't be coy. I know very well that you have been hunting me. You chased me out of Lisbon, you destroyed my network, you and that tart Roberta and her bloody interfering uncle. I saw the two of you together. Oh, yes, not so observant after all, are you." He laughed. "Tell me, are you still fucking her, Michael? And does she know about that posh tart in London? Were you fucking her as well?" Michael's surprise clearly showed on his face. "Oh, yes, I know about her, one of Musgrave's lackies. I found out later." Renard stepped closer. "I have contacts, you know. I know what passes in

London. If I had known," he kicked at Michael's leg, catching him on the thigh as he tried to wriggle away, "I would have taken more time with her. Just like I will with the grand Senhorita Roberta when we take Lisbon." Renard aimed another kick at Michael's head, which he just managed to catch on his arm as he tried to roll away. "And I owe you for driving me out of Lisbon all those years ago, you bastard. My father was furious, you know. It nearly ruined his career."

Michael managed to get up on his hands and knees. "I'm going to kill you, Renard!"

A foot caught him in the mouth and he fell back, stunned, spitting blood. Renard laughed. "Oh, really? And just how are you going to do that?" As Michael lay on the ground another kick caught the side of his head, and his vision closed in, everything going black. "If anyone is going to die, I rather think it is you."

Another voice cut in, speaking French. "Lieutenant, you cannot do this, it is wrong, he is under a flag of truce."

Renard spun towards the voice. "I don't bloody care, sergeant, this man is a spy, an enemy of France, my enemy, and I am damn well going to see him dead!"

"But, monsieur," the sergeant began.

Michael's head hurt, but the sergeant's intervention gave him a moments respite, his vision cleared, and he managed to get back to his knees, swaying as he fought to stand. His sword was too far away, he was surrounded by French infantry, their muskets ready, bayonets fixed.

"Do you know who I am, sergeant? Do you? I am Lieutenant Renard, on Marshal Massena's staff, and that means, sergeant, that you will do exactly what I tell you to do." Renard was almost screaming, spittle flying from his lips as he screamed at the sergeant. "But, I know, sergeant, if it makes you happy we will do this properly. Seize the prisoner, your men can shoot him, a proper execution, which is more than he damn well deserves!" The last was shouted in the sergeant's face.

The sergeant's men looked at him, and he nodded. They closed in on Michael and seized his arms, dragging him to his feet. As they hurried him towards a wall, the sergeant of dragoons appeared with a few men. "What's going on," he shouted.

Renard spun to face him, "The execution of a bloody spy, that's what sergeant."

The sergeant looked at Renard, at his uniform, at his snarling face. He was a veteran, but in all his years he had never known anything like this. He didn't like it; he didn't know what to do. He turned to one of his men, "Pascal, ride and get the Colonel, quickly." He addressed Renard, "Lieutenant, I think we should wait for my Colonel."

Renard saw the indecision, and turned back to the infantry sergeant. "Stand him against the wall, and form a firing party."

Michael felt the rough stonework against his back, he squinted against the bright sunlight. He pushed himself away from the wall, tried to step forward, but a musket butt in his stomach slammed him back. The infantry, hesitantly, began to form a loose line a few yards away, Renard to one side, grinning like a maniac, shouting at them to hurry up. There was a clatter of horses' hooves, and a voice, honed on the battlefield, roared out, "What the damnation is going on here?"

Michael slumped back against the wall, and peered in the direction of the voice, he saw the infantry, the dragoons, all coming smartly to attention, he saw Napier, and next to him he saw a man in a dark blue coat, with gold embroidery and epaulettes, a bicorn on his head, his face ruddy, his hair dark and curly.

"I said, what in damnation is going on?" He pointed at Renard, "You, you, sir, what is this about?"

Renard stammered, "This man is an English spy, sir."

Napier called out, "Marshal Ney, he's not a spy, damn it, he's my escort, he's an English officer."

"He certainly looks like that to me," the Marshal replied. He addressed Renard. "And you, who are you?"

"Lieutenant Renard, Excellency, Marshal Massena's staff."

"Oh ho! One of Massena's brood, eh? Well, Lieutenant Renard, I suggest you get on your horse, and that you leave now, and you tell the good Marshal that Michel Ney does not execute anyone under a flag of truce!" Renard hesitated, and Ney shouted, "Dupont, escort this, this, this person away from here." Michael realised that behind Ney and Napier was a sizable escort of dragoons. An officer came forward, with two men. Renard turned on his heel, and with a look of pure venom at Michael, he walked away.

Michael swayed slightly, and the dragoon sergeant told two of his men to help him. Gently they lowered Michael to the ground. One of them produced a flask of wine, and held it to Michael's lips, he drank, thirstily, the wine stinging his cut mouth, causing him to cough violently. Napier appeared at his side.

"Good God, Roberts, what was that all about, if it wasn't for Ney you would be a dead man by now."

"Just an old friend," Michael coughed and spluttered.

Lieutenant Colbert appeared, "Sergeant, help him inside, out of the sun, then see to his injuries."

Michael was gingerly washing his cheek and mouth inside the farm house, when the door opened and Ney walked in followed by Napier. Ney addressed the soldiers, "Leave us." Once the three men were alone, Ney spoke again. "The two sergeants have told me what happened. I will not ask you if you are a spy, clearly you are an English officer. I gather, however, that there seems to be some personal animosity between you and Renard?"

Michael could not help but laugh, and then winced at the pain in his ribs. "You could say that, sir. It is my intention to kill him." Ney looked a bit taken aback. Michael went on, "But I thank you, sir, for saving my life. I am indebted to you."

Ney shook his head. "I do not begin to understand, nor, I think, do I want to. As for your debt, I think it unlikely that I will hold you to it, Lieutenant, but I appreciate the sentiment. Napier, I think we had better get you both on your way. I shall ride with you to the river, you shall have a Marshal of France as an escort, to keep you safe." He laughed." In any case, I want to see the bridge."

Marshal Ney rode down to the Marialva bridge between Michael and Napier, his squadron strength escort just behind. Ney halted about fifty yards from the river. "I think that is close enough, for the moment." He nodded across the river, "Your outpost is getting quite excited."

The dragoons had formed, and Michael could make out Henry van Hagen at their head. A dust cloud showed that a galloper was on his way to Gallegos. The small infantry detachment were already marching quickly away.

Ney called out to his escort, "Dupont, wait here. Major Napier, allow me to escort you." Together the three men rode to end of the bridge, halting at the wagons. Ney looked down at the water. "The river level is falling." He looked thoughtful for a moment, then turned back, a smile on his face. "Major Napier, it was good to see you again, and I thank you for coming to see me." Napier nodded. "And Lieutenant Roberts, take care, who knows," he laughed," I might need you to redeem your debt one day?"

With that he wheeled his horse and rode back to his escort, and on, up the road, followed by his escort.

"Come on, Roberts," said Napier, "lets go home."

"Yes, sir. And thank you, sir."

"Oh, don't thank me Roberts, thank the Marshal. He was on his way to look at the river crossing here, we met him a very little way towards Ciudad Rodrigo. Just as well, eh?"

At the top of the hill they found a very relieved van Hagen. "Who was that?" he asked, and then, "Damnation, Michael, what happened to you? I beg your pardon, Major."

"That's quite alright, Lieutenant. That was none other than Marshal Ney, looking at the river level. I imagine he intends to cross it quite soon." Napier replied. Michael just smiled, hugging his bruised ribs, and he Napier kept their horses walking towards Gallegos.

They rode on quietly, cresting the hill they could see Gallegos in the distance, and a squadron of dragoons trotting towards them. "We seem to have created quite a stir, Roberts. I don't suppose you would care to tell me what it was all about?"

"I beg you pardon, sir, but I would rather not." Napier looked askance at him. "As the Marshal said, sir, it's personal, but it is also a confidential intelligence matter, sir, Viscount Wellington is aware, sir."

"Hmm, I see."

The squadron was getting closer, and Michael could see the officer in front. "Oh, damn, it's Stanhope."

Stanhope halted the squadron, and rode to meet them. "Napier," and then, "What the devil happened to you, Roberts? Explain yourself, man."

The devil indeed, thought Michael, then Napier spoke up. "Ah, Stanhope, there was a rather unfortunate misunderstanding, with an over enthusiastic French staff officer. Fortunately Marshal Ney was able to sort it out, and send us on our way." He smiled broadly at Stanhope. "I'll explain everything to General Crauford. Come on Roberts." And Napier calmly walked his horse on, past a silenced Stanhope.

Michael gently squeezed Johnny, and rode with Napier, back to Gallegos.

Chapter 13

As Michael and Napier rode down the slope towards Gallegos they could see the other two squadrons formed up in the wheat fields in front of the village. Beyond the village, they could just make out the lines of the infantry battalions.

"My friend the Marshal seems to have caused quite a stir. I can see Crauford, we had better push on and report, don't want him getting vexed. Can you canter, Roberts?"

"I think so, sir." Napier pushed his horse into a canter and Michael followed, wincing.

Crauford was sitting in front of the squadrons, one of hussars, and Ashworth's of the 16th. They reined in in front of him and saluted. "Well, Napier, what the devil is going on?" asked Crauford, an irritated tone in his voice.

Napier recounted all that had passed. Crauford looked askance at Michael when he heard about his narrow escape, but he was more concerned by Ney's interest in the river. "Looking at the river was he? And you say the level is dropping? Then, no doubt, he will be coming to pay us a visit soon." He eased himself in his saddle, and addressed Shaw-Kennedy, sitting nearby. "Pass the word, stand down." Shaw-Kennedy rode off. Crauford turned his attention to Michael. "And you, sir, I have no doubt, will wish to get to headquarters and report what has passed?"

"Yes, sir."

"Then you had better get on your way."

It was mid-morning when Michael and Lloyd left Gallegos. By the time they had covered the fifty odd miles to Celorico the sun was just setting, but Michael's ribs now only hurt if he breathed too deeply, his face was still sore, and he could feel all the other bruises. Michael rode straight to headquarters, dismounting, he sent Lloyd to their billet, and went in search of Colonel Murray. He found Captain Reynett, who he had met several times while acting for Sir Stapleton.

"Captain Reynett, sir, I need to speak with Colonel Murray urgently."

"Hello, Roberts. You do, do you, well, he's with Wellington at the moment. It will have to wait."

"I beg your pardon, sir, but it is urgent, and I believe his Lordship will want to hear this as well."

Reynett stared at Michael for a moment. "Very well, follow me, but on your own head be it."

Reynett led the way down a corridor, knocked on a door, opened it, stuck his head in and spoke. "Begging your pardon, my Lord, but Lieutenant Roberts is here and says he must speak to the Colonel urgently." There was a muffled response. Reynett opened the door wide, ushered Michael in, and then closed the door behind him.

Wellington and Murray were seated at a table, covered with maps and documents. "Mister Roberts," began Murray, "I trust this is important?"

Michael told them about his run in with Renard, what he had said, and then how Ney had intervened. Finally he spoke about Ney's interest in the water level in the Azaba. Wellington had listened carefully, and now he spoke. "That man Renard seems to know far too much. As for Ney, I have no doubt that he is planning some thrust against Craufurd, but Craufurd knows very well what he is about." He paused thoughtfully. "Murray, will you ensure that Mister Roberts' intelligence about Renard gets back to where it needs to in London?" Murray nodded his acquiescence. "Then," continued Wellington, "I think you may return to Sir Stapleton, and I thank you for the news about Ney and the river. Be so good as to share that with Sir Stapleton, Roberts, but no more. D'ye understand?"

"Yes, sir."

"Then, good evening to you, Roberts."

Michael was able to get cleaned up before he saw Sir Stapleton. His face was bruised, his ribs ached, but he decided he was reasonably presentable. Sir Stapleton made no comment, and in response to the news of Ney's reconnaissance merely grunted, "Not much we can do about that fifty miles away."

The following day headquarters moved to Almeida, and five days later, at the end of June, to Alverca, closer to the border. Michael returned to his work as a staff officer, often away visiting the various cavalry regiments under Sir Stapleton's command, but never, he realised, back to Gallegos. He was also kept away from the rest of the Sixteenth who were not at Gellegos. Sam Dudley was almost completely recovered from his broken arm, and had fully returned to his duties, but there was no indication of Michael being returned to the regiment. Michael was frustrated, he felt like an exile. It got worse when the French did advance against Gallegos. By all accounts the Light Division with the Sixteenth and the German hussars executed a fine withdrawal back to the river marking the Portuguese Spanish border. Once again the regiment had been in action and Michael had not been there, but his friends, Tomkinson and van Hagen had done well.

It got worse. A few days later the Sixteenth were in action again. There was a small skirmish under the direction of Crauford, but it had not gone well. Colonel Talbot of the Fourteenth had been killed, and rumours got about that the Sixteenth had not behaved well. These were soon squashed by Sir Stapleton, Crauford and Wellington himself, but Michael felt even more estranged from his friends and his regiment.

A few days later the inevitable news came of the surrender of Ciudad Rodrigo, and Michael was suddenly told by Sir Stapleton to "Get along to headquarters and see Colonel Murray, he has a job for you."

Murray was to the point. "You know Don Julian Sanchez?"

"Yes, sir."

"Good. He was part of the garrison of Ciudad Rodrigo, and now that has fallen he is unattached, and unsupported. Wellington wants him, and you are to go and find him, and persuade him to join us. We will undertake to pay and supply him and his men. The last we heard he was at Fuentes. Tell him his Lordship would like to know what is coming down the road from Salamanca. You are to go with him, see for yourself, see how Sanchez does. Got that? Then off you go, Mister Roberts."

An hour later Michael and Lloyd were on the road, Michael had chosen to ride his favourite horse, Johnny, who was well rested and in excellent condition. Lloyd was riding Rodrigo, who was likewise in fine condition, good feed and regular exercise had worked wonders with him, and Lloyd was delighted to be riding out on him. Fuentes lay some forty miles to the east, towards Spain and the French. Their route took them to the river Mondego and around the mountains of the Serra da Estrela, rising high on their right hand. Then it was almost due east, over hills and valleys, broken terrain, poor land, sparse vegetation, and sparsely populated. As night was falling they came to a small village, more a collection of run down hovels and broken walls. With some difficulty Michael managed to find them a billet for the night, but the food was poor, and the wine thin, and the houses infested with fleas. After a restless night, they were glad to be on their way again at first light.

Gradually the country and the going got easier, but then they dropped down into the rugged Coa valley, crossing the river on a high bridge. Another two hours beyond the Coa, and they were riding into Fuentes. As they entered they were greeted by some of Sanchez's lancers who recognised them. Sanchez himself was in one of the larger houses, overlooking the small square and the church. As they dismounted he appeared in the doorway and greeted them.

"Lieutenant Roberts! This is an unexpected pleasure. Strenuwitz! See who is here!"

"Hello, Don Julian, it's a pleasure to see you again," Michael replied, and as Strenuwitz appeared he added "and you, Strenuwitz."

"Now, come along in." Sanchez ushered Michael in, leaving Lloyd with the horses and already in conversation with some of the lancers.

Inside, Sanchez led the way into a large dining room, with heavy furniture, and tapestries on the wall. He called for wine and food, and waved Michael to a seat at the table, where he and Strenuwitz joined him.

"So," began Sanchez, "what brings you here?"

Briefly Michael explained what Viscount Wellington was proposing. Sanchez seemed pleased by the offer, glanced at Strenuwitz who gave a nod, and accepted. "I would be honoured to place myself and my men under Wellington's command. I have to admit that I was wondering what we should do, now Ciudad Rodrigo has fallen. Two hundred lancers need a lot of supplies, and pay. And as for watching the Salamanca road, we planned to visit it tomorrow. Why don't you come along with us?"

This was exactly what Michael had hoped, and he agreed readily. After a pleasant dinner with Sanchez and Strenuwitz, Michael went in search of Lloyd to let him know they would be leaving at first light. As he expected, Lloyd was at the stables, where their horses were already installed, fed and watered. Watched by a small crowd of lancers, Lloyd had a local turning a grindstone while he sharpened up the edge on his sabre. He was explaining to the men around him that sharpest part of the blade need to be the last six or eight inches, because that is the ideal part of the blade to strike with, it's moving fastest and least likely to stick in an opponent. Lloyd pointed to an old leather strap hanging on a nail, and got two lancers to hold an end each. The strap was a couple of feet long, Lloyd made a regulation cut at it, and neatly severed it. The lancers were impressed.

"Lloyd!"

"Yes, sir?" Lloyd snapped to attention and saluted with his sabre.

"Perhaps you might give mine a bit of attention as well?" Michael drew his, with its blued and gilt decoration along the blade, and passed it to Lloyd. Then he strolled into the stable to make a fuss of Johnny, who nuzzled his chest and snorted. Outside the lancers were watching Lloyd at work, and as soon as he had finished Michael's sabre they started on their own, Lloyd giving them tips.

By first light the next day they were ready to march. Sanchez invited Michael to ride with him, and Lloyd followed along. The weather had improved and it was a fine day, but not too hot as they rode into the hills to the south of Fuentes. They were taking a long, circuitous route to avoid French outposts and patrols. The terrain was rugged, the vegetation sparse, but the road more or less followed the contours, and the going was not too strenuous. Small villages were cautiously by-passed, with patrols continuously scouting ahead and regular reports coming in. They crossed the Azaba and the road began a steady climb up towards Fuenteguinaldo. Through the scrubby trees that grew everywhere it was occasionally possible to see for miles, as vistas opened up. Then the road crossed a rolling plateau, completely devoid of trees. In the distance ahead, Michael could see mountains rising up, the heat haze making it difficult to tell how far away they were. Then they crested a rise and Fuenteguinaldo came into sight, built on a low hill and dominated by a massively built church.

They skirted the town to the south, and a little later forded the Agueda. Robleda was passed to the north and their direction swung more north-easterly. As the sun began to drop, and the air chilled, they approached the small town of Martiago. Scouts came in and declared it empty of French. Tired and weary they rode into the town where the townspeople greeted them with enthusiasm. The priest rushed out of the low, simple church, and set about organising billets for them. He assured Don Julian that there were no French in the vicinity, but Ciudad Rodrigo was a little more than a dozen miles to the north, so pickets were posted, and they slept fully dressed with the horses saddled and ready to ride.

The following day was a hard day. Their route took them across country, down into steep valleys, and then up and out again. On the hill tops the going wasn't too bad, but there were more and more frequent valleys with precipitous slopes down and up again. There were frequent halts to adjust saddles as they slipped forward or back, and rucked up the blankets under them. Eventually the ground levelled and they rode across open pastures. Finally, a last climb took them up and onto a wide open plain. Just as it was getting dark again, they dropped a little off the plateau and into a small valley.

"Lieutenant Roberts," Sanchez spoke, "we will bivouac here, there will be no fires, the Salamanca road is about two miles north of us. The French do not usually patrol at night, they stay close to the road, but we must be careful, and it will be better if they do not know we are here."

Bread, cheese and wine were shared around to make a frugal dinner, followed by a cold night, wrapped in cloaks. There was the same for breakfast, eaten hurriedly before daybreak. Then they mounted and rode north, cautiously, dropping in and out of the few depressions on the plateau. At the edge of the plateau the trees began again, effectively screening any view of the road, but ahead and to the left was a spur off the plateau with three small summits along it. A shallow valley fell down the southern side of the spur, and the lancers rode down, into the trees. Sanchez quietly ordered the lancers to halt, and they dismounted, making themselves comfortable on the scrubby grass under the trees.

Sanchez had indicated to Michael that he and Lloyd should stay mounted, now he spoke, "Lieutenant Roberts, we will go and look at the road."

"Is it far?"

"Perhaps half a mile." Michael's look of astonishment made Sanchez laugh. "Do not worry, Lieutenant. We have vedettes out, and we are going up there". He pointed up the high spur next to them.

They climbed the slope, following a slight depression that led towards the centre of the ridge, the trees gradually thinning out, until they arrived just below the crest. There they dismounted, leaving the horses with Lloyd and a lancer. Sanchez led the way on up, and, suddenly, below them, at the bottom of a much steeper slope than the one they had just climbed, was the Salamanca road, snaking away to the north east. It was empty.

Sanchez sat down in the shade of one of the few scrubby trees that clung to the hill top. "We should make ourselves comfortable, Lieutenant, and see what passes."

It was an hour before there was any activity. Michael was dozing gently in the slowly increasing heat when Sanchez prodded him. "Here, Lieutenant, here comes the French army."

Michael said, "I'll get my telescope."

Sanchez stayed him with his hand. "No, Lieutenant, no telescopes, they can catch the sun and give away our presence. There is no danger to us, we can disappear very quickly, but it is better if they do not know we are here."

As Michael watched a battalion of blue coated French infantry with their distinctive white lapels and waistcoats came down the road. They had a company strength advance guard, but it was only a hundred yards or so ahead of the main body.

"You see, Lieutenant, they keep very close together, they know what happens to small detached bodies." He smiled and pulled a finger across his throat.

Following closely behind the battalion was a long line of wagons, and then another battalion. Michael took his notebook and pencil from his sabretache and began to take notes. There was a pause of half an hour and a large body of several squadrons of dragoons came in sight. They were escorting wagons, fifty by Michael's count, but he couldn't tell what was in them. The day passed, and so did the French, every hour or so another group, marching towards Ciudad Rodrigo.

In the mid-afternoon Sanchez suddenly sat up and pointed. "Now this is interesting."

Michael raised himself to look. Coming down the road was a small body of dragoons, their brass helmets with black horse hair tails glinting in the sun, Michael counted fifty, followed by a coach, then two wagons, and another fifty dragoons. They were perhaps a mile and a half away, and moving slowly because of the wagons. Sanchez grinned at Michael. "I think we should take a closer look, see what's in that coach, eh, Lieutenant? I think we can manage a hundred French dragoons." Sanchez took a quick look in both directions, but nothing else could be seen on the road. Then they scrambled to their horses and rode quickly down the steep slope.

In ten minutes the whole of the lancers were moving cautiously through the trees towards the road. Michael and Lloyd drew their sabres, wrapping the sword knots tightly around their wrists. Suddenly they emerged from the trees. In front, some two hundred yards away across an open pasture, was the French convoy. There was no finesse, no tight, knee to knee formation, no carefully regulated advance, building speed. Sanchez simply shouted "Charge", and the whole body went straight into a flat out gallop, every man spurring his horse on. The lancers were shouting and screaming, waving their lances aloft. The dragoons on the road started to turn to face the attack, drawing their long, straight swords. Michael saw the carriage door open, and a man leapt out, bareheaded, in blue, with gold epaulettes, making for a horse tied to the carriage.

Within seconds they were across the intervening ground and onto the road. The lancers rode past and around the dragoons, keeping out of reach of their swords, but thrusting at them with their longer lances. Michael and Lloyd found themselves closely engaged with the head of the dragoons behind the coach. Michael parried a thrust from a dragoon who came straight at him, pulled Johnny left, and spurred him forward. As he shot past the Frenchman he cut backhanded, horizontally at head height and saw the blade slash the man's neck open. Blood spewed out and the man crashed from his horse. Then he was through to the other side of the road, and turning Johnny sharply about to his right, keeping his sword arm closest to the enemy. A few yards away he saw Lloyd, his sabre bloody, engage another French dragoon. A rapid series of cuts directed at the man's face put him on the defensive, but he was too slow, and Lloyds sabre cut upwards and into his jaw. Michael just had time to think, damn, he's good, when another French dragoon came at him, fast, arm and sword straight, aiming at Michael's chest. Michael parried him, and cut as he passed, but his sabre only struck the cloak rolled across the man's back and did no harm. He saw the man from the coach mounting, saw him trying to get his horse under control, saw a lancer spear him through.

In a few minutes it was over. The remaining dragoons were riding hell for leather back towards Salamanca. There were not many. Michael looked around and saw that the dragoons had been completely scattered and broken by the ferocity of the lancers attack. He saw a Frenchman, his leg bleeding profusely, trying to crawl under a wagon, watched in horror as a lancer killed him. Then he heard Sanchez shout, "Lieutenant Roberts, come here!"

Sanchez was off his horse and standing by the coach, its door open. Michael rode the few yards to him. He saw Lloyd looking aghast as French wounded were simply finished off. Across the road a dismounted man was running, hampered by his long boots and empty scabbard. A lancer rode him down, driving his lance into the middle of his back. There were no prisoners.

Michael had heard the rumours, had thought he understood, but to see it was different, he had to speak. "Don Julian, you are killing the wounded, taking no prisoners, it's wrong."

Sanchez turned and stared at him. "And tell me, Lieutenant, what should I do with them? Burden myself with them? Or perhaps I should let them go free to rape and kill more women and children?"

Michael looked for a moment in silence, and then sagged in the saddle. "No, Don Julian."

"No, Lieutenant. Now, dismount and see what we have here."

Michael dropped down from Johnny and walked the rest of the way to the open coach door. Inside were the remains of a half eaten meal, cheese on a plate, a discarded knife, an open bottle of wine lay on the coach floor, its contents soaking into half a loaf of bread. On the seat was an open document case. Sanchez said, "I think we will just take that as it is, look through it later." He closed it and passed it to Michael. "Perhaps you should have it, take it to Wellington. But now we must be quick."

Around the coach the lancers were moving quickly and efficiently, some rounding up loose dragoon horses, others checking the dead for valuables, going through the wagons, unhitching the horses from them and the coach. Strenuwitz appeared, "Nothing much in the wagons, Don Julian, tents, bread, fodder for the dragoons' horses." He shrugged. "We can burn it when we go."

Sanchez nodded. "Yes." A quick look around. "Did we lose anyone?"

"Two men, Don Julian, and three wounded."

"Can the wounded ride?"

"Yes."

"Then let's be on our way before more French turn up."

An hour later they had left the dead and the burning wagons well behind, and they were a good six miles to the south of the Salamanca road, back in woodland, and feeling secure. Sanchez slowed the pace and they rode on for another hour. At a small village they buried the two dead lancers who had been brought away tied over their horses. Nearly half the lancers were leading a captured horse. Lloyd had been quiet. As they stood to one side while the lancers buried their comrades, he spoke quietly to Michael.

"Begging your pardon, sir, but that was a hell of a thing, sir, killing all those Frenchmen like that. I can't say as I hold with it." He paused, and Michael waited. "But I suppose it's not my country, is it, sir? I expect I would feel different if the French came to the valleys, raping and killing." He paused again. "A fair fight is one thing, sir, but then war isn't fair, is it, sir? So I think we must just go along with it, let them do their killing their way, and do our killing our way, sir. Begging your pardon."

Michael turned to look at Lloyd, whose gaze was fixed on the funeral. "D'ye know Lloyd, I couldn't have put it better myself." He looked back to the funeral. "Of course, there's one Frenchman I'd cut down under any circumstances, without any hesitation, fair fight or not."

"Yes, sir, and I'd be glad to make an exception for him, sir."

"Thank you, Lloyd."

The two men stood in silence, side by side in the heat of the late afternoon, and watched the funeral.

That night they bivouacked around an isolated farmhouse. The Spanish family who lived there crowded themselves into the kitchen, leaving the single other room for Michael, Sanchez and Strenuwitz. Michael slept fitfully, wrapped in his cloak on the bare earth floor. During the night one of the wounded lancers died, and was carried on his horse until they found another small settlement with a church and a priest. While the lancers buried their comrade, Michael sat under a tree and started to look through the papers they had captured.

The officer appeared to have been an infantry Brigadier on his way to join Junot's Corp. The papers included his orders, details of his expenses, and returns of the units in his brigade. Those would be useful, thought Michael. Then, at the bottom of the case, Michael found a bound volume. He opened it and read the title, 'Emplacement des Troupes de L'Empire Francais', and its date, 1st June 1810. He started to flip through the pages. With growing astonishment Michael realised that it contained details of every unit in the French army. Not just in Spain, but everywhere. Their location, their strength, what brigades, divisions and corps they belonged to. Michael's mind was almost overwhelmed by the implications, what it could mean to Viscount Wellington. He looked up to see that the funeral had ended, and Sanchez was walking towards him. Michael scrambled to his feet.

"Don Julian, Look at this," he waved the book at Sanchez, "we need to get this to Wellington as quickly as possible."

Sanchez quickly understood the significance of the book. "Quickly, and safely, Lieutenant Roberts." He thought for a moment. "I will give you a small escort, the best men on the best horses, if you ride hard, the way we came, you should make Alverca in two days, and avoid the French, it's about thirty five leagues."

Michael nodded his agreement, a hundred miles and more, over rough terrain, and in the heat of July. It would be tough, but it was necessary. "Then we will leave now, Don Julian, it has already been light for two hours."

Late in the evening of the following day, Michael, Lloyd and their escort rode wearily into Alverca. They had lost two of the lancers on the way, one with a lame horse, another whose horse fell and broke its leg as they had pushed fast down into a valley. They had been left behind. With luck Don Julian would pick them up on his more leisurely return. Michael left Lloyd to look after the tired horses and the escort, and sought out Colonel Murray.

Murray greeted him cheerfully. "Hello, Roberts, how did it go with Don Julian?"

"Very well, sir, but, look, we took this off a French brigadier on the Salamanca road two days ago." He held out the book to Murray.

Murray took it and started to look through it. "Good God!" He looked up at Michael. "This is tremendous, Roberts, we must see Wellington at once."

Viscount Wellington was equally astonished. "Murray, this means we can work out exactly what strength the French have against us, and, just as importantly, if they are likely to be reinforced at all." He turned to Michael. "Mister Roberts, just how did you come by this?"

Briefly, Michael recounted what had happened on the Salamanca Road, adding that Sanchez was very happy to place himself and his men under British command.

"It was well done, Mister Roberts, very well done. It would seem that Sanchez will be quite an asset." Wellington looked at him. "And now I think you had better go and rest and freshen yourself up."

"Yes, my Lord. I have some of Don Julian's lancers with me, sir, they acted as an escort, they need a billet, sir."

Wellington laughed. "Well spoken, Roberts. Murray, can you help him?"

"I think so, my Lord, I shall get de Lancey to arrange something."

"Excellent. Now, off you go, Mister Roberts, and well done, very well done. Oh, and, for the moment, keep this little book to yourself, eh?" Wellington returned to leafing through the book.

Chapter 14

As soon as he made arrangements for the lancers, Michael returned to his billet, going first to the stables. There he found Lloyd rubbing down Rodrigo, with Parra looking after Johnny.

"Hello Parra."

"Senhor."

"How are they, Lloyd?"

"Well enough, sir, well enough, nothing a day's rest won't put right."

Michael strolled around to where Duke was munching contentedly on some forage, Lloyd's Edward and Harry in stalls next to him. "We can ride Duke and Edward tomorrow," he laughed, "or they'll start to get fat."

Lloyd chuckled, "Chance would be a fine thing, sir, on this forage."

"Yes, it would. Rodrigo did well these last few days."

"Yes, sir, diolch yn fawr, I think Edward might have struggled a bit."

"Parra, do you know where Francisco is?"

"He went to get some food for you, Senhor, when he heard you had returned. Everyone else has already had dinner. I think he is also getting something for Senhor Lloyd."

"Good, good. Then I shall leave you both to get on. Lloyd, we had best be up and about early. Bring me some hot water to shave at first light." Michael rubbed his stubbled chin. "I fear I am beginning to look like one of Don Julian's lancers."

In the dining room Michael found Francisco laying out a plate of cold beef and bread for him, along with a bottle of wine. " Senhor, I am sorry it is only cold food; dinner was a little while ago."

"That's alright, Francisco, it will do."

He had barely sat down when the door opened and Sir Stapleton Cotton came in.

"Roberts! Good to see you back. No, sit down, sit down." He pulled up a chair and sat down. "Francisco, get me a glass as well. Now, tell me what you have been doing?"

When Michael had finished his story, Sir Stapleton said to him, "That's good work, Roberts, and Sanchez and his men will be useful, very useful from what you say. Now I have some news for you," he smiled, "Stanhope has gone home."

"What?" Michael was astounded. "I beg your pardon, sir."

"No, no need." Sir Stapleton smiled at Michael. "I thought you might like to know."

"Yes, sir, thank you." Michael paused for second. "Does that mean you will send me back to the Regiment, sir?"

Sir Stapleton's expression turned serious. "Ah! No, I'm afraid not."

"But, sir, Dudley is fully fit again. Surely you don't still need me?"

"Err, no, but you are proving useful to have round, Roberts, like with this business with Sanchez. Your Portuguese and Spanish are far better than anything Dudley can manage. And, frankly, Wellington wants you here, told me so himself, so you will just have to put up with it."

The following day Sanchez rode in with a small escort. He spent some time with Wellington, and Michael only managed a few words with Sergeant Hernandez, who was one of the escort. From him he learnt that they had only found one of the lancers left behind from Michael's escort. What had happened to the other one was a mystery.

In Ciudad Rodrigo, in General Harrasti's former office, Marshal Andre Massena, Duke of Rivoli, Prince of Essling, commander of the French Army of Portugal, drummed his fingers on the table, and thought hard. His senior aide de camp, Chef de Battalion Pelet stood silently and waited. The news he had just given Massena was troubling. He had picked up a rumour that the British were building fortifications outside Lisbon.

Massena looked again at the map lying on the table, and waved his hand across it, dismissively. "I see no natural obstacles before Lisbon, nowhere to build fortifications." He paused. "If there are fortifications they can only be to delay us while the British embark their army." He paused again.

Pelet felt emboldened to speak. "Your Highness, there are three main roads to Lisbon, the British cannot defend them all. Fortifications can be turned, by-passed. The maps show no difficult terrain, nothing to stop you manoeuvring the army around any defences."

Massena grunted. He rose from his chair and walked to look out of the window. Outside was a ruined Ciudad Rodrigo, in and around which his army was preparing to advance towards the Portuguese frontier fortress of Almeida, take it, and cross into Portugal. He had to drive the British out of Portugal, the Emperor demanded it. If there was anything that might cause difficulties, he needed to know. He turned back to face Pelet. "Find Renard, tell him to go and find out the truth of the matter. It would be good to send him off, Ney has taken a great dislike to him, and, for once, I can't say I disagree with him. Let our spy earn his keep somewhere else."

In Alverca Michael was chatting with Sam Dudley when Sir Stapleton strode in to their shared billet. "Roberts, tell your people to start packing, you're leaving us for a while, new orders for you, and as soon as you've done that, get along to see Murray, he'll brief you and give you your written orders. Off you go now, and good luck."

At headquarters Michael made his way to Murray's office, which had become familiar to him. He knocked, walked in, and checked. "I beg your pardon, sir, I didn't realise…"

Murray cut him short. "Come in Roberts, come in." Wellington was standing by the window, and turned to look keenly at Michael. Murray went on. "You are off to Lisbon again, with a special task." He glanced at Wellington who spoke for the first time.

"Tell him, Murray, best he knows everything, if he hasn't already worked it out."

Murray paused, thoughtfully, for a moment. "You see, Roberts, we are dreadfully outnumbered, which you will be well aware of." Michael nodded, wondering what this was all about. "And, as things stand at the moment, we cannot hope to stop the French and beat them here, on the frontier. They are intent on driving us into the sea, and taking control of Portugal. We have to stop them." He paused again. "You are, of course, well aware of the construction work that has been going on to the north of Lisbon?"

Michael nodded again, "Yes, sir'."

Murray went on, "However, you may not be aware of the full extent of those works?"

"Err, no, sir, I am not. I have only seen those near the Tagus, but I read about the materials and rations sent out elsewhere in the papers that I recovered and destroyed."

"Well, Roberts, there is a line of fortifications, more than one line, actually, that runs from the Tagus to the

Atlantic." Michael's surprise was evident. Murray smiled at him. "Yes, right across Portugal, two lines, and a third on the southern coast to protect an embarkation point, should we have need of it. The plan is to withdraw before the French, to encourage them to follow, to let them think we will abandon Portugal. At the same time a proclamation will order all Portuguese citizens to evacuate the countryside in front of the French, and to remove or destroy all food supplies and anything else that might be of use to the French. We will end our retreat once we enter the lines, and turn to face the French, who will be faced with a continuous line of strong defences with the army behind it, while they are stuck in a country that cannot feed them. They must attack, and be beaten, or stand and starve, or retreat. In any case their army will be destroyed."

"Roberts," Wellington spoke, "it cannot be stressed too much that the whole plan depends upon the French following, and believing they are going to drive us into the sea. To that end it is essential that they do not learn of the existence of the lines. The Portuguese government is in ignorance, our government at home is in ignorance, our army, never mind the French, is in ignorance, Ambassador Stuart is in ignorance. It must stay that way. Fortunately, you stopped one man who might have given the secret away. You also know the man who is probably the biggest threat to that secret." Renard, thought Michael. "So, Roberts, we are sending you to Lisbon to make sure neither he nor anyone else discovers the lines until we enter them, and the French see them for themselves. I don't care how you do it, or what you have to do. Murray?"

"Yes, my Lord. Now, Roberts, we are sending you, ostensibly, as liaison between the Lisbon garrison and the Portuguese authorities, which will, of course, particularly include General de Silva and his people. You speak the language like a native, you know de Silva, you are the obvious choice. That should allow you the freedom of action you might need. However, you are also to work with Captain Jones of the Royal Engineers who is in charge of the construction work, help him with security, smooth things over if he has any problems with any authority in Lisbon. But, above all, discretion is the order of the day. You are not, under any circumstances, to discuss the lines with anyone, except Captain Jones, not the Portuguese, and not even with Ambassador Stuart. D'ye understand, Roberts?"

"Yes, sir." Michael was stunned.

Murray picked up a document from the table and held it out to Michael. "Here are your written orders. They make it clear that you are in Lisbon on detached duties from headquarters, and answerable to me, and me alone. They are very unclear about what those duties are." Murray turned to Wellington. "Is there anything else, my Lord?"

Wellington was looking at Michael. "No, Murray, I think Mister Roberts is well aware of the considerable responsibility we have loaded on to his shoulders. Eh, Mister Roberts?

"Yes, my Lord, thank you." I think, Michael added to himself.

Late the following day Michael and his party arrived in Coimbra after a very long, hot, and hard day's ride of over seventy miles. Michael's orders quickly secured them an adequate billet for the night.

"Lloyd, Parra, you look to the horses, Francisco, you know what to do, I shall be back within the hour to eat." Michael strode off, leaving the rest of his party exchanging silent glances before getting to work. In fact, Michael was back in half an hour. Sofia was not to be found. Her neighbours had nothing more to tell him than the last time he had enquired. Michael was not surprised, and only a little disappointed. He had enjoyed his brief affair with Sofia, but that was all it had been, all it could be, while his heart and his love belonged to another. He wondered, briefly, what had become of her. He wondered if he would ever know. Then he turned his attention to the matter in hand, and how he might manage to fulfil his orders.

Pushing on towards Lisbon, Michael took the road to Leiria where they put up for another night, and then on to Torres Vedras, where Murray had told him he should find Captain Jones. As they approached Torres Vedras the terrain grew more rugged, the road twisting and winding, with steep hills covered in trees rising up in front of them. Coming around a bend they suddenly came face to face with a road block formed by a wagon pulled across the road, and manned by Portuguese Militia. An officer carefully checked Michael's orders, before giving him directions and allowing him to proceed. As they rode on, Michael could see a massive fortification sitting on top of a hill to his right. It was to there that the directions took them. A road climbed up the steep hill, and took them around behind the fort to its entrance, past a long, low earthwork, pierced with embrasures with the black muzzles of cannon visible. Between the road and the fort was a deep and wide dry ditch, its sides faced with dressed stone. Michael began to grasp the scale of the Lines; this was far more impressive than the field works he had scorned.

At the entrance the party was again halted and checked, before a Portuguese sergeant led them inside. Only then did Michael see the huge size of the fortification. A Royal engineer officer came striding towards him, and Michael quickly dropped off Duke to greet him.

"You must be Lieutenant Roberts? I was told to expect you. I'm Captain Jones." The man was in his mid-twenties, with a slightly gaunt look to him, but a strong jawline.

Michael saluted, "Yes, sir, I am."

"Come along then, we can give you a billet for the night, and you can have a look at the plans of the Lines, something not everyone can see, but I gather you have to be fully briefed." He smiled at Michael, "It's quite a big undertaking, and tomorrow I have to go over to Sobral, to the other large fort, you can come along and get a better idea of what this is all about. And then, I suppose, you will be wanting to get to Lisbon?"

"Yes, sir, I will."

Inside a small hut built in the middle of the great redoubt, Jones unrolled a map for Michael. It showed the location of all the forts that made up the Lines. Michael was stunned. "There are dozens of them!"

Jones smiled. "Yes, it is rather impressive." He pointed to the map. "This is where we are now, in front of the main line, which you can see runs from the Tagus at Quintella across to the coast at Ribamar. This forward line is concentrated on the Tagus at Alhandra, blocking the road to Lisbon along the Tagus, and here at Torres Vedras and also at Sobral, blocking the other two main roads from the north. It's a huge undertaking, but I have a free hand, I just order whatever I need and send the bills to the Commissary in Lisbon." He paused thoughtfully. "As I said, you should come with me tomorrow to see Sobral, and then, from there, you can take the road to Lisbon through Bucelas, that will give you an idea of the second, main line of defences." He gave a little laugh. "We had to survey the whole lot, both lines of mountains, would you believe they don't appear on any of the printed maps?" He unrolled another plan. "Now this," he said, "is the real jewel, the fort of Saint Juliao da Barra." Michael winced at his pronunciation. "This, as you can see is on the coast, its about ten miles west of Lisbon." Michael could see that it was a large and extensive fortification.

"Would that be the embarkation point, sir?" he asked.

Jones looked sideways at him. "It is."

"Colonel Murray mentioned it, sir, when I was given my orders."

"I see. Well, then, let me show you around."

Captain Jones gave Michael a quick tour of the fort, pointing out that it was, in fact, three separate forts, joined by a continuous parapet, and supported by another four forts in its immediate vicinity. Between them they completely dominated the road from the north. At Sobral the situation was much the same, and again, closer to Lisbon, at Bucelas. As Michael and his party rode south, two days later, leaving Jones and the lines behind him, he could not but marvel at the immense undertaking, and feel pity for any troops thrown against them, particularly since, if they did break through, they would find the main British army waiting for them. He shook his head in admiration for Wellington's plan. It was simple, and could result in the destruction of the invading French without the need for a battle. A few miles out from Lisbon, Michael passed the city defences, he saw four artillery redoubts overlooking the road, with work going on the complete and strengthen them, and he knew that there were others in a long curve around the city. They were nowhere near as impressive as the Lines to the north.

Lisbon in early August was hot, a huge change from the cooler north and even the mountains around Torres Vedras and Sobral. Arriving at his house, the horses were quickly taken care of by Parra and Lloyd, and the mules unloaded. As Senhor Santiago and Francisco carried the baggage into the house, Michael sat in the cool of the kitchen with a glass of Senhora Santiago's lemonade, and listened contentedly to her chatter, bringing him up to date on affairs in the house, while she busied herself making meals for them all. It was good to be back home.

In the morning Michael rode across to Belem, and presented himself to the British commander in Lisbon, Brigadier General Peacocke. Peacocke was somewhat taken aback by Michael's sudden appearance, but Murray's orders were explicit in giving Michael free rein, answerable only to Murray for his actions. Peacocke could have taken umbrage, Michael more than half expected it, but he grunted, shrugged, and dismissed Michael with the comment that he was one less thing to worry about, and he would be pleased if Michael could smooth over matters with the Lisbon authorities concerning the recent behaviour of some officers at the opera. Michael promised to do what he could. His next call was on Ambassador Stuart, who was expecting him. He was happy to see Michael, because, as he put it, he could leave him to deal with de Silva and any situation in Lisbon as he had more than enough to do with intelligence from the rest of Spain and Portugal. He expressed his confidence in Michael, and bid him good day.

Michael's next call was on General de Silva, his welcome was warm. "Lieutenant Roberts! It is good to see you again. I knew someone was being sent to liaise between your army and our authorities, well, me, really. It's all about intelligence and making sure we keep French spies in ignorance, if there are any left." He chuckled. "Frankly, Lieutenant, I don't expect you to have much to occupy your time, not since we destroyed Raposa's network." He used Renard's Portuguese name. "Of course, I heard about your success in Ciudad Rodrigo. Very well done. But, tell me, what did the spy have that was so important?"

Michael had half expected the question, and was ready. "Well, sir, it was all a bit of an anti-climax in the end. All he had was a list of types of supplies being sent, and where to." He laughed. "I think the French know exactly where the army is at the moment, so it was all a bit pointless."

De Silva looked disappointed, then smiled. "Better safe than sorry, I suppose, and it was a very good piece of work on your part. And it is one less spy to worry about."

"Yes, sir, it is."

"Any news of Raposa? We have heard nothing."

"Not recently, sir. We know he was with Massena at the siege of Ciudad Rodrigo, and is presumably still with him." Michael briefly told de Silva about his run in with Renard at Marialva, and his meeting with Marshal Ney.

"Madre de Dios!" exclaimed de Silva when Michael had finished his story. "That was close." He looked closely at Michael. "This really is personal, isn't it, you and Raposa?"

"Oh, yes, sir, very."

"Then be very careful, Lieutenant, such passion can cloud one's judgement and lead to mistakes, fatal mistakes." He rang a handbell on his desk. "But enough, will you take coffee with me?"

"Thank you, General, but I do have another call to make, if you will forgive me?"

De Silva laughed. "Of course, Lieutenant, and, please, give my cousin a kiss for me." He winked at Michael who felt his face redden, making de Silva laugh even more.

Michael had already sent Francisco to see his sister and tell Roberta that he would call as soon as he could. The late afternoon found them taking a light dinner in the shade of the courtyard of Roberta's house. Michael told her about Stanhope, and his time on Sir Stapleton's staff. She already knew about the taking of Soares the spy, but listened intently as he described the breakout with Sanchez from Ciudad Rodrigo.

Then he surprised her, when, as casually as he could muster, he said, "Oh, and I had a little run in with Renard."

"What!", exclaimed Roberta, her face a picture of shock and concern. "Renard? How, where, what happened? Tell me, now!"

Once again Michael retold the tale. As he did, Roberta reached across the small table and took his hand in hers, squeezing it, tightly. When he finished she sat silent for a moment, and then spoke, quietly. "This isn't going to be over until one of you is dead, is it?"

Michael looked at the stone flags of the courtyard for a moment, before raising his eyes to meet hers, unblinking. "No, Roberta, it isn't. There's too much for it to be any other way. That man needs to be put down like a rabid dog." Michael's voice, cold and hard, sent a shiver down Robert's spine.

"Then," she replied, "make sure it's him that dies, not you, do you hear me?"

He smiled. "That is the plan."

"And just how do you propose managing that?"

"To tell truth, Roberta, I have absolutely no idea." He took a mouthful of his wine. "I suppose it is hoping for too much that he might return to Lisbon, but a man can hope." Dusk was falling. "Anyway," he went on, "enough of that. It's getting dark, shall we go in?"

Roberts laughed. "Oh, Michael, you are so transparent. Yes, we shall, but you must go home and be patient for a few days."

"What?" Roberta smiled, covered her face with her fan, and arched her eyebrows at him. "Oh! Ah, yes, I see." Michael reddened, and Roberta laughed more.

Michael wasn't sure exactly what he was expected to do, so he fell quickly into a routine of visiting the embassy and de Silva's headquarters every morning to see if there were any developments that concerned him. Sometimes he saw

Stuart, more often than not his clerk, who simply told Michael, "Nothing today, Lieutenant." At de Silva's the General frequently invited him into his office for coffee and an inconsequential chat. Every other day he rode out to Belem to see if there was anything there for him. He was able to tell Peacocke that he had smoothed matters over with de Silva concerning the behaviour of officers at the opera. In fact, de Silva had told him which regiment they were from, and Michael knew they had left Lisbon to rejoin their regiment. He rode out to the lines regularly, in his civilian clothes, to test the security of the Portuguese pickets between the lines and Lisbon. He discovered no problems. Riding out to Alhandra he met the engineer in charge there, a Lieutenant Forster, who gladly gave him a tour of the defences. By late morning Michael had done all that was needed, and was a free agent. Then, in the cool of the evening, he exercised Johnny and Duke on the small parcel of land behind his house, and practised the Sword Exercise with Lloyd.

After a week had passed he received an invitation from Roberta to dinner.

As they relaxed after the meal, and finished the fine bottle of wine, Roberta spoke, hesitantly. "Michael, why are you here?"

He smiled, "Because a beautiful woman asked me to dine with her."

"No, Michael, you know very well what I mean. Why are you here in Lisbon? You aren't really doing anything except ride off into the hills a lot. My cousin is a little perplexed, he wants to know, and asked me to find out."

"Has he been keeping an eye on me?"

"No! Well, yes, a little, of course he has. It is what he does. Now, why?"

Michael looked down and fiddled with his wine glass. He had feared something like this. He decided to tell her, not the truth, but a truth. "Roberta."

"Yes?"

"Do you remember, when I first returned to Lisbon, that neither of us was able to tell the other about our secret activities?"

"Of course I do." She thought for a moment. "So," she spoke slowly, "you are here for something, but you cannot say what it is. Am I right?"

He looked up and gave her a slight smile. "Yes, you are."

Roberta stared hard into his eyes, and Michael held her gaze. "Is this something that might come between us? You English, me Portuguese?"

"No, no, not at all." Michael was somewhat shocked by the thought.

"You know that I must tell my cousin what you have told me?"

"Yes, of course."

"I suppose something like this was going to happen sooner or later."

Michael reached for her hand, half afraid she would pull it away, she didn't. "I will tell you, and the General, as soon as I can, I promise."

"Oh, Michael, you know what happens when you make promises to women."

Michael had no answer.

Roberta rose from the table and moved to Michael's side, still holding his hand. "Hold, me, please, Michael."

Michael stood and clasped her in his arms. After a moment, Roberta pushed back from him, and smiled at him. "I'm alright now, take me upstairs, please?"

August passed slowly. There had been a little excitement when new tarletons arrived in Lisbon for the regiment. Michael had procured a new officer's one for himself, and Lloyd had sorted out a good one for himself before they were sent on after the regiment. The old ones they were wearing were warped from the rain and the heat, and had lost most of their silver trim, real silver on Michael's. In the middle of the month a remount of fifty-four horses arrived for the regiment from England, and there were a few activity filled days getting those fit and sent on their way. Michael settled into a dull routine.

He made courtesy calls on Furtado and Rodrigues, and asked both if they had any news on the identity of the mysterious Augusto. Both were sympathetic, apologetic, they had nothing. Michael despaired of ever recovering the missing half of his inheritance. Surely his presence in Portugal, in Lisbon, was now generally known in his father's circle? So why hadn't Augusto come forward?

One hot, August evening, Michael was standing under a portico in Black Horse Square, watching the hustle and bustle going on all around. He was at a loose end. Roberta had some social event she was attending. All his Regimental business was concluded. De Silva and Stuart had nothing for him. He leaned against a pillar, wondering where to go for a cold glass of wine. Suddenly, he felt the prick of a knife at his neck, and froze.

A quiet voice in his ear spoke. "Who is the most beautiful woman in Lisbon."

He hesitated, disbelieving for a second, and then, "The woman in your arms," Michael replied. The point of the knife disappeared from his neck, and he whirled around, to confront a stocky, young man, with sparkling, laughing eyes, dark curly hair peeking out from under his broad brimmed hat, and a huge grin from ear to ear.

"Antonio?"

"Ah, Miguel, you remembered the old password!"

Laughing the two men embraced, and slapped each other on the back.

"Antonio, how are you, it's been so long."

Antonio shrugged. "It's been nearly five years, Miguel, I'm thirsty."

Michael laughed at his old friend. "You haven't changed. Come on, I'll buy us a bottle of something good."

Over the next hour the conversation flowed with news, good and bad, as Michael caught with what had become of the boys he had run with in the streets of Lisbon. Antonio was coy about what he was doing, but Michael worked out that he was involved in smuggling, although quite what and to where remained a mystery. Antonio had heard about Michael's parents, and commiserated with his friend. He was frankly amazed when he learnt that Michael was now a British cavalry officer.

"Had you been in uniform, my friend, I would probably not have known you, let alone held a knife to your neck."

They talked about old friends. Ricardo, their leader, was now a sergeant in an infantry regiment, Marco, always the clever one, a militia officer. Little Jorge was working as a tailor, Carlos was working on a mule train supplying the army, and big, slow Bernardo was a gardener, saved from military service by a badly broken leg that had left him with a severe limp. And then there was Jean-Paul. Antonio mentioned him first.

"Remember that French boy, what did we call him?"

"Raposa Negra"

"Yes, that was him. Utter bastard. We should have let you knife him."

"Perhaps you should have."

Something in Michael's voice caused Antonio to raise his eyebrows and stay quiet. Michael went on.

"Turns out he became a French spy. He was here with Junot, and has been back since." He took a mouthful of wine. "I tell you, Antonio, the man is a spy, a killer, and needs to be put down like a rabid dog."

Antonio was taken aback by Michael's vehemence, and was left speechless. Michael went on. "I don't think he is in Lisbon now, but you and the others would know him wouldn't you?"

"Yes, I think so, but…"

Michael cut in. "Just keep an eye open for him will you? Ask the others to do the same? You never know, one of you might see him."

"Of course, Miguel, for you, because of him, of course."

"Thank you. If you do, you might find me at home, my parents house, you remember it?" Antonio nodded. "Or, if I am not there…" He paused and thought. "If I am not there, you remember Roberta?"

"Oh ho, of course, Miguel, we were all very envious, and…"

"Yes, alright." Michael smiled. "Anyway, her cousin is General de Silva."

"Really? Oh!"

"Don't worry, Antonio, I doubt the General would be bothered by your activities, whatever they are. Anyway, a message to her will get to the General, he will know what to do about Raposa."

"Consider it done, Miguel, if he is seen. It was bad when the French were here before, no one wants to see that again. But, tell me, from what you say, I think that you must be back in touch with Roberta, eh, Miguel?"

Michael smiled. "And tell me, where can I find you?"

Antonio laughed. "Here, there, but, if you remember where my mother lives," Michael nodded, "you can always leave a message with her."

"And your father?"

Antonio's smile faded. "He went to fight the French with the Ordenança. He did not return."

"I am sorry."

"Thank you. So, you see, Miguel, we both have cause to hate the French."

And with that, the conversation went back to more general reminiscence and gossip.

Chapter 15

Renard blinked in the sudden sunlight as the tarpaulin was pulled off the barrels he was hidden amongst. The captain of the small cargo boat, an afrancesado, looked down on him, "We are coming into Lisbon now, senhor, it is safe to come out, no one will notice you."

Renard squeezed out between two barrels, and into the heat and glare of the early afternoon sun. He blinked and took a deep breath, glad to be out from the hot, airless hiding place he had been stuck in since first light. The skipper was right, there were very few people on the dockside as many slept or relaxed through the hottest part of the day. No one was paying any attention to another small boat coming into dock. Even if someone did see him, he was dressed as the sort of clerk frequently seen around the port on the business of some merchant or other, he might as well have been invisible. The boat was soon moored, and Renard handed the captain a purse. He knew he could rely on the captain, he had been well paid, and Renard had let it be known that he knew where the man lived. He had no idea, nor if the man had any family, but the look in his eye had told Renard that the comment had struck home.

He stepped ashore, and into the shade of a colonnaded building. For a few moments he scanned the surroundings, before heading off to the home of another afrancesado. He wasn't expected, he expected the man to be surprised, and terrified, in that order, but his rooms were in an old quarter of Lisbon where no questions were asked. Renard expected the French to occupy the city by early October, but he had a lot to do in the next few days if he was to give Massena the reassurances he wanted about defensive works, and he would need to find reliable couriers to travel into Spain and north to the army. Then, once Lisbon was back in French hands, he would deal with that tart Roberta once and for all. He should have taken care of her when he was in Lisbon with Junot. That had been a mistake, he had simply underestimated her role in Portuguese intelligence, taking her for a mere gossip. He had since learnt enough about the destruction of his network in Lisbon to know otherwise. As for Roberts, he would see if he couldn't have his house seized for himself. He smiled at the thought of taking possession of that fine house.

Renard's unsuspecting host, Pereira, was a clerk, and Renard intended to pass himself off as a fellow employee sharing the man's rooms. He took himself into a disreputable looking coffee house to pass the afternoon until he could be sure Pereira would have returned from work. He ordered coffee and food, and settled himself to wait in a corner that gave him a view of the door and a section of the street outside.

Once Renard was confident that Pereira would be at home, he set off. Pereira's rooms were in a tall tenement block, in a poorer part of town. There was nothing to pick it out, it was anonymous, which was what Renard liked. The main door to the building was open, and Renard quietly made his way up to the second floor. The rooms were at the front of the building, the windows gave a good view of the street below, but were high enough up to avoid the glance of passers-by. He tapped on the door, and waited for a moment. A voice inside called out, "Just a moment". Then, as the door opened he threw his weight at it, it crashed inwards, sending the man behind it staggering back. Renard slipped quickly in, glanced behind him at the empty passage, then shut the door behind him. He smiled, coldly, at the shocked man before him.

"Hello, Pereira, I have come to stay for a while."

Renard had harboured doubts about the fortification rumours from the beginning. He passed a few days just going around the taverns and coffee houses, listening to the talk and the gossip, but hearing nothing useful. Before he went blundering around the countryside he wanted to get some idea of where he should be looking, and if there was anything to look for, which he doubted. He thought Massena was jumping at shadows, he wasn't the man he had been, and he didn't trust Pelet one little bit. Still, they had sent him, and here he was back in Lisbon, for which he had to admit to a little fondness. It wasn't Paris, but it would do. Then he began to pick up rumours about construction work going on, but not where, or how big. In the taverns there began to be mutterings that the English were preparing to leave Portugal, to abandon it to the French. But he needed something more than tavern gossip and rumour. Then Pereira came home with news that was of great interest.

Pereira worked for a chandler, and had been instructed to deliver a very large consignment of rope and pulleys, apparently for a signalling station, to a construction site on the bank of the Tagus some three or four leagues towards the Atlantic. It was a large order, and would take a couple of days to prepare.

Renard asked Pereira, "What sort of a site is it? Where is it? Is it just some signal relay station?"

"It is beyond Belem, senhor, I am not sure what it is," Pereira was nervous, "I haven't been before, but one of the other clerks has, and he called it the fortress. He said it is a massive construction, senhor. I thought perhaps it would be of interest to you."

Renard said nothing for a moment, letting Pereira stew. "Very well, I will meet you just outside the city, on the Belem road. I will come with you; another clerk will not be noticed."

Pereira was nervous about the arrangements, but when Renard appeared from trees at the side of the road, a few miles out of Lisbon, the muleteers transporting the supplies didn't give him a second look. What he found at their destination was a massive series of very strong fortifications, some still under construction. On their way along the road they first passed a group of three smaller forts, then another two larger ones, a third single, even larger fort, and finally a huge, strongly built fortress with stone bulwarks, and bristling with cannon. They were superficially checked by bored Portuguese Militia sentries, and then waved into the site, it helped that they were expected. Renard kept in the background, and kept his eyes open as the mules were unloaded and the consignment checked. He was, frankly, astonished. It was indeed a massive fortification, built right on the coast, covering a large area, but clearly built with one object in mind, to defend the English army while it boarded its transport ships. It overlooked a small, curved bay where ships could get in close, and smaller boats could run up on a gently sloping beach. It was exactly what Massena needed to know about, it was the clearest evidence that the English were preparing to abandon Portugal.

The following day Renard walked through the city, heading north. With the knowledge that the English were building an evacuation point, he needed to see if there was any truth in the rumours about the fortifications to the north of the city. A little beyond the suburbs he found a line of scattered fortifications that appeared to run in a curve around the city. Construction work was continuing on those as well. Renard could hardly avoid laughing out loud. God knew, he was no real soldier, but he knew that while the defences he saw might slow an advance by the French army, they would be only a minor inconvenience, particularly if the English army was embarking three leagues away. The Portuguese army was laughable, and would never hold Lisbon, just as they had failed at Oporto.

Now he knew the truth of the matter, he needed to get the information to Massena. He could, of course, go himself.

But that was risky, it had been difficult enough getting into Lisbon. And the information needed to be sent by a number of different ways, in which case he might as well send a few others and stay safe in Lisbon. He would continue to keep his eyes and ears open, and Massena would need up to date intelligence when he entered Lisbon, who was trustworthy, who should be dealt with, like de Silva. And, he thought, he deserved a little fun. There were one or two houses in Lisbon, very, very discreet houses, where he could get the fun he preferred.

With the help of Pereira he found a smuggler, a man accustomed to carrying goods through the mountains between Portugal and Spain. He agreed to carry a letter in cipher to the French, who, Renard hoped, would be on the Portuguese border, if not already in Portugal. His price was high, but worth it. A day later Renard and Pereira found another man, a tinker who travelled up and down the border, to carry another letter. At least one of them should be successful. He also found, and employed, a couple of ruffians he had used before, he felt more comfortable with a little muscle to hand. They could watch his back while he was out and about, and also run errands for him, while he stayed in during daylight hours. Pereira was increasingly unhappy, but could do nothing but go along with Renard's demands.

By the beginning of September Renard felt well satisfied with his efforts, he had discovered the truth of the rumours about the defences around Lisbon, and sent the information to Massena. He learnt nothing new to change his opinion that there was nothing to stop the French army gaining Lisbon while the English army abandoned Portugal. The frontier fortress of Almeida had fallen, Massena and his army would be on their way. All he had to do was lay low and wait.

By the beginning of September Michael was getting bored and frustrated. He had spent the best part of a month riding around the defensive lines, looking for breaches of security and finding none. He regularly called on the British commander at Belem, but it was a mere formality. Similarly with the Ambassador and de Silva. He told Roberta about Antonio and the other old friends. She remembered them, and thought it was worth asking them to watch out for Renard. Michael told her that they all knew that de Silva was her cousin, and she laughed at his description of Antonio's reaction. The frequent time he was able to spend with Roberta was delightful, but, dearly as he loved his friend, he could not help but feel that he would be better employed with the army, preferably with his regiment. With the fall of Almeida he knew there would be a lot more fighting, and he wanted to be with his Regiment. Then things changed.

By the beginning of September General De Silva was feeling quite pleased with himself. He had not been idle. He had been hard at work with informers and his own intelligence gatherers, endeavouring to identify and deal with any individuals sympathetic to the French and Republicanism. With the fall of Almeida and the French expected to advance on Lisbon, it was a pressing matter to deny them any possible assistance. He had identified around fifty suspects who were believed to be actively aiding the French. They were mainly of the middling sort of professionals, lawyers, doctors, minor officials, a few employees of merchants. When he was ready, de Silva had them all arrested.

Questioning them all took time, and de Silva left it to men more experienced at extracting information than he was. He had to be careful, some had powerful friends who immediately protested at his actions. He issued strict instructions that no violence was to be used, which was a handicap. It slowed the process down, and the results were disappointing. After a week, it was beginning to look as if over enthusiastic informers had exaggerated claims of activity in support of the French. He was a worried man, he needed something to justify his actions, or he could be in trouble himself. He had enemies in high places.

He was sitting in his office, in a comfortable armchair wondering what to do. On a low table next to him was a list of those arrested. He looked at it again. He ignored everyone except the handful who worked for merchants. Something, possibly recent experience with Renard's network, suggested to him that if there was anything to be found, it would be amongst them. The lawyers, the doctors, even the few government officials arrested, could talk all they liked. He couldn't see anything that they could actually do. Those in trade had the opportunity to act.

Running through those associated with trade he decided to question them himself. The first two took up the rest of the morning. It was an unproductive exercise, they clearly knew nothing, and were guilty of no more than careless talk. Then one name caught his eye, or rather the name of the man's employer, Baron Quintela. He knew full well that the Baron was in the Brazils, which meant that the man was effectively employed by Rodrigues, Quintela's head clerk. He decided to pay a visit to the Palacio Quintela. Some fresh and air and exercise might sharpen him up. He roused himself from his chair, seized his hat and cane, and, calling for a couple of men to go with him, he set off.

Rodrigues was more than a little surprised when General de Silva opened his office door and stepped in. Outside his two men stood at the door, having persuaded the porter that the General did not need to be announced. Rodrigues leapt to his feet.

"General de Silva! This is a surprise; how may I be of service?"

De Silva settled himself in the chair opposite Rodrigues, waved him back into his own chair, and came straight to the point.

"Senhor Rodrigues, you were very helpful over the matter of Serrano. I believe that I can trust you?"

"Of course, General. Is this about Teves? I know he has been arrested." Rodrigues raised his hands in despair. "It was bad enough when Serrano was exposed, but the idea that we might have two traitors here is terrible."

"Whether or not Teves is a traitor has still to be established. It may well be he is just a young man with foolish ideas that he will grow out of. If he has committed no act of treason…" De Silva shrugged dismissively.

"Then how can I help, General?"

"Simply tell me what you know about him."

Rodrigues blew his cheeks out. "There's not a lot I can tell you. He hasn't been with us all that long. He is an intelligent young man. Very quick, perceptive. I think he may find the work of a clerk a little lacking in stimulus." He shrugged. "I don't expect him to stay long."

"Does he have any particular friends?"

"Amongst the other clerks? I don't think so. He is amiable enough, gets on well with everyone, but a particular friend? Not that I am aware of."

"So, how did he come to work for you?"

"He was looking for work, could read and write well, taught by priests at an orphanage. Came in off the street and asked for a job. I admired his initiative, tried him, kept him. Now I wonder if I made a mistake, if I was fooled?"

"We will see about that Senhor Rodrigues. Now thank you for your time, unless there is anything else you can think of?"

"No, General. Perhaps I might speak to the other clerks, see if any of them have any information?"

De Silva shrugged. "It can't do any harm. Send a message if you learn anything."

De Silva walked back slowly to his headquarters, deep in thought. When he got to his office he looked over the information on Teves that had led to his arrest. An informant had said that he was seen in a tavern that was known as meeting place for French sympathisers and Republicans. It had been left alone, better to know where such people met, where a discreet eye could be kept on them. According to the informant he had been heard talking, advocating action to help drive the English out of Portugal. De Silva sighed; it wasn't much, but potentially enough. Still, he felt a sense of unease, and sat and thought, and listened to his instincts.

Damn it all! Sitting and wondering wasn't going to achieve anything. He rang a small handbell to summon his secretary. When the man entered he said, "The suspect, Teves, I want him brought here, now, and I shall want coffee for two."

Teves was a very ordinary looking young man, dressed in shabby clothes, exactly the sort you could overlook, thought de Silva. He had a very worried look on his face.

"Sit down," de Silva instructed him. "You can leave us," he spoke to his secretary and the two men that had brought Teves. They hesitated. "Go! You can wait outside."

De Silva sat opposite Teves, and poured two coffees. Teves looked nervous, and he smelt after his days of incarceration. De Silva handed him a coffee, he took it, his hand trembling.

"I think" began de Silva, "that you have been a careless and foolish young man." He paused as Teves stared at him. "I do not think that you are a traitor." He saw hope flicker on Teves' face. "Which does not mean that you are not. However, this is your chance to convince me."

"H…, how do I do that," Teves stammered.

"Tell me what you were doing in the tavern on the east corner of Praca das Flores?"

Teves gaped at him. "Again? I have already explained."

"Please, explain again, to me."

"I was there with someone I knew from the orphanage; he invited me to join him for a drink. Kept asking me what I thought about the French and the English."

"And what did you say?"

"I said I didn't bother about such things; I was more concerned with making a living. Then he asked me if I would like to make more money. I asked him how. He said he couldn't tell me, but there was a man I should meet, who was interested in what merchant's clerks knew. I said I wasn't interested and left."

"Is that all? He didn't give you the man's name?"

"No, General, he didn't, that is everything."

De Silva thought for a moment. "Tell me, what is your friend's name, and do you think that tavern is where he usually drinks?"

"Veiga, General, and yes, he said that if I change my mind I could usually find him there."

"Very well." De Silva looked at Teves, and decided to follow his instinct. "Senhor Rodrigues tells me that you are an intelligent young man, and that he thinks you are getting bored with being a clerk?"

"No, General, I…" De Silva raised his eyebrows questioningly. Teves, sagged. "Yes, General, but it is a living."

"Hmm. What if I gave you a chance to do something much more interesting?"

"General?"

"This what I propose, and I need an immediate answer."

As dark fell the following evening, a cleaned up, but rather nervous Teves walked across Praca das Flores, and entered the rough looking tavern on the far corner. Inside he stood for a moment while his eyes got used to the gloom.

"Hey, Teves! You came back, come, join me."

Teves saw his friend Veiga waving at him, and went over. Veiga was sitting on his own, the tavern was quiet so early in the evening, only a couple of the other tables were occupied.

"You're lucky to find me so early, let me get you a glass, you can share this bottle with me, eh?"

Teves settled on a stool, and in a moment Veiga was back, pouring a drink.

"So, have you thought about my offer?"

"Yes, I have, and I'm not sure. I mean, more money would be good, but I don't know."

Veiga's speech was slurred, and loud, it was his second bottle. "Now listen," He draped a companionable arm around Teves, "It's good money, and all for a little inside information."

"Like what?"

"Oh, just where stuff gets sent, where the mule trains go to, that sort of thing."

"But they supply the army, ours and the English."

Veiga giggled. "Exactly. Then we know where they are."

"Who is we?"

"Me and my friend, my very good friend who pays me. Senhor Raposa."

A scruffy looking man who had been sitting nearby with three burly companions rose from his seat. "I think I have heard quite enough, take him!" ordered de Silva.

Early the following morning, Michael was at the back of the house, with Lloyd and Parra, readying the horses for a ride out to Belem, when Senhor Santiago appeared with a man Michael recognised as one of de Silva's. He brought an urgent summons from de Silva. Leaving Parra to deal with the horses, he and Lloyd hurried to de Silva's headquarters. When Michael entered de Silva's office, the general wasted no words. "Renard is back!"

"What? How? When? How do you know?" Michael was staggered by the news; he had assumed Renard was in the north with Massena.

"Please, Lieutenant, sit down, and I will tell you." Michael lowered himself into the chair indicated by de Silva. "We have, in the last few days, arrested a number of people suspected of being afrancesados." He paused. "We have, of course, interrogated them. One of them turned out not to be an afrancesado at all, in fact he has been exceptionally helpful. I am sorry to tell you that your friend Senhor Rodrigues has lost another clerk, to me. He is an intelligent young man, and perceptive, I have given him a job. He led us to a man who has been working for Raposa. Unfortunately, he couldn't tell us exactly where Raposa is. However, he did say that he thinks, thinks mark you, that he is staying with someone called Pereira.

"Pereira!" Michael interjected. "That's not much help. There must be dozens of men by that name in Lisbon. It's like looking for a man called Smith in London." A thought struck him. "It is a man, I suppose?"

"Yes, no doubt about it. The man said he thought Pereira was a clerk of some sort."

"I suppose that might narrow it down a bit."

There was a knock at the door, de Silva's secretary opened it to admit Roberta, and then closed it behind her. Roberta sensed the serious tension in the room, saw the look on Michael's face. "What has happened?" she asked.

Quickly, de Silva filled her in on the news. She was equally shocked. The three of them sat in silence for a while. Then de Silva spoke. "Clearly, we need to find him, do either of you have any idea how?"

Michael and Roberta both shook their heads. Michael didn't have any idea why Renard might be back, but he knew what he didn't want him to discover.

Roberta looked at him, "Michael, could Renard be anything to do with why you are here?"

Her words broke in on Michael's train of thought. "What?" He was startled by the question. "No, I don't think so." Even as he spoke he realised how inadequate that answer was. He tried, but failed to meet Roberta's gaze.

De Silva coughed. "I think, Roberta, that we must not press the Lieutenant on the nature of his duties. It would not be fair." He turned his attention to Michael. "However, it could help if we had some idea of why Renard might be here. Lieutenant?"

Michael took a deep breath and answered. "Sir, I honestly do not know why Renard might be here. I can only suppose that he is trying to gather what information he can about Viscount Wellington's intentions with regard to the defence of Portugal."

"And will he defend Portugal?" De Silva's voice had a hard edge to it. "I am well aware of the fortifications being built at Saint Juliao da Barra. They appear to be for the purpose of defending an embarkation point. And there are rumours, Lieutenant, rumours that I have heard every day for the last few weeks, brought to me by people I can rely on. They all tell me that the English intend to retreat before Massena and abandon Portugal."

"No, sir, I do not believe that is Wellington's intention at all." Michael spoke with a hard formality.

"Cousin, Michael, please," Roberta broke in, "this thinking will not help us. Whatever might, or might not happen, it will help nobody if Renard is at large to do who knows what."

De Silva sagged back in his chair. "Of course, you are quite right, Roberta. They are only rumours."

"Perhaps, sir, that is why Renard is here, to spread such rumours to drive a wedge between Portugal and Britain." Michael was keen to change the subject, and get back to the problem of finding Renard.

"Yes, of course," de Silva rang a bell to summon his secretary, "but first, I think we need coffee, and then we can discuss how to proceed."

The ordering and arrival of the coffee resulted in a calmer atmosphere. Michael did not want to fall out with de Silva, and he was grateful to Roberta for her intervention. The pause in proceedings also gave him time to consider the problem. Something someone had said was tickling at his memory, it was there, but wouldn't come to mind.

"I suppose", said de Silva, "that we had better start sending men around all the businesses, particularly the merchants, looking for a clerk called Pereira. Ha! If we arrest every clerk called Pereira the commerce of the city will grind to a halt! Unless either of you have a better idea?"

Roberta shook her head, and Michael shrugged. "No, sir, but if anything occurs to me…"

Michael and Roberta left de Silva in his office and walked out of the headquarters, followed by Lloyd. It was only mid-morning, so Michael escorted Roberta home, arranged to have dinner with her, and then set out for his own house. He and Lloyd were both wearing civilian clothes, and looked like a Portuguese gentleman out for a stroll with his manservant. Michael followed a slightly indirect route that took them across the landward side of Black Horse Square. He was hoping he might bump into Antonio, and could tell him Renard was back in Lisbon. There he saw a small group of men, labourers by their clothes, gathered around listening to another who appeared to be haranguing them. His curiosity piqued, Michael drifted closer to listen.

"You've all worked on the new fortifications at Sao Juliao. Tell me, how do you think those are going to defend Lisbon from the French? You don't know? Of course you don't, because that is not what they are for." Michael got a little closer to better hear what the man was saying, he seemed to be giving voice to the rumours de Silva had reported. The man went on. "I will tell you what they are for, they are to protect the English while they board their ships and sail away, leaving us to the mercies of the French." The man paused to sense the mood of his audience. They were muttering amongst themselves, clearly not happy at the idea of what was being suggested. "And who is paying for it all? We are, Portugal is, we are paying for our own betrayal!"

Michael had heard enough, and with a nod to Lloyd to follow him, he moved slowly away. He didn't believe that Wellington intended to abandon Portugal, and he knew that Britain was subsidising the war to a huge amount, there was plenty of complaint about that from the newspapers that came out regularly. There was a fortune in British money being spent on the Portuguese army and the mountain of supplies going into the building of the fortifications. Then he remembered what had been tugging at his memory. The supplies, of course! Jones had told him he ordered whatever he needed, and sent the bills to the

Commissary in Lisbon. That meant that there was a complete record of all the suppliers, one of whom might just employ a clerk called Pereira, who might just be Renard's agent, and able to supply him with useful information, just as Soares had tried to. It was a slim chance, but it would narrow the search a little, it was somewhere to start. Someone in the Commissary Department might even know of Pereira. He turned to Lloyd.

"Come on Lloyd, we need to get into uniform and get out to Belem!"

Chapter 16

The man in Belem that Michael wanted to see was Deputy Commissary General Dunmore. He found him in a crowded office, papers everywhere, and a handful of clerks scribbling away, or scurrying about on errands. He read Michael's orders, and frowned.

"These are a little vague, Lieutenant? However, Colonel Murray is not a man to be trifled with, how may I help you?"

Michael had given some thought to how he might answer this inevitable question. "It is a difficult and sensitive matter, Mister Dunmore, it involves the possible defrauding of the army by a Portuguese supplier, thousands of pounds are at stake."

Dunmore paled. In his shock it didn't occur to him to wonder why a light dragoon officer would be investigating possible fraud. "I trust, Lieutenant, that there is no suggestion of impropriety in my department, sir?"

Michael smiled to himself; this was just what he wanted to ensure the man's fullest cooperation. "No, not at all," now Michael gave the man a reassuring smile, "far from it, but Colonel Murray believes that you may be able to provide the information we need. He was quite complimentary about your work here." Michael hoped that Murray would forgive him, if he ever heard about this.

Dunmore positively glowed. "Of course, Lieutenant, whatever you need, the resources of my office are at your disposal."

Michael nodded in appreciation, "Thank you, Mister Dunmore. Perhaps you can tell me if you or any of your staff have come across someone called Pereira, he is possibly a clerk?"

Dunmore looked thoughtful for a moment. "No, I can't say that I have, but let me ask the office." He turned to the room, "Gentlemen, gentlemen," he called. All present ceased whatever they were doing and turned to face Dunmore. "Gentlemen, have any of you come across anyone by the name of Pereira, a clerk, possibly? It is important that we trace him."

Michael looked around the dozen or so faces, all blank, one or two shaking their heads.

"Come along now," encouraged Dunmore, "anyone?" He waited a moment more and turned back to Michael. "I am sorry, Lieutenant, but there you have." He shrugged, and gave a little wry smile, then a voice said, "Yes, sir!"

Dunmore spun to look at the man who had spoken. "Well, Jenkins."

"Sir, there's a Pereira as works for Mister Sealy, sir, of Evans, Offley and Sealy."

Michael looked questioningly at Dunmore who answered his unspoken question. "A large trading house, lieutenant, mostly concerned with the port trade. I believe they keep an office in Lisbon, but we don't deal with them."

"I doubt that's our man," Michael was disappointed, "but thank you anyway, Mister Dunmore."

At that moment the door opened and two clerks bustled in, laughing, sharing some joke or other. They pulled up short at the scene before them.

"Ah, Simmons, Ellis. Do either of you know a clerk called Pereira?" Dunmore asked them brusquely.

The two men hesitated, frowned, then one said, "There's a Pereira that works for Rocha, the chandler, sir."

The other clerk suddenly spoke out. "I say, is that the fellow who was out at Sao Juliao, about two weeks ago? I saw him delivering some tackle. For signalling, I think. I remember because it was such a large consignment. I beg your pardon, Mister Dunmore, I didn't know his name, sir, Richards dealt with him."

"That's alright Ellis, no harm done."

Michael broke in, "What can you tell me about him, either of you? Anyone?"

Simmons shrugged, "Nothing, sir, he's just another clerk. Seems to keep himself to himself, not friendly at all."

"That's as may be," chipped in the other clerk, Ellis, "but he had a friend with him when I saw him."

"Did he? What did he look like?" asked Michael.

"Well, nothing special, sir, and I was a little way off, checking a delivery of palisades."

Michael felt thwarted, but then Ellis spoke again. "You could ask Richards, sir, he took receipt of the delivery."

Before Michael could ask, Dunmore spoke, "Richards? Where is he?"

"Still out at Sao Juliao, sir."

Michael cut in quickly. "Mister Dunmore, it is important that I speak to Richards, immediately. Could one of your people take me to him?"

"Of course, Mister Roberts. Ellis, you know the way and the fort best, take my horse, off you go."

Within a few minutes Michael, Lloyd and Ellis were on their way. Once clear of Belem Michael pushed the pace to a canter where the road was good, a trot the rest of the way, and the six or seven miles were quickly covered. Arriving at the fort, Ellis quickly gained them admittance, and leaving Lloyd to deal with the three hot and sweat soaked horses, he and Michael found Richards in conversation with an Engineer officer. The officer turned towards them and Michael was relieved to see it was Captain Wedekind, of the King's German Legion, who he had met s few times before, during his visits to Belem. Michael saluted as he approached, and a surprised Wedekind returned the salute with a "What the devil are you doin' here, Roberts?"

"Beg pardon, sir, but I need to speak with Mister Richards, urgently."

Wedekind waved at Michael to carry on, and he turned to a rather bemused Richards.

"Mister Richards, two or three weeks ago you received a consignment from Rocha, equipment, tackle for signalling?"

"Yes, sir, that's right."

"Delivered by an employee of Rocha's called Pereira?"

"Yes, sir, he's been out a few times with materials."

"And I believe there was another man with him, another clerk, perhaps, not one of the transport drivers?"

"Yes, sir, there was. I just assumed he was a new fellow, with Pereira showing him around."

"Can you describe him?"

Richards puffed his cheeks and blew. "It's a while ago, now. Quite a dark complexion, as I recall. Black hair. Didn't say much."

"How old would you say?"

"About our age, I suppose, and your height, a little taller than me."

"And he has only been here the once?"

"As far as I know, sir, but I don't necessarily see everything that arrives."

Michael was already turning away, and he called over his shoulder as he started to run to the horses, "Thank you!"

Lloyd had unsaddled and was rubbing down the horses when Michael reappeared, shouting. "No time for that Lloyd, get the saddles back on, we have to get to Lisbon." He turned to the bemused clerk who had followed him. "Thank you, Ellis, and, please, thank Mister Dunmore for me."

It was a twelve mile ride to Lisbon and de Silva's headquarters, and they pushed the pace hard all the way. By the time they arrived, Michael and Lloyd, and Duke and Rodrigo, were all bathed in sweat. Once again leaving Lloyd to deal with the horses, Michael quickly gained admittance to de Silva and told him what he had learnt, finishing with "It sounds like Renard to me, General!"

"I agree," said de Silva, leaning forward to ring the bell that summoned his secretary. "And, with luck, we shall have him before the night is over."

By the time dusk was falling all was in readiness. Michael and Lloyd had returned home, changed into their civilian clothes, left the horses with Parra, and returned to de Silva's. There a body of some twenty police officers in civilian clothes were assembled. Pereira's address had been obtained from Rocha, and it was already under surveillance. In twos and threes the plain clothes officers were sent to take position around the building, a four floor building with apartments and rooms on each floor. Pereira was understood to have rooms on the second floor, overlooking the street, which made any approach difficult. There was, apparently, a single staircase, and once de Silva's men were in there would be no escape by any back entrance. De Silva had taken personal charge of the raid, and, dressed again in shabby clothes, waited with Michael some hundred yards away in another street.

"We will wait until it is darker," he said, "it will make it easier to approach the building, and we may see a light to tell us if anyone is actually at home."

At that moment a vagrant came up to them and spoke quietly, "Pereira is at home, General, a light has just appeared. He seems to be alone." Just as quietly the man shuffled off, back the way he had come.

De Silva turned to speak to Michael. "If Renard is there he may just be laying low. We will wait another half hour and then go in." He addressed one of his men waiting with them. "Take a slow walk around everyone, don't go near the house, let them know we will move in on the half hour, when the church bells chime." He turned back to Michael, "We will wait here until my men have secured the building, they know what they are doing, it is best to let them get on with it."

Michael agreed, and settled back to wait as time ticked slowly by.

De Silva spoke quietly, "You will miss your dinner." He chuckled at Michael's startled reaction. "Don't worry, I have sent a message to my cousin, you will not be in trouble like you were with Senhor Barros. I asked her to keep a little supper for us both."

"Thank you, General, that will be most welcome," Michael replied, although he wasn't too sure about finishing his evening with de Silva.

The bells of Lisbon's churches began to strike half past eight, and the ringing had not ended when the sound of shouts reached them. A few minutes later one of de Silva's men appeared.

"We have Pereira, General, but there was no one else in his rooms."

De Silva swore softly. "That is unwelcome news. Come, Lieutenant, lets us see what we can find." Followed by Michael and Lloyd, de Silva led the way towards Pereira's rooms.

Pereira was sitting on a chair, securely bound, and with two of de Silva's men watching over him. Others were carrying out a search, while a third group were asking questions of Pereira's neighbours. Pereira's eyes widened when he saw de Silva, in fact he looked absolutely terrified. As they walked in one of de Silva's men handed him a handful of papers. The General looked through them and passed then to Michael.

There were a dozen or more sketches, of fortifications, with place names. For a moment Michael thought the worst, then he almost smiled. There were a couple of sketches of Sao Juliao, the rest were of the ring of defences around Lisbon itself, there was nothing about the lines being constructed to the north. If Renard had been able to send this information to Massena it would only encourage him to advance.

De Silva approached Pereira; he did not beat about the bush. "Where is Raposa?"

Pereira looked frantic, and gabbled, "I don't know who you mean."

De Silva nodded and one of his men struck Pereira a fearsome blow on the face. He asked again, "Where is Raposa?"

Tears began to trickle down Pereira's face, and he stammered, "I don't know!"

De Silva nodded to his man, and another blow whipped Pereira's head to the side.

"Where is Raposa?"

"I don't know, I swear, I have no idea."

Michael could stand by no longer. "General de Silva!" De Silva looked at him, an eyebrow raised in question. "Perhaps, if I might make a suggestion?"

"Yes, Lieutenant?"

"Perhaps, sir, you and your men might leave me alone with him for a few minutes? And Lloyd, sir."

De Silva stared hard at Michael for a couple of heart beats before speaking. "All of you, out now." He addressed Michael. "I hope you know what you are doing Lieutenant." He followed his men out and left the room.

So do I, thought Michael. He caught Pereira's gaze, and held it. "Lloyd?"

"Yes, sir?"

"Do you remember Ciudad Rodrigo?"

"Yes, sir."

"Do you remember Soares?"

"Oh, yes, sir," Lloyd answered with a chuckle. He hadn't been sure what Michael was up to, but now he had an idea.

At the mention of Soares' name Michael saw an emotion flicker across Pereira's face. "I see that you knew him." Pereira remained silent. "I had him hanged, you know." Michael nodded to Lloyd, who stepped behind Pereira and seized him by the hair, holding his head in place. Pereira's eyes bulged as Michael produced his knife from inside his coat, opened it, and locked the blade. Once Pereira had had a good sight of the knife, Lloyd pulled his head right back, exposing his throat. Michael stepped up close, placed the blade against Pereira's throat, and bent to speak quietly into his ear.

"Senhor Pereira, I need you to listen to me, very, very carefully. I need to find Raposa. I know he was here. I know you took him out to Sao Juliao. You are going to tell me where he is now. And you should know this, I am all that stands between you and the gallows, if you help me I will help you." Michael lifted the knife slightly.

With the blade away from his throat, Pereira gulped and licked his lips. "Senhor," he gabbled rushing his words, "he went out, two hours ago, he didn't tell me where."

"Now, why do you think he did that?"

"Senhor, he likes…," Pereira swallowed and looked even more scared.

"Pereira, tell me, you cannot be in any more trouble."

"Senhor, he likes young girls, senhor, very young." Michael fought to keep his expression impassive. He saw Lloyd's grip tighten, and Pereira winced. "I think he was going to a house where…"

"Spare me the details, Pereira. Where is this place?"

"I don't know, senhor, somewhere in the docks, I think."

Michael laid the blade of his knife on Pereira's throat. "Now, I want you to be very sure about that. If I find that you are lying…" He drew the blade gently across the exposed neck.

"Senhor, I swear, I don't know, in the docks somewhere, that's all I know." Pereira gabbled, his eyes fearful.

Michael looked into those eyes, saw the fear, saw no lies. He straightened up, closing the knife. "Let him go, Lloyd." He went to the door and through to where de Silva was waiting.

"General, he thinks Renard has gone to a brothel in the dock area, somewhere that specialises in young girls. Do you know of such a place"?

De Silva looked shocked. "Yes, there is one." He called down the stairs. "Frasco! Get up here." A weedy, scruffy man appeared.

"Yes, General?"

"The brothel in the docks, specialises in young girls, do you know where it is?"

"Yes, General."

De Silva rattled out his orders. Pereira was to be taken to Police headquarters by four men. The rest were off to the docks to visit the brothel.

Michael was impressed by de Silva, he hadn't really thought of him as a man of action, but the raid was quickly and effectively planned and executed. Doors were broken down, young girls screamed, men ran, futilely, and were rounded up. The brothel was an old, ramshackle place, a warren of filthy rooms. It was cleaned out, Renard wasn't there.

De Silva was seething with frustration. "Bring me whoever is in charge of this cesspit." Two of his men dragged in a woman in her thirties, long, black hair straggling over a ripped dress. She was the oldest female in the place by some distance. He paused for moment, weighing her up. "Would you like me to go away, for this to have never happened?"

The woman looked startled. "I can't pay very much." She clearly didn't know who she was speaking to.

"I don't want money," de Silva answered. The woman waited, silently, but hope flashed across her face. "I am looking for someone, a man called Raposa, he comes here, where is he?"

"You will go, leave me alone? Leave the girls here?"

"Yes."

"He was here an hour ago, I was just talking to him, when he suddenly said he had changed his mind, that he had to go. He just left, Senhor, I swear."

Michael had been watching silently, this was de Silva's territory, but now he spoke out. "What were you talking about?"

"I was telling him that one of the Militia regiments had just returned from the north."

"And?"

"Nothing else Senhor, I saw a lot of them down near Black Horse Square, they were drinking and complaining about being used as labourers. They were really unhappy about the eight league march to get home." She paused. "It was the length of the march that seemed to surprise him."

Her words sent a cold shiver down Michael's spine. Those were the militia that had been sent to labour on the fortifications, on the Lines, the real ones, not the ones just around Lisbon. If Renard found out about those from the militiamen…

"Lloyd, follow me." He started for the door.

"Where are you going?" de Silva asked.

"Black Horse Square."

"I'll send men down there; I need to finish here."

"But you said…" the woman exclaimed.

De Silva spun on her. "I lied."

The situation around Black Horse Square was difficult and confused. Earlier a fire had broken out, and the militia had moved to tackle it. The fire had been quickly contained, but then men and officers alike had then taken to the coffee houses and inns. By the time Michael and Lloyd were approaching the area, a lot of wine had been taken, and not a lot of food. It was getting noisy, and there was a feeling of barely contained anger and frustration. There were occasional shouts about traitors and the English.

Michael spoke quietly to Lloyd, "Keep close to me, and best say nothing, you simply wouldn't pass for Portuguese, and I have a nasty feeling about the cause of this."

As they turned the corner into Black Horse Square itself, Michael's suspicions were confirmed. The man he had seen earlier in the day was again haranguing a crowd, but these weren't the labourers and idlers from then, this was a crowd of militia, including officers, and they were all armed. The man's theme was much the same, that the English were going to abandon Portugal, fleeing to ships protected by fortifications they, the militia, were labouring to build, and would be expected to defend.

Passing deeper into the square they came to a large tavern. It was one of the more respectable establishments, and looking in through the window, Michael could see a large gathering of militia officers engaged in animated conversation. "Lloyd, I'm going in here, I want to know what they are talking about. You wait here, try and stay in the shadows." Lloyd nodded, and Michael pushed his way in through the doors.

The officers were gathered together in the middle of the large room, and Michael found an empty table near the door, and spoke to a worried looking waiter. "What's going on, and a bottle of your best?"

"They are not happy, Senhor. They say they have been away from their families building defences up at Sobral and Torres Vedras, all along the mountains from Alhandra, to stop the French, but then they find the English are building a fortified port to leave Portugal while they fight the French." The man shrugged, "I understand how they feel. Let me get you your bottle Senhor."

At that moment one voice in particular carried to Michael. One of the officers, a major, was shouting. "Then let us occupy Sao Juliao, then the English will not be able to leave, they will have to fight the French in the defences we are building. See if they can beat them at Alhandra, or Torres Vedras, or any on of the roads to Lisbon." There were general, supportive shouts at this.

The waiter returned with Michael's bottle and a glass. Michael paid, and said to him, "They really don't sound happy. Do you think they will try to occupy Sao Juliao?"

The waiter replied, quietly, "Who knows, Senhor, perhaps after they have slept off the wine they will change their minds. As for these fortifications, I have never heard of them. I am not even sure where these places are. That gentleman over there was asking me same earlier."

Michael glanced over to where the waiter indicated, and looked straight into the eyes of Renard.

Chapter 17

For a moment neither man moved, each as surprised as the other, then Renard was on his feet and running towards a door at the back of the tavern. Perhaps he was readier to have to fly for his life, but it gave him a second or two start on Michael. Then Michael was also on his feet and going after Renard, but between him and the door through which Renard vanished was the crowd of militia officers, and they were in no mood to make way for a mere civilian. The door slammed as Michael pushed and shoved, and was pushed and shoved in turn by the militia officers. An outstretched foot tripped him, bringing him crashing to the floor. He scrambled to his feet to the sound of laughter. He crashed through the door into a short corridor and then into a kitchen, a couple of surprised women jumped away from him, screaming. A dark, open door stood opposite him, and he ran towards it. It took him out into a dark alleyway, it was empty. Renard was nowhere to be seen. Cursing, Michael turned back into the kitchen. The women had been joined by three men, one of them his waiter.

"Where did he go?" Michael shouted at the two women. "The man who just ran in here, before me, where did he go?"

"Senhor, there was no man."

"What? I saw him come through this way!"

"No, Senhor, there was no one."

Michael's waiter spoke, "A man came back out of here as I came in, he was in a hurry."

"What?" Michael pushed past the men, and back down the short corridor. Then he saw the narrow door off the corridor, standing open, he had missed it in his rush, but

Renard hadn't. Back in the tavern's main room the militia officers were still arguing and shouting, and drinking. Michael made his way around them, and out of the front door. As he emerged into the square, Lloyd appeared from the shadows.

"Lloyd, has a man just come out of here?"

"Well, yes, sir. He went that way, and a couple of right rough looking coves joined him. There he is now, sir, look you, just at the corner." Lloyd pointed, and Michael just caught a glance of three dark figures disappearing around the distant corner.

"Damn it, Lloyd, that's Renard, come on."

"Uffern gwaedlyd," Lloyd swore. "Sorry, sir, I didn't realise it was him."

The two men went running towards the corner where Renard had disappeared. "You couldn't have known, Lloyd, but would you know him again now?"

"I think I might, sir, but it is dark."

They tore around the corner, but there was no sign of the three men. "Come on, they can't have just vanished."

At the next street junction Michael glanced to his left, and shouted, "There, there they go."

Fifty yards away they saw one figure dart sideways into another turn, while two figures turned to face them. Slowing down, Michael and Lloyd walked towards them. Light glinted off steel and Michael could see that both men had drawn wicked looking knives. They were standing, confident, grinning.

"Hey, run away while you still can," one of them shouted, "and take your ugly footman with you." They both laughed.

"Lloyd," Michael spoke quietly, "can you take the one on the left, I'll take the one on the right. Don't let them see we are armed, yet, let's back off, draw them on a bit." He raised his voice. "Senhors, there is no need for that, I simply want a word with the man you were with."

Michael and Lloyd edged back a yard, encouraged, the two men came on towards them, closing the gap. "Err, now, look gentlemen," Michael tried to sound nervous, "'I am sure this is just a misunderstanding. I think we will just leave." He turned left, towards Lloyd who also turned to his left, his right hand going under the cape thrown casually on his left shoulder. Michael turned his back, one of his hands on the top of his cane, and gave what he hoped was a nervous glance over his shoulder. The two men were now striding confidently towards them, only a few feet away.

"Now!" shouted Michael, spinning to face the threat, and drawing the wickedly thin blade from his cane. A rasping sound followed as Lloyd also turned, and drew his sabre that had been hidden under the cape. The two men stopped, but it was too late. Lloyd stepped forward and his blade bit deep into his opponents knife hand, severing fingers, the knife clattering to the ground as the man screamed in pain, then the blade reversed, flicked across, and the man fell to his knees, clutching at his throat before pitching face down onto the street.

Michael whipped the tip of his blade across his man's forearm, and his knife dropped from his hand. He turned to run, and as he did Michael plunged the blade into the back of his thigh, bringing him to the ground as his leg failed him.

The sound of running feet came from behind them, and Michael and Lloyd spun towards this new threat.

"Senhor, Senhor, it is alright, General de Silva sent us."

In the gloom of the street Michael recognised some of de Silva's men. "These two were with Raposa," he said, "but he's gone, I don't know where. That one is dead, but this one may be able to tell us something."

The man was lying on his side, moaning and holding his leg. Michael walked to stand by his head, and placed the tip of his blade on the man's cheek. "Where has Raposa gone?" he asked, putting a little pressure on the blade, so a small trickle of blood appeared. The man had gone rigid with the touch of steel on his face.

"I don't know!" Michael pressed a little harder. "I don't know, Senhor, I swear I don't know!"

Michael removed the point, and squatted down to look at the man. "It's a funny thing Lloyd," he spoke in Portuguese, Lloyd's was good enough to understand him, "there seem to be a lot of men swearing they don't know where Raposa is. They were lying, I wonder if this one is?"

"I wouldn't be at all surprised, sir," Lloyd replied.

"Neither would I." Michael addressed the man again. "It looks like we don't believe you, so, I am going to count to three, and then, if you haven't told me where Raposa is, I shall put out one eye. And if you still don't tell me anything, I shall put out the other eye. Do you understand?"

The man nodded. Michael began to count, "One, two,…"

"He went for a horse!" The man almost screamed in his fear.

Michael was surprised. "Not to Pereira's?"

"No, no, senhor, no, the police are there!"

"And how does he know that?"

"He told him, senhor." His eyes flickered in the direction of the dead man. "He came to us in the square and told us."

"And where would Raposa find a horse?"

"The other side of the castle, senhor, just off the Alhandra road. There is a stable kept by a friend, an afrancesado."

"Damn!" It made sense, it seemed to be the road Renard normally took in and out of Lisbon.

"Did he say where he was going?"

"No, senhor, he just muttered something about going to see for himself. He wasn't even really speaking to us, senhor."

Michael rose to his feet and turned to de Silva's men. "You can take him away, He can tell you where this stable is, but I don't think he is any more than a hired ruffian."

He thought hard for a few moments, while the man was gathered up and carried away. Then he decided what he would do. "Lloyd, back to the house now. I need my uniform and Johnny, quickly."

As they hurried to his house Michael went over his reasoning again. Renard already had a head start on him, and he wouldn't catch him on foot. By the time he could get mounted, Renard would be at least half an hour ahead of him, and it was only some twenty miles, or less, to Alhandra. He stood little chance of catching him before he got beyond the Lines. But the man had said that Renard was going to see for himself. After hearing what was being said in the tavern, that could only mean one thing, he was going to see the Lines for himself. So, the chances were that he would ride out to Alhandra, get just beyond the Lines, hide, wait for daylight, and then turn west along the outside of the lines, probably as far as Sobral. By then he would have seen more than enough. From there he could turn north, and disappear into the mountains to find his way to Massena. If Michael went straight after him, and he saw Michael first, he could just make a dash to the north and the mountains, where Michael would never find him.

He had no doubt that Renard would be looking behind him, fearful of pursuit. Instead, Michael decided, he would ride direct to Sobral, try to get ahead of Renard, wait, and hope to surprise him on the road. It was a shorter distance, and he knew the road, he had ridden it several times in the last few weeks, and he wouldn't be slowed by a need to wait for daylight or to observe and take notes.

The church bells had rung out for midnight as Michael started out for Sobral on Johnny. Lloyd had wanted to come with him, but Rodrigo was tired after the day they'd had, and it would be too much for an ordinary troop horse like Edward. Most of all, Michael wanted Renard for himself, so he left a frustrated Lloyd at the house. Once clear of the lights of Lisbon, he let Johnny have his head, and trusted to him to pick his way through the dark. It wouldn't be the first time, numerous night time pickets and patrols had given him complete confidence in Johnny's vision in the darkest conditions.

It was still dark when he passed through the pickets in the Bucelas area, over half way to Sobral. Dawn had not long broken as he passed by the great fortifications just south of Sobral. There he was held up for a frustrating quarter of an hour by an officious Portuguese militia sergeant. Eventually an officer appeared, and Michael was allowed to pass. He managed to beg some bread from a passing commissary. Sobral itself was quiet, there were not many people about, and shuttered shops and houses showed where inhabitants had already abandoned the town in the face of the expected French invasion. A mile beyond the town, the road ran along the side of a long ridge. Here the road forked, and either road was away from the Lines, heading north. It was here that Michael hoped to meet Renard. He turned Johnny off the road and up the slope to a small copse of trees. From there he could see most of the road back into Sobral itself. He eased himself out of the saddle, sat back against a tree, holding Johnny's reins in his hand, and settled down to wait.

It had got light at about half past six. If, Michael thought, Renard had started out then from near Alhandra, he would probably get to Sobral in about four hours. Michael looked at his watch, another hour or two then, if he was right. And if he was wrong? What if Renard had just ridden north from Alhandra, heading directly for the French Army? Michael relaxed. If that were the case, then he wouldn't see the Lines save a small section by Alhandra, he wouldn't be able to tell Massena anything definite. Massena would still come. He would kill Renard another day. Michael forced himself to relax and enjoy the stunning view that lay before him.

The sun climbed higher behind him, and the day gradually began to warm. The traffic on the road was sparse, an occasional group of labourers passed by, heading to work on the Lines. A small patrol of Portuguese infantry went past, without seeing him. Michael chewed on his bread, took a drink of water. Then he checked his pistol. He sat down again, and chewed some more bread. Johnny was quietly stripping leaves off a tree. Time passed slowly. Michael began to feel drowsy as the temperature continued to rise. He was tired after his busy day and sleepless night. The chomping sound of Johnny eating was rhythmic, hypnotic. His eyes began to close and his head to fall.

The long, piercing whistle of a red kite brought him jerking awake. He shaded his eyes and saw the bird, a small, black shape, circling, high in the cloudless sky. Struggling to his feet he reached for the wineskin of water hanging from Johnny's saddle. As he did so he looked down the road towards Sobral, and froze. There was a rider coming, a civilian, on a grey horse, trotting along briskly. Michael couldn't make out any details, but he pushed Johnny back under the trees, and swung himself into the saddle. He was no more than fifty yards off the road. The rider came closer, two hundred yards, one hundred, and then Michael was sure, it was Renard. He had guessed right.

Michael gathered up the reins and drew his sabre. He felt Johnny tense as the horse realised something was happening. Then, as Renard was almost level with him, he touched Johnny with his spurs and the horse shot forward. Within a few strides Johnny was at a flat out gallop, tearing down the slope, covering the ground fast.

Renard suddenly looked in their direction, and tried to spur his horse on, but it was tired, and stumbled and spooked at the sudden jab of the spurs. A pistol appeared in Renard's hand, and there was a flash, a puff of smoke, a bang, and the whizz of a ball going God knew where.

The distance between Michael and Renard was down to a few yards, when Michael reined in Johnny, and turned him slightly. Johnny crashed into the other horse, shoulder to shoulder, Michael tried to cut at Renard, who struck out with his pistol, catching Michael on the shoulder. Both horses were falling, and he missed with his cut, catching the grey across its neck instead, he heard it scream as the sabre sliced into it. Then he was out of the saddle, and hit the dusty surface of the road, rolling to get clear of the horses.

For a moment he lay on the road, stunned, his tarleton had gone flying, he'd lost his grip on his sabre, but it was still attached by the sword knot. His right hip hurt like the devil where it had hit the road first, he could feel blood trickling down his cheek. He got to his hands and knees and looked around. A yard or two away Johnny was climbing to his feet, apparently unharmed. Beyond him he could see the grey, struggling, trying to rise, and screaming in agony. Where was Renard? He couldn't see him. Michael staggered to his feet, and as he did he heard a man shout out in pain. Then he saw a hand clutching at the grey's saddle.

Michael limped across to the grey. It had a broken foreleg, and Renard was pinned under it by his left leg. His right leg was still in the stirrup, but the leather was twisted and he was caught in it. The horse kicked again, and Renard screamed, "My leg, I think it's broken."

Michael took a long look, then hobbled over to Johnny. As far as he could see he was alright apart from gazed knees and a nasty looking cut on his muzzle, but he was standing quietly enough. Michael scratched him on the forehead. "Alright, lad, alright now," he spoke soothingly. Then he pulled his pistol from its holster and hobbled back towards Renard, cocking it as he went, his sabre trailing on the ground from his wrist.

Renard saw him coming, saw the pistol. "No, please, no, Michael, don't shoot me. Please, I beg you."

Michael ignored him. He placed the muzzle against the grey's head, in the middle of its forehead, halfway between eyes and ears. Then he pulled the trigger. The horse convulsed once, bringing another scream from Renard.

Only then did Michael look at Renard. "That's the only pistol I have." He looked at it. "I suppose I could reload it." He looked thoughtful. "No." Michael tucked it into his sash, and gathered up his sabre. Still limping he walked around the dead grey to where Renard lay.

"Shooting is too good for you, Jean-Paul."

"No, Michael, no, I surrender, I am your prisoner, you cannot hurt me."

"Mercy? You expect mercy? Did you show Lady Travers any mercy when you shot her down?"

"What? Her?" He sneered." What was she to you. She was just one of Musgrave's people, his tame tart, nobody."

Michael felt his anger building. Up to now he had managed to remain in control, calm in the face of the challenge of taking Renard, but now, Renard's words released his anger, and he felt himself grow even calmer, even colder, as his hate of Renard consumed him. He stepped closer.

"What was she to me? She was everything, you bastard, and you took her away from me."

"What?"

Michael's burning cold anger freed him of all restraints, and he carefully placed the point of his sabre on Renard's throat. Renard froze and his eyes were full of fear, and Michael smiled at the sight.

"No, Michael, you can't! You mustn't! Please."

"You're going to Hell, Jean-Paul." Michael leaned all his weight on his sabre until he felt the point hit the surface of the road. Renard convulsed, his leg kicking, his hands grabbed at the razor sharp blade, slicing them open, pink frothy blood spurted onto his white neckcloth, his eyes glazed over, and he died.

Michael stood upright, and pulled his sabre free. He stood there, he didn't know for how long, looking at Renard, as his anger finally drained away, and he felt very, very tired. Eventually, he wiped his sabre on the tail of Renard's coat, returned it to its scabbard, and set about searching the body. In a coat pocket he found a small notebook, flipping through it he saw scribbled notes and sketches of the fortifications of the lines. He stuck it in his sabretache. There was a small purse, a fob watch, he left them. He left Renard's pistol where it had fallen, he left the horse, he left Renard, he left everything else.

He picked up his tarleton and put it back on. He stuck the pistol back in its holster. Slowly, painfully, Michael mounted Johnny. Then he turned towards Sobral, and began the long ride home.

In Almeida, Pelet handed Marshal Massena a decoded letter. "It's from Renard, he says the only serious fortification is protecting an embarkation point. The fortifications around Lisbon are not significant."

Massena read the letter for himself, and smiled. "Renard seems to have done well." He looked up at Pelet. "Now we can march on Portugal, not too hard, let the English take to their ships, and we will take Lisbon."

In Sobral Michael stopped at a pump in a small square. Watched by a few curious onlookers, he took a long drink, and then washed his face and Johnny's cuts and scrapes. Sitting on the edge of the trough, he got out Renard's notebook, and had a more thorough look through it. Renard had made quick, but accurate sketches of the fortifications from Alhandra all the way to Sobral. There were lists of amounts of money, they appeared to be a record of Renard's expenditure. Then there was a single page with a few names. He wasn't entirely surprised to see his own and Roberta's. What did surprise him was the name of one of Lisbon's more prominent, and wealthy Fidalgo's. Michael could think of only two reasons why he might be in Renard's notebook, as a particular enemy, or as a friend. Thoughtfully, he returned the notebook to his sabretache, mounted, Johnny, and rode on, wondering what to do with it. He couldn't show it to de Silva without revealing the existence of the Lines. Passing by the forts south of Sobral he saw smoke, and found a forge. While a bemused blacksmith watched, he tore out the page with the names, and shoved it into his pocket. He threw the notebook into the fire and stood there while it burned to ashes.

It was late afternoon and almost dark when he rode up to the stables behind his house. Lloyd, Parra and Francisco all rushed out to meet him. Lloyd caught him as he almost fell out of the saddle. He smiled at Lloyd. "It's done. Renard is dead. Francisco, go and tell Senhorita Roberta that Renard is dead. She can let de Silva know." Francisco nodded and ran off towards the house. "Parra, I'm afraid

Johnny took a tumble, nothing serious, I think he is alright." Parra led Johnny away, fussing him as they went.

Michael eased his tarleton off and gave it to Lloyd. "Lloyd, I shall need a little help, but I am going to bed."

Senhora Santiago fussed over him, and made him drink a large glass of brandy before she allowed him to go to his room. There, Lloyd helped him out of his sword belt and boots. "Thank you, Lloyd, I can manage the rest."

Slowly, carefully he undressed. The page from the notebook he put carefully away in a drawer. He lay on his bed, then stretched out to pick up Elaine's picture. He held it on his chest, and stared, the candlelight catching the gold of the lock of hair. "I did it, Elaine. I killed him." Then he took out her letter. He knew every single word of it, but to see it, to see her handwriting, gave him a connection. He read it again, as if for the first time.

'My dearest Michael,

If you are reading this it means that I am dead, how, I cannot guess. I hope that this gift will keep my memory fresh in your mind for many, many years to come. I hope that I have had the time, and the courage to tell you what you have so very, very quickly come to mean to me. I never thought that I would love again, you proved me wrong, something I don't usually take kindly to, but in this instance I am only too, too happy to be wrong. My darling Michael, I love you.

I hope that you have loved me, I hope I know that you do before I die. If not, I hope you will remember me as a dear, dear friend. If you do love me, do not, my love, do not make my mistake of thinking love comes only once. I hereby, most sincerely, release you of any ties, real or imagined.

Remember me, your ever loving Elaine.'

Tears began to roll down his face, and with the picture clasped to him, he sobbed himself to sleep.

Michael slept long and late. When he finally woke he found his uniform gone, and his civilian clothes laid out for him. He stirred, and put his feet to the floor. He ached all over, not least his hip. He heard a distant shout, "Senhor Lloyd, he is awake," and smiled to himself. A few minutes later Lloyd and Francisco appeared with fresh coffee and hot water for shaving.

"Bore da, sir. Senhora Santiago is cleaning up your uniform, and Parra says there's nothing wrong with Johnny that a couple of days won't see right."

"Good Morning, Senhor, Senhorita Roberta said that you are to call on her as soon as you are able to," Francisco grinned, "she seemed very pleased with the news, Senhor."

Michael scratched his head and rubbed the stubble on his face. A shave would be a good start to the day. He saw Elaine's picture was back in its usual spot. He glanced at Lloyd and Francisco, but they were busy around the room. He smiled, and set about shaving.

Once he was fit to be seen, and had breakfasted, Michael's first port of call was the Embassy. Stuart was surprised to see him, but delighted at the news he brought. At Michael's request he agreed to let Musgrave know as soon as was possible, and to send a courier to inform Colonel Murray. "Perhaps, sir," asked Michael, "you would be so good as to ask him if I might rejoin my Regiment?"

From the Embassy Michael went to call on Roberta. She threw herself into his arms and hugged him.

"Oh, Michael, Michael, tell me it's true?"

Michael released himself from her grip and held her at arms length, smiling. "Yes, Roberta, it's true. Renard is dead."

"Thank God, but how, you must tell me? Are you hurt at all? What's that scratch on your face?"

"It's nothing, it's just where I landed awkwardly when my horse fell, I have a bruised hip as well."

"Oh, no! Come, come, you must sit down. Constanca! Coffee and brandy for the Lieutenant, hurry!"

"Roberta, Roberta, it's alright, I'm fine." Michael laughed. "Sit down, and I'll tell you what happened." And he did, leaving nothing out, save the existence of the Lines. He hated to do that, but it was orders, and direct from Wellington.. It was a brutal tale, but he knew his friend, his lover, would understand, and not judge him. When he had finished she leant across to him, and took his hand.

"Michael, thank you." They sat and looked into each other's eyes for a moment. Then Roberta broke the spell. "Come, finish your coffee, we must go and let my cousin know!"

De Silva was, naturally, delighted, although Michael did not give him the full version of events, again he omitted any mention of the Lines. The General broke out his best brandy, and insisted on toasting Michael's health.

"So, Lieutenant, what will you do now?" the General asked.

"I am not sure, sir. Just carry on here as before, I suppose."

"But have you not done what you were sent here to do?" The General smiled, mischievously.

Michael laughed. "Possibly, sir, possibly, but it is not for me to say."

Later that night, Roberta lay with Michael, her head on his shoulder, his arm around her shoulders. A single candle illuminated the room.

"Michael?"

"Hmm?"

"Do you think things will be different now?"

"Different? How?"

"Now that Renard is dead. Does it change things for you?"

"I don't know." He thought for a moment. "I am glad, relieved that Renard is dead. He was a nasty, vicious, dangerous man, and I do feel better for having avenged Elaine. Much better." Another pause. "But I still love Elaine, I miss her, she was everything to me, and I hope Renard is burning in Hell."

"You still can't let her go, can you?"

"No."

"She let you go, Michael."

"I know, but I feel I need something more than a letter. What, I have no idea." He paused, thoughtful for a moment. "Right now, I just want to get back to my Regiment, things are simpler there." He rubbed a hand across his face. "Perhaps, with Renard dead, Wellington will be done with me." He gave a little, hollow laugh. "Somehow I think there's little chance of that."

Roberta turned towards him, held him in her arms, and they lay together, silent.

Brindle Books Ltd

We hope that you have enjoyed this book. To find out more about Brindle Books Ltd, including news of new releases, please visit our website:

http://www.brindlebooks.co.uk

There is a contact page on the website, should you have any queries, and you can let us know if you would like email updates of news and new releases. We promise that we won't spam you with lots of sales emails, and we will never sell or give your contact details to any third party.

If you purchased this book online, please consider leaving an honest review on the site from which you purchased it. Your feedback is important to us, and may influence future releases from our company.

Also by

David J Blackmore

Published by Brindle Books Ltd.

To The Douro

Wellington's Dragoon; Book One

A young man's decision to fight leads to a war within a war…

To love…

To loss…

…and a quest for vengeance, as he plays a vital role for the future Duke of Wellington.

To by this book from Amazon, you can scan the QR code below

Printed in Great Britain
by Amazon